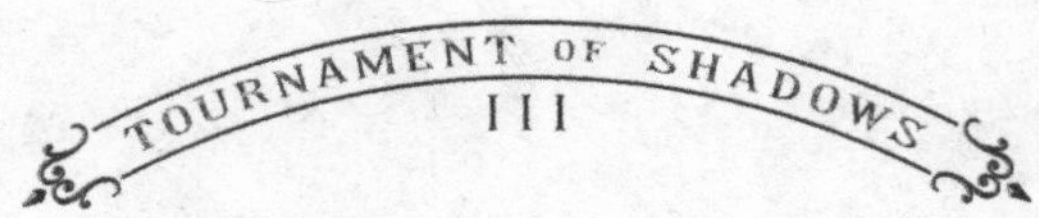

SHADOW SCHEMES

TILLY WALLACE

v02102022

ISBN 978-0-473-65638-6

Published by Ribbonwood Press

To be the first to hear about Tilly's new releases, sign up at:

https://www.tillywallace.com/newsletter

One

London, *Autumn 1788*

Like a summer rain drenching parched land, Seraphina Winyard's magic returned and filled every part of her. She drank up the tingle running from the roots of her hair to her toenails. For all that she worried about depleting herself, she rose from bed each morning more powerful than ever. Just as a regularly exercised muscle becomes stronger, so her magic relished being used and pushed to its limits.

Not surprisingly, in her correspondence box awaited a summons to appear before the council.

"I am to be told off, no doubt, for besting their show pony," she muttered as Elliot held her hat and cloak.

The council believed Lord Tomlin to be the best and brightest mage in all of England, and Sera had doused his light as he sought to outshine the sun in a recent performance for the king and queen. Not to mention the fighting that had broken out in the city that night, as Londoners argued over what her victory meant to them.

"If they lock you up, do we still get paid for the whole month?" Elliot asked.

She dug deep to find a weak smile for him, but no retort came. Worry gnawed at her. While she had no regret over her actions, nor in proving her greater ability, there would be consequences. Only now did she consider what they might be. Harsh words couldn't harm her—they could yell and bluster all they wanted and it would be but wind blowing at a mountain. But what if they curtailed her freedom?

By the time she reached the mage tower in Finsbury, anxiety swirled inside her. Mentally, she clad herself in armour, both to protect herself and to confine her temper. Sparks danced along her skin and under her clothing. Her ability was jubilant at being tested and urged her to do it again and again. A seductive voice whispered that the more she pushed herself to the limit, the more powerful she would become.

The oak she had grown in the courtyard rustled in greeting, and Sera murmured to the sapling. A jolt of excess magic surged through the tree's trunk and into its root, adding nutrients to the surrounding soil.

Before her eyes, it grew at least two inches in girth and six inches in height. At its base, autumn crocuses pushed through the grass and added much-needed colour with their vibrant purple flowers. The appearance of the bulbs proved that once the soil was nurtured, all sorts of things would flourish.

Sera swept into the council chamber and nodded to the assembled mages. Only Lord Pendlebury greeted her with a returned nod and smile. A grimace was plastered on Lord Tomlin's face as though he was either in pain or attending the meeting under duress. His complexion had a dull grey cast to it. Sera suspected he had not yet fully recovered from their performance.

As the clock chimed the hour, the mages shuffled to their seats. Sera's bottom had barely touched the padded chair when Lord Ormsby, Speaker of the Mage Council, launched his attack.

"Lady Winyard, your recklessness and inability to follow simple instructions nearly resulted in the death of Lord Tomlin and caused a riot along the banks of the Thames." To emphasise his point, he thrust out his arm and drew a circle in the air before her.

Sera drew a slow, deep breath and centred her thoughts. She had anticipated this accusation on the journey to the tower, and had considered a hundred replies. Now the moment had come to choose one. "Lord Tomlin and I were tasked to entertain the king and his honoured guests. From the reaction of King

George and the accounts in the newspapers, we achieved our goal in grand fashion. Were the people not entertained?"

A deep red flush bloomed over Lord Ormsby's face. The raised arm swung to point at Lord Tomlin. "It would have been on your head if England lost its most powerful mage."

"If Lord Tomlin were truly so powerful, how is it he could not best me in the performance?" she asked. "Why, even now, he looks as though you dragged him from his sickbed, whereas I suffered no ill effects."

Spluttering came from around the table, and Lord Ormsby's face turned from red to puce. Lord Tomlin stared at his hands, a tight set to his jaw. This was one unfortunate outcome of Sera's revealing the extent of her power, then—any overtures of friendship between them were ended for good.

"Surely, gentlemen, we can now admit we were wrong in our assessment of Lady Winyard's ability?" Lord Pendlebury said. "She amply demonstrated that she is a force to be reckoned with and the equal of any man at this table."

"You perverted my schedule of events to your own selfish ends." Lord Tomlin's hand curled into a fist.

"Night should *never* triumph over the light. It upsets the natural order of things." Lord Gresham glared at Sera.

An odd comment from him, given his preference for wearing black like a storybook evil sorcerer.

"Why are so many people afraid of the dark?" Sera asked. Light and dark were not inherently good or evil. That was defined by actions. She had enjoyed channelling the persona of the goddess, but yet again, the idea of a powerful and shadowy woman struck fear into the hearts of many. People had rallied to her defence that night—did the council believe they had only swelled the ranks of her dark army?

The newspapers contained conflicting accounts of her. Some drew comparisons to how Sera's existence disrupted the order of things for the council and that perhaps a change was long overdue. Others prophesied that, like her portrayal of Nyx, darkness would sweep over England if Sera were not curtailed.

"In Europe, they confine women mages to institutions of learning. The question has been raised in Parliament that England should follow the example set by our European colleagues." And with that, Lord Ormsby gave voice to Sera's worst nightmare.

She drew a quick, shallow breath and focused on tracing a pattern among the mosaic pieces composing the table's clock face. Her eyes burned, and she blinked back tears. *Never* would she cry in front of these men. "I did exactly as tasked by this council. Do not judge me harshly because Lord Tomlin wasted his magic on maintaining illusionary clothing. I had my gown physically sewn, so that it would not drain me during the performance."

"An excellent point, Lady Winyard. It was an unfortunate choice by Lord Tomlin." Lord Pendlebury poured himself a glass of water and the pitcher tapped against the tabletop as he replaced it.

Lord Tomlin scowled, but seized on the opportunity to save face. "Of course, if *I* had commissioned a set of appropriate clothing, Apollo would have defeated Nyx as we scripted it. As we all know, it is far easier to extinguish a light than it is to create one."

Sera bit her tongue. Let him believe that, if it defused some of Lord Ormsby's anger.

"You will be given another chance to follow instructions, Lady Winyard," Lord Ormsby said. "There are reports of disturbances at Bunhill Fields and an attack on someone passing through. Locals claim the dead are unquiet in their graves. You are to get to the bottom of it and tell the departed to be quiet."

"You want me to investigate the dead at the cemetery?" This was a punishment, but it could be worse. She still had her liberty and had not been shut up in a nunnery—or a university.

"A fitting task for the goddess Nyx, is it not?" Lord Ormsby's lips pulled back in his grimace-smile.

Oh, well played, my lord. She harboured a strong suspicion that the men around the table feared both the dark and the dead. Her remarkable performance as the night goddess had given the Speaker the perfect next move in their game. "What of an aftermage who can converse with the dead? Surely they would be more effective at getting to the bottom of the disturbance?"

"Given that a man has been assaulted, this council believes a mage is required to determine the source of the physical manifestation." Lord Ormsby spread his arms wide to deflect blame on the other mages for selecting Sera for the task.

"I am sure it will allay the fears of the common folk if the goddess of the night had a good talk with these restless spirits." Lord Pendlebury raised his glass to her.

His words echoed through her and cooled a little of her anger.

"Given that you will need to be at Bunhill most nights until the matter is resolved, you will not be required to perform any duties during the daylight hours. This council believes it would be best if you spent your days in quiet study and reflection." A chill look dropped over Lord Ormsby's face and the grimace widened.

They removed her from the public eye and shoved her into the dark. If the Speaker thought he had placed her in checkmate, he was in for a surprise. A queen could move in many ways, and Sera would find inspiration in Nyx and claim the shadows as her own.

"Of course I will do as instructed by the council." In this instance. "I shall seek my Aunt Natalie's advice as to the best way to tackle the task you have set me during the long night hours, while maintaining the required degree of propriety." She added the last as a pointed reminder that they were giving her free rein to prowl the city while everyone else slept. Who knew what mischief she might get up to?

She might even wear breeches.

Lord Ormsby thinned his lips to a tight line. "Your aunt is a rather...forceful woman. She refused to admit me when I paid a call after the display. I sought reassurance on this council's behalf as to your condition."

"I apologise for her enthusiasm in her task. I found myself quite inspired after the performance, and was cloistered in my study working on new spells. You had stressed the importance of a mature woman to advise me, one not prone to magical charms. My aunt fills that role rather well, don't you think?" Sera plastered a sweet smile on her face. At least she had blocked the council's attempt to force a housekeeper in their pay upon her.

Lord Ormsby sighed, and the rest of the meeting passed without incident.

When she returned to her home, Elliot waited in the foyer. Sera handed her hat and cloak to him. "How would you like to join me on another nocturnal adventure?"

His dark eyes lit up. "About time. What is it?"

"Apparently the dead are unquiet in their graves at Bunhill Fields and they attacked someone. I am to investigate." She scratched her nails into her hair and dug out a wayward pin.

His hand froze in the act of hanging up her cloak

on its hook. "You want me to trail you in the cemetery at night with vicious walking dead about?"

"Yes." She didn't think the attack could have been *too* vicious. Spirits weren't corporeal, after all. They couldn't throw a punch or use a knife. Could they?

He finished placing the cloak and hat on their hooks. "Nah. Thanks. I'd rather go to the pub."

She crossed her arms and stared at him. "I thought you were supposed to be assisting me in illicit activities?"

"I'm not getting involved with the dead. Why don't you ask Mr Miles? Dead bodies are more his bailiwick." He waved her through to the parlour.

Sera didn't have to wait long to ask the surgeon, as he called on her while she was drinking a cup of tea and paging through a book on ancient magical rites that she had acquired in a small, dim bookstore the previous day. Such books could not leave the hidden library, but the council's magic had no control over those that had never been entombed there.

While Elliot fetched a tray from the kitchen for Hugh, Sera told him of her instructions to stay out of the light and wander the cemetery. "I shall have to ask the contessa for tips on how to be a proper vampyre, since I am to adopt the habits of one."

Not all the habits, mind you. The contessa didn't drink wine, and Sera would have to ask if the Italian Unnatural could stroll in her garden while the sun was high in the sky.

"The council's reaction cannot surprise you—you have given them a reason to fear you." Hugh occupied his favourite armchair. With his elbows on the arms, he touched his fingertips together and gazed over them at Sera.

"Good. At least they will no longer refer to me as *that feeble girl*." Sera's grand performance at the diplomatic banquet had been, in her mind, a complete success. She had proved to the gathered audience that she possessed greater magic even than Lord Tomlin.

"But in doing so, you have created a greater enemy," he said in a soft tone.

Sera fidgeted with the edges of the book in her hands. Frustration bubbled under her skin. Could she not do anything right? "I am either a useless girl or a terrifying witch. Why can I not simply be *me*?"

A smile broke over Hugh's face and crinkled his eyes. "There is nothing simple about you, Sera. You must find a way to put their fears to rest while reminding them of your power and position."

Sera tossed the book to the padded seat and threw up her hands. "I do not know how! I will ask Abigail and Kitty to ponder that one. They are far more politically minded than I."

The names of her friends Lady Abigail Crawley and Katherine Napier reminded her of something else—a promised engagement. Blast. There were too many commitments to cram into her evenings now.

"You seem to have recovered from your exertions

remarkably well." His gaze assessed her, and a shiver of delight ran over her skin at the thought of his doing so if she were in a state of undress.

Sera held out her hand, and a silver flame burst into being, dancing an inch off her palm. "I course with more magic than I did before that night."

He selected another small pie from the tray. "Is that a common phenomenon when mages push themselves to such an extreme?" He popped the savoury morsel into his mouth.

She extinguished the flame by curling her fingers. "I don't know. The others all wield their magic conservatively, as though they dipped a glass into a bucket that can never be refilled. Yet my magic not only returned, it now overflows. As though my container has grown larger for being emptied. It whispers to me to do it over again, that each time it will increase my ability. Imagine what I could become after draining myself a half dozen times." Her mind was crammed with images of how powerful she would be. Even if the other mages banded together, they would be no match for her.

"You might grow in strength, or you might never recover. How do you know when you might stretch yourself to breaking point? Has any mage permanently exhausted themselves?" His words carried a dire warning.

The only tales she recalled of mages draining themselves to breaking point came from history books, and were men who had to act in times of war or great disaster to save the lives of others. She couldn't recollect any incidence of a mage doing it deliberately to make their magic stronger. "Possibly. That might be why the others do not cast to the point of collapse."

Sera leaned back on the settee and stared at the ceiling. Lord Branvale had told her little of testing her limits, except to warn against it. Lord Rowan had asked if she had tested herself. Had he meant emptying herself completely, or was there some other assessment of her capabilities? "What if my age has something to do with it? When I turned eighteen, I came fully into myself. What if, when a mage pushes to their limits while younger, the magic recovers more fully than if an older mage does it?"

Hugh huffed and tapped his chin. "An intriguing hypothesis. But again, I must urge caution, at least until you have further information. I would not wish to see you drained with no hope of replenishing your magic, like a well that has gone dry."

Neither would she. To be devoid of the magic in her veins seemed a horrible existence, like lopping off a limb and losing a fundamental part of herself. "I will be careful. But I cannot promise never to do it again. It calls to me, Hugh, whispering of the wondrous things I could do." She leaned forward and wished she could find the words to share what it felt like.

"Be careful, Sera, please. I do not want to see you

harmed." He held her gaze, worry and affection combining in his eyes.

"There is something I would ask, if you are brave enough to accompany me. The council is hiding me from view and has tasked me to investigate a nocturnal disruption at Bunhill Fields cemetery." Sera picked up a cushion and plucked at the braid around the edge.

"I would be delighted to accompany you. I must admit to some familiarity with the nocturnal activities at Bunhill." He glanced down at his hands.

"Ah. I hope you weren't on one end of a shovel?" Medical schools were notoriously undersupplied with what they needed to teach new doctors in the fields of human biology and anatomy. A few enterprising individuals were eager to earn a few coins by providing what the students required.

"No, although I admit I never ask too many questions about the origins of the cadavers on my table. I was fortunate to study anatomy under Doctor Husom, who has an amazing and detailed knowledge of the human form. But even in the official anatomy classes, some bodies had a rather distinctive earthy aroma about them that warred with the scent of decomposition and preservative spirits." He continued eating, while telling her of his dissection studies.

Sera shuddered at the images his words conjured. She didn't want to contemplate how students revealed the secrets of a body, even if it were the only way for surgeons to gain the knowledge they needed to help the living. But she agreed with him about one thing. "Grave robbers seem the most likely answer to the disturbances and attacks at night."

"The more innovative resurrection men employ an aftermage to assist them, one who can make spirits materialise to terrify anyone who investigates the noises. It keeps all but the most determined watchman from investigating and buys them time to escape." Hugh rose to his feet.

"Your company will be much appreciated. I shall start my enquiries during daylight to determine if the phenomenon is confined to one area. I also need to find out more about the attack. Then we shall pay a midnight visit to the cemetery." Better to determine a course of action in the sunlight, before the cemetery put on her night-time disguise.

He took her hand and then bent his head for an all-too-brief kiss. "What are friends for, if not to join you on such adventures?"

Two

The next day, Sera hired a horse from the mews and rode out to find the sexton at Bunhill Fields. Before she wandered around in the dark carrying a magical light like a figure from one of Mrs Radcliffe's novels, she wanted to find out exactly what sort of disturbance was upsetting the locals and where it was happening.

She tied the horse to a stout rail by the gate and trudged along a path to the sexton's cottage. Birds twittered in greeting from the trees, and a faint breeze stirred the air, bringing the aroma of freshly turned soil. She found the sexton sitting outside in the pale sunlight, sorting through an assortment of shovels and picks used by his grave diggers. He appeared to be putting aside those that needed repairs. Of average height, he had the hearty appearance of a man used to laughing long and often. A cloth cap perched toward the back of his head and exposed a swath of greying hair at the front. He wasn't at all the sort of person she thought to find in charge of overseeing the burial grounds.

"I am Lady Winyard, sir. The Mage Council sent me to investigate your disturbance." She leaned one gloved hand on a post supporting the gate.

He put aside the shovel in his hands and looked her up and down as though she were applying for a job. "They sent me the night witch?" A hearty laugh came from his barrel-shaped chest, and he rose to his feet to sweep her a bow. "That's just what the job requires."

The compliment and his good humour balanced his insult. Sera would let it pass.

"The council was somewhat vague, saying only that there was some unrest and an attack. What exactly is occurring?" She hoped Elliot's jest about the walking dead wasn't accurate. The dead could not rise from their graves and molest the living. Such things only happened in tales told around a fire at night to terrify children. Unless heinous dark magic was being used. But most likely, it was the resurrection men—those who dug up the recently departed to sell their bodies to the medical schools.

"Jim was the fellow who claims it attacked him. He lives on the other side of those trees." He gestured to the northwest, where smoke curled from behind a dense hedge. "Then there's moaning and lights waving back and forth." He gestured off into the distance.

She arched one eyebrow. The answer seemed simple to her. "Grave robbers?"

He huffed and shook his head. "I've been sexton here for over ten years and I'm telling you, milady, I know a grave robber when I spot one. Usually we find the graves they tried to enter the next morning. Whatever is making this commotion doesn't seem to touch a single grave."

Oh. That sounded more intriguing. "Can you show me where these lights and noises are manifesting? Then I shall talk to Jim."

"Of course, milady." He wiped his hands on a cloth and gestured for her to accompany him.

They strolled along the paths littered with leaves. A sense of peace washed over Sera. Here there was no bustle of the living, only the silence of those in eternal repose. Or at least, they *should* all be silent.

"Do you have an aftermage who speaks to spirits, and who comes to the cemetery?" While the council thought the job more appropriate for her, there were others who had an affinity for restless souls due to the generational trace of magic in their veins.

"Ethel often comes to talk to them. She lives up the hill from Jim. Haven't heard if she has been out to have a chat with this one." As he spoke, he pointed beyond the treetops. Sera gathered there was a small community nestled beside the cemetery.

"This is one of the older areas of the cemetery. The graves here are all about a hundred years old. Shouldn't be anything to entice the grave robbers, and there's been no sign of them trying to enter the larger tombs." He patted a headstone with faded lettering and lichen spreading over its shaded surface. Protective branches stretched over the tombs and the trees created a sheltered glade.

The sexton had a point. Fresh bodies were best for the medical schools. Why would grave robbers dig up those that were decades old? Or not, since he had just said there was no evidence of any disturbances.

"The lights were seen over here. Bobbing between the trees and those mausoleums. One of my lads that came to have a look says there was a moaning, like a spirit with something to say. He also heard flapping, like big wings." He walked to one of the squat mausoleums and laid a hand on the iron door.

Sera recalled Hugh's mention that some grave robbers employed an aftermage to convey just such an effect as the moaning, and the wings could have been any night hunting bird, like an owl or a nightjar. "Is the phenomenon seen anywhere else in the cemetery?" Most likely the nocturnal thieves had passed through on their way to more recent burials.

"No. Just here." He spread his hands wide and then crossed his arms.

Sera surveyed the quiet landscape. Late-blooming flowers pushed up through the grass. Dappled light filtered through the surrounding trees. A faint breeze caressed her cheek. Even the stench of London's streets and chimneys faded, to be replaced by the sweeter scent of earth and grass.

What about this section attracted lights and noises? She would reach out to each grave and look for disturbances.

"Where was Jim attacked?" She turned and tried to orient herself to the cottage the sexton indicated.

"Coming through hereabouts. He was returning home from the tavern and taking a shortcut." He drew a line with his arms from one side of the cemetery to the vague location of Jim's home.

The trees here were gnarled with age, roots jutting up from the soil like arthritic knuckles. In the dark, one might easily catch a boot on such a root and trip, then cry out or groan.

"Do you need anything else, milady? It's just that I have three burials to organise today," the sexton said.

"No. I shall find my own way back when I am done, thank you." She waved him away as she approached the first grave. The soil had shifted over the years, and the marker had lurched to one side. The movement caused a jagged crack through the stone. Perhaps the unquiet dead wanted to complain about the sad state of their lichen-covered headstones, or the fact that they no longer received visitors.

Sera rested her hands on the rough surface of the headstone and closed her eyes. Anchoring her body, she let her magic trickle down through her palms and into the earth. Tendrils burrowed through the soil until they found the remains of the wooden casket.

With a gentle touch, she skimmed over the contents to find a woman with skeletal hands clasped over her chest.

"Hmm. You seem content to slumber on," she murmured to the occupant. "Rest in peace."

Or did the physical form remain undisturbed, but the spirit form experienced some agitation? Before trying to summon the soul of every person in the area, she did a quick tour and took a head count. At least fifty people were in the graves, tombs, and mausoleums. She would exhaust herself trying to contact everyone in the next realm. Better to return at night and see if the phenomena manifested at one particular grave.

Part of her believed it was a fool's errand and that the culprit would turn out to be bored youths. But she could not deny that the peaceful grounds made a welcome change from tending to London's sewers.

A crow fluttered down and perched on a squat plinth topped with flat stone carved in the shape of an open book. The bird hopped from one granite page to another as it called to Sera. The man who had heard wings might have heard such a bird in the trees.

"Hello. Are you following me, or did you have work to do here today?" Given its familiarity, she assumed it was the crow that Elliot spoke to. She held out one hand to the bird, and it rubbed its head against her crooked finger. "I will be back tonight if you wish to join me."

The crow squawked a brief noise that could have been either acceptance or a polite refusal, then took flight once more. As she pondered her course of action, Sera settled at the base of a large elm. She pulled her knees to her chest and clasped her hands around them. Then she leaned back against the bark and closed her eyes.

In this relaxed position, she sent out strands of magic. She pushed through the grass and skimmed over the graves, searching for any trace of magical residue that might explain what had happened. In the silence, she stayed alert to any whimper or cry from the supposed unquiet dead. But she couldn't detect the faintest whisper. Why would the deceased only rouse at night, and how did they know dark had fallen?

With no immediate answers to her questions, Sera stood and brushed leaves and twigs from her skirts. Around the area, she scattered the dirt with magical spores to plant mushrooms in the dense leaf matter. When they erupted through the soil, she whispered a spell over them. When night fell, they would emit a faint yellow glow and turn red if anyone walked past them.

On her way back to the sexton's cottage, Sera sprouted mushrooms along the path. Each received a tickle of magic to make its cap glow once night fell. When darkness blanketed the city, the cemetery would transform. Shadows would claim the paths and headstones would hide from view, and she wanted to find her way back to the troublesome spot.

She took her bearings once more before heading through the trees to find Jim. They opened up to reveal a cluster of cottages built haphazardly with an assortment of materials. Working-class homes, made from whatever they could scavenge to provide shelter for their families. A lone cottage perched on the hill behind them.

"Where could I find Jim, who had an encounter with a ghost?" Sera asked a woman pinning clothes to a rope strung between two cottages.

"The one with a yellow door, ma'am," she answered.

The sunny colour made the dwelling easy to spot. On closer inspection, though, she could see the paint was peeling. It reminded her of a sunflower whose seeds had been pecked out by hungry sparrows. Sera rapped with her knuckles and waited.

A scrabble and cough came from within. Then the door swung open on a man with bleary eyes and a red nose laced with swollen veins and broken capillaries that spread across his cheeks. His shoulders were slumped, his frame gaunt. A whiff of stale sweat and cheap gin tickled Sera's nose.

"Jim?" Sera asked as he gazed at her in confusion. "I understand you were attacked in the cemetery? I am here to find out who was responsible."

"It was a spirit, I tell you, wanting to suck the life

from me," he said, and held the door open further for her to enter.

From the state of Jim, any *life* within him would have proven an unsatisfying morsel.

The one-room shack contained a single cot pushed against one wall. Two mismatched chairs sat before the hearth. A table with a single chair stood beneath a window on the other wall. Her heart ached for the man. No one should see out their last days in such a place. London needed adequate housing for everyone, regardless of their station in life. At least she could mend the holes in his walls and the leaks in his ceiling.

"Tell me about that night." While he cleared his throat, Sera turned a slow circle and sent her magic to find every gap in the walls and roof. One by one, she closed them over and made his home windproof and watertight. At least his winter would be fractionally more bearable.

"It was late, and I wanted to get home, you see." He dropped into a chair and his body slumped as though his spine could no longer support his torso.

"Were you alone?" she asked, taking the chair next to him.

"Oh, yes. I often cut through the cemetery. That lot don't mind, do they?" he wheezed.

"How did you encounter whatever attacked you?" Given it was early afternoon, and he appeared deep in his cups, she wondered that he could have seen anything at all after an evening of drinking.

He rubbed his jaw. "It was dark and drizzling. I saw a light. Blue it was, and swinging. Like a lantern. I followed 'em, hoping we could share the light."

"Then what happened?" Having fixed the roof and walls, Sera sent a gust of magic up the chimney to clean away the soot.

"I called out, didn't I? Asked 'em to wait up." He raised his arm, as though gesturing *stop* to the unseen figure.

"Did they?" It could still have been a grave robber, interrupted on their way to find a fresh burial.

He nodded, and his eyes shone bright. "I walked a bit quicker, to catch 'em. I came through the trees and saw it wasn't a lantern, but a man glowing all over."

"What made you identify it as a man?" Many things could make a lantern's light distort and appear different, from a reflection in something, to a simple spell teasing out the light given off.

Jim sucked on his top lip and narrowed his gaze. "I could be blind drunk and still spot another fella. Head, arms, feet." As he spoke, he mimed the shape in the air with his hands. "Come to think on it, can't recollect seeing any feet, but he had legs, so there must have been feet."

"How did the attack happen?" Sera had yet to be convinced that the assault was spiritual in nature.

"I called out again. Thought he was being rude not to share his lantern. I swiped at him and my arm went right through him. I stumbled. Then I heard wings and something hit me, clawing at my face. That's when I realised it wasn't no man, but a spirit. He screamed at me and I hightailed it back to me cottage after that. Talking to the others round here, some of them have seen the wavering light and all." He crossed his arms, as though to defend himself against derision.

"Has anyone else been attacked or injured?" A flurry of wings could certainly have been a disturbed owl. Sharp talons could cause serious damage to a person wandering around in the dark. Especially if the bird was startled by some arm waving. From Sera's inspection, Jim didn't seem any the worse physically from the attack.

"Nah. Just me." He shrugged bony shoulders.

"Has this been going on long?" Had a lonely soul been wandering the old part of the cemetery for a hundred years, trying to get a message through?

"That depends. We get used to the sights and sounds of that lot." He gestured with his thumb toward the cemetery. "But this one is blue and they ain't usually. This week has been different. We can all feel it. Gives you a right chill. Those of us what normally ain't bothered by that place after dark are staying in our cottages."

Sera mulled over his words. Those living close to the cemetery had pegged this phenomenon as different from what they usually encountered. What had changed in the last few days? A disturbed grave, perhaps, or another event linked to one of the interred?

"Thank you, Jim. You have been most helpful. Could you tell me where Ethel lives?" She may as well enquire with the aftermage while she was here.

He pointed behind where they sat. "Cottage on the hill. But she ain't there. Saw her leave earlier. Has work at the funerals—there's three today."

Some families found comfort in the presence of an aftermage to pass on any last words from the recently deceased. Sera would have a go at finding the spirit herself, then seek Ethel.

Taking her leave of Jim, Sera returned to her home. Since Lord Ormsby preferred her to stay out of the public eye, she spent the rest of the day in her study, painstakingly seeking out the Fae runes on the bracelet she'd once worn. She noted each rune on a piece of paper before hunting out the next and hoped there was some order in how they appeared within the engraved tree.

After some hours of the microscopic work, her eyes complained, and her back ached. Sera stood and stretched her arms over her head.

"Rosie is dishing up supper," Elliot said with impeccable timing from the doorway.

"Brilliant. I am famished." To emphasise her words, her stomach rumbled.

After a delicious meal with her odd family, and once night had settled over London, Sera donned men's garb to wait for Hugh. Elliot shook his head, but remained oddly silent.

"I saw your friend the crow today," Sera said as she paced in the parlour.

"She's following you. Pay her no heed." He waved her comment aside.

Something linked the crow and her footman, but Sera had not yet uncovered what. Elliot avoided such questions except to confirm he was no crow shifter or some other type of Unnatural. "I will not ignore her, not when she is obviously making the effort to converse with me."

"Oh? 'Bout time she started talking to you and stopped muttering in my ear." Elliot leaned on the parlour doorjamb and crossed his arms.

"I have the feeling there is something she wishes me to know. Perhaps she saw whatever is making the lights at Bunhill Fields." If she touched her mind to that of the crow, would they be able to talk to one another? Her sparrow friends replied in images, sharing what they had done each day. But she had not tried with a more intelligent creature, perhaps it was time.

People thought the crow, a carrion bird, was a harbinger of death.

THREE

"Here comes your surgeon." Elliot gestured out the window.

With Hugh's arrival, any further talk of secret messages from crows was set aside for another day. The surgeon rode one horse and led another. He jumped down as Elliot opened the front door and Sera hurried out.

"Don't wait up!" she called to Elliot and then skipped down the path.

While more comfortable aside than astride, Sera could ride as a man. Since she would be exploring the cemetery at night, Sera reasoned there would be no one to see her wearing breeches who might object to her manner of dress. Except for Hugh, who merely raised both eyebrows at her choice of attire.

"This would explain why you wanted an astride saddle," he said.

"Breeches are more practical for chasing spirits in

a cemetery at night, don't you think?" She took the reins from him and placed her left foot in the stirrup.

"I thought one of us was supposed to wear a white nightgown and wave a lantern?" He chuckled.

"Well, we can decide on that while we wait for the spirits to appear." Sera grinned back. She must remember to thank Lord Ormsby. He had given her an adventure with breeches and midnight escapades.

At Bunhill Fields, they tied the horses to a tree and passed under the wrought-iron gates. Sera dug into the satchel slung her over shoulders and gave Hugh a glass jar with a wire handle. When she tapped the side, the mist contained within lit up a pale blue and cast a light better than any lantern with a wick.

"That is handy. It would prevent fires from candles in the home," he said as he waved the lantern back and forth to admire the light.

"The process to make them is rather slow and time intensive. I am tinkering to improve it so they can be freely distributed." When the next batch was ready, she would give them to Jim and his fellow residents.

They walked in silence, following the faint trail from her mushrooms that led them to the troublesome area.

"This is where the sexton said the disturbances have been." Sera entered her circle of mushrooms, each changing to pink and then red as the vibrations from her footsteps reached it. They faded back to deep yellow as she passed.

Hugh examined a few headstones and then returned to the open bit of lawn. "What now?" he asked.

As this was Sera's first attempt to settle a restless spirit, she wasn't sure what would happen. "I assume we simply have to wait until it appears, and ask what it wants."

Hugh set his lantern at the base of an ancient tree. Then he removed the rolled blanket he carried over his shoulder and undid the strap holding it closed. He spread it under a tree and bowed to her. "My lady."

Sera sat and crossed her legs. From the satchel, she removed a stoppered earthenware bottle of hot tea and slices of cheese and bread wrapped in a cloth for Hugh. "Rosie didn't want us starving while we waited." She poured tea into two tin mugs. "It is possible the spirits might not appear with our light illuminated. We might douse it, if you are not afraid to sit in the dark with me."

Hugh grinned. "I think I can manage." He tapped his lamp, and the night swallowed them up.

As their eyes adjusted, shapes became more distinguishable around them. The moon broke through the clouds occasionally and swept a silver beam to caress a headstone before disappearing once more. At first, Sera thought the cemetery utterly silent. But minute by minute, her ears became attuned to the activity going on around them. An owl hooted. Wings flapped in the branches above. Nocturnal creatures nosed through the fallen litter.

They sat in companionable silence for what could have been minutes, or hours, when the air in one spot lightened. As it grew in size, it took on a silver hue. Edges became more defined and distinguished it from a stray moonbeam.

Sera nudged Hugh, not wanting to speak in case she frightened it away.

He sat up, his body tense beside her. The ability to throw a punch was no defence against a spectre, but if grave robbers had conjured this image, she would be grateful to have the surgeon at her side to deal with any spade-wielding men.

The light continued to swell and grow, the silver deepening to the blue of a clear summer's day as it stretched to some five feet in height. Sera let her magic drift over the grass and tease out more details about the shape. The floating object appeared to be a genuine apparition, and not a human wearing a glamour or other form of disguise. The mushrooms glowed yellow and did not register human footsteps nearby. Next, she brushed over the surrounding trees and shrubs, searching for anyone hiding in the dark. Nothing.

A low moaning came from the spirit as it drifted in a regular pattern between two sets of trees. Back and forth it went, the noise growing in pitch as it moved.

"Do you think it is here for a reason? I have heard that unfinished business can tie a soul to an area," Hugh whispered.

"I can try talking to it, but I've not encountered a shade before." A few people were sensitive to the other realm, where departed spirits lingered, but they preferred to practise their gift in warm parlours, not cemeteries at night.

Sera considered how to reach out to the lost soul. She wrapped the spirit in tendrils of magic, mainly to still its constant movement. It expended energy to make itself visible with the ghost equivalent of pacing and she wanted it to use its resources to converse. When it hovered before her, she noted Jim was right —there didn't appear to be any feet.

"Who are you?" she called out, once the soul hovered in the middle of the glade.

"Merr..." It screeched like a startled crow.

"Mary?" Sera tried to match a name to the uttered syllable.

"Merr..." It cried out again, this time with such a shriek that it pierced Sera's ears enough to make her wince.

"That is French for *the sea*. Perhaps it is trying to tell us it drowned?" Hugh suggested.

Sera had only a rudimentary grasp of French, but it seemed as good a guess as any. "Did you drown in the ocean?" she called out.

The light pulsing around the shape intensified.

"Merr..." The lone syllable wailed around the glade and birds rustled in the trees above them.

"Murdered!" Hugh shouted with enthusiasm, as though this were a game of charades.

The spirit fell silent and the pulsing blue light dimmed a little.

Sera huffed in surprise at the lack of reaction. "I would have thought murder would be the most compelling reason for a restless spirit," the surgeon said.

"Perhaps we need a different approach." Sera murmured to her magic, asking it to help the trapped soul find a way to share its message. She crafted a mist and blew it over the apparition. It shimmered and sparkled. The blue changed to moonlight silver, then a pale cream shot through with blue. As it pulsed, the edges became clearer.

"It's a woman." Hugh leaned forward as the spirit took on the vague semblance of a woman with long wild hair and a gown with a trailing hem. "I told you someone had to wear a nightgown."

"Who are you?" Sera asked again, hoping the more solid appearance meant the spirit might communicate.

"Merr...dit," she croaked. A spectral arm rose and seemed to point back toward London.

"*Dit?* Isn't that French for *said*? So we have *sea* or *ocean* and *said*." Sera tried to piece together the message from the other realm. Just her luck to encounter a foreign spirit who could only speak in her native tongue.

"Perhaps she is trying to convey that the ocean compelled her to do something. Or could she be the shade of a water-loving Unnatural, like an undine or selkie?" Hugh followed Sera's line of thought.

"Or it might not be French at all. What if she is trying to name a place that is of importance?" They had so little to try and determine what the spirit wanted. "Is Merr-dit a place?"

"Merr...dit!" the spectral woman wailed and jabbed a finger into the distance.

"Is that a yes to its being a place, or a no?" Hugh asked.

The spirit let out another ear-splitting wail and then her form burst apart into a hundred fireflies that darted off into the trees.

"I think we upset her." Sera tapped the lantern. The departure of the glowing spirit and her fireflies had plunged them into an inky dark that seemed more menacing than when they had waited in silence.

"And we are no closer to knowing what she wants." Hugh rolled up the blanket while Sera put the mugs and bottle in her satchel. "But I shall try again tomorrow night with, I hope, the assistance of the local spirit aftermage."

As they walked back to their horses, Sera slipped her hand into Hugh's. When they stopped at the entrance gate, she tugged his hand. He turned with a curious gleam in his eyes. Standing on her tiptoes, Sera kissed him and, somewhere in a tree, an owl hooted.

The next morning, Sera allowed herself the luxury of taking a breakfast tray in bed. Since Lord Ormsby wanted her off the streets during the daylight hours, there would be no tasks waiting in her correspondence box. She read the scandal sheets as she chewed her toast. People were still speculating about what it meant that Nyx had defeated Apollo and plunged the banqueting room into velvet night.

Some sought to link the appearance of Sera at court with the recent deterioration of the king. She tossed the paper to the coverlet with a snort. "If the plague returns, will they attempt to burn me at the stake to appease the old gods?"

After dressing, she decided to try again to find Ethel, who much frequented Bunhill Fields. She hoped the other woman could help in finding the source of the spirit's agitation. After the events of the previous night, Sera doubted the departed soul had physically assaulted Jim. Most likely, he had tumbled into a headstone when he tried to punch it.

Sera donned a long cloak with a deep hood and pulled it over her forehead before leaving the house.

"You know, each day you're looking more like a witch," Elliot murmured as he opened the door.

She glanced at the garment made of soft grey wool. "This isn't black and everyone knows witches only wear black. Nor do I have a cat. But thinking along that line, if you see your crow friend, tell her I want to talk to her."

Elliot pursed his lips. "You sure about that? Once she starts, you'll have a devil of a time getting her to shut up again."

"I will ferret out your secrets along with Lord Branvale's." She waggled a finger at him and the footman paled. Sera was not deterred. Quite the opposite. Each time they met, the importance of the crow dug a little deeper into her mind.

She walked to the mews to hire a horse. They were a more convenient mode of transport, and she preferred the large animals over a stuffy and sweat-stained carriage. On the ride north to Bunhill Fields, she considered how magic manifested itself in the descendants of mages.

Her friend Lady Abigail Crawley, with her gift of song, was a rarity. A few souls were born with the ability to reach beyond the veil and converse with the departed. The gift caused much titillation at society gatherings should a lady among those present be able to take questions for dead relatives. It was second in popularity to fortune telling. A young lady who could read the tea leaves was always in demand, as eager debutantes wanted to know if they would make a match during the Season.

She guided the horse around the burial grounds to the community on the other side, where she dismounted and tied the horse to a low-hanging branch with lush clover underneath. As she passed Jim's home, she left a lantern by his door with a note to tap it (laid out in pictures in case he could not read) to activate the light.

Ethel's cottage sat on its own, perched on the hill and overlooking the rest of the village. It conjured to mind the legend of Baba Yaga and her rickety cottage with chicken legs. Except this one was nestled in the grass and facing her. No need to whisper *Hut, hut, turn your back to the forest and your front to me* as she approached.

An ancient woman with a deeply lined and tanned face sat on a ladder-back chair by the door. Her arthritic hands were wrapped around a steaming tin mug. Watery eyes regarded Sera. A faint floral whiff of bergamot gave away the drink as a blended tea.

"I am Lady Winyard, in search of your wisdom, Ethel." She hoped for a friendlier greeting here. One witch to another.

The woman nodded. "They whispered you'd be paying a call." She gestured to the vacant chair beside her.

Sera took a seat and gazed out at the landscape. She assumed the *they* who had heralded her arrival were the souls lingering around the cottage. Or possibly the sexton or Jim, since she had mentioned to both that she wanted to find Ethel. "I have no experience in talking to spirits, and I am supposed to help one move on. I could use your advice on the matter."

Ethel slurped her tea in such a way that Sera wondered if she possessed any teeth. "Odd things they are to talk to. Very few of them say what needs to be said. It's like they want you to puzzle it out. Instead of saying they love someone, they say only one holds their heart or some such rubbish."

"This one seemed most intent on saying something. It kept repeating the same two syllables. *Merr. Dit.* It could be a name, a place, or a phrase in French." Sera would not be defeated so easily. The spirit's determination to try to speak increased her certainty that it would resettle in the afterlife once its message was understood and acted upon.

"I don't know any French. But there are ways to get it to confirm if it's a name or place." Ethel picked up the kettle sitting on the ground beside her and poured strong tea into a clean mug. Then she handed it to Sera.

She inhaled the woody but floral aroma. Wherever Ethel bought her tea, it smelled divine and far better than anything she'd had even at Kitty's or Abigail's homes. One sip brought a sigh of contentment from Sera's lips. "This is the best tea I have ever had." Although they drank it black and strong, the tea had sufficient floral notes to lend it sweetness.

"A very satisfied lord has it delivered once a month from some warehouse he owns. His father died unexpectedly and he and his brother argued over who got some country estate and other things. I told him where the will was hidden." Ethel let out a chuckle.

Barter had its advantages. Sera would gladly trade a few spells for a monthly delivery of such a brew. "You must tell me who. Perhaps I can find a way to make him indebted to me."

Sera winked at Ethel over the mug. The old woman let out a raucous laugh and slapped her knee. "Lord Thornton. He's a few years older than you and unwed. You could get more than tea out of him if you smiled the right way." Ethel sniggered and returned to slurping her drink.

Tea would suffice, but Sera tucked the name away. It sounded vaguely familiar. "Jim says the disturbance is recent. Do you know when this particular spirit appeared?"

Ethel drew in a sigh and held it. It appeared she had to stop drinking, breathing, and talking to think. Then she swallowed her mouthful. "No more than a week. She's an old one, but I've not sensed her before in all the years I've rambled over that place."

"I would appreciate it if you could accompany me tonight. Perhaps between the two of us we can figure out her message." While they talked, Sera rendered Ethel the same service she had given Jim. Her magic sought out gaps and drafts in her little cottage and coaxed the wood or iron to mend itself.

"I've never worked with a mage before, but I'll not say no to the chance to walk among the dead with Nyx at my side." Ethel grinned and revealed that she was indeed missing most of her teeth.

"Thank you. I'll return at nightfall." Sera rose and handed her empty mug back to Ethel. The window behind her had a too-small piece of glass wedged in the frame, allowing the weather to reach inside the cottage. She placed both hands on the cool sheet that had once been sand. Murmuring under her breath, Sera encouraged it to stretch and grow. Soon, the glass fit tightly in the frame.

"Thank you, milady. That will keep the winter rain out." Ethel poured more tea into her mug and gave no appearance of moving any time soon.

"I do what I can to help. Until tonight." Sera walked slowly back to the horse. She touched a broken window here, a badly cured board there, or picked up a fallen slate. Each was a small repair to a cottage, but Hugh's words echoed through her. *Do one small thing. Small things build into big things.* Her tiny actions would combine to make a warmer community come winter. Especially when she added her magic lanterns that didn't require a wick or flame, and some form of heating.

FOUR

That evening, Sera rode again out of the city as twilight descended, with the hood of her cloak pulled low over her face to disguise her feminine features. In her satchel, she carried four of the glass jars filled with mist. By the time she dismounted at the higgledy-piggledy settlement and tied the placid horse to a tree, darkness was settling over the rooftops.

Two girls watched her approach, both with similar sharp features and tawny hair, but one appeared a few years older. Siblings, Sera assumed.

"Who are you?" the oldest girl asked. The younger curled closer, her hands clutching at the rough wool of her sister's skirts.

Sera pulled back her hood and added a dusting of stars to her dark hair. "I am Nyx, goddess of the night. Ethel is going to help me with a troublesome spirit."

The older girl snorted. The younger girl's eyes widened and her mouth made an O.

"I have a present for you. It will light your way at night." Sera reached into her satchel and pulled out a jar. Then she held it out to the younger girl, who seemed more curious. Sera tapped the side and the mist within obeyed, glowing a soft silver blue.

The young girl gasped and let go of her sister. One hand stretched out for the jar. "Are they fireflies?" she asked in wonder.

Sera shook her head. "I wouldn't trap fireflies in there. It is a magical mist. When you tap the jar, it will either glow, or stop glowing." She slid the wire handle over the child's outstretched hand.

The girl peered closer, watching the swirling mist in the jar. "Thank you, Nyx," she whispered.

Sera bit back a grin. Removing another jar from her bag, she offered it to the older girl. "I have another, if you would like one?"

"It'd be handy, I suppose. Or I could sell it." The older girl shrugged and took the jar by the handle.

Her younger sibling reached up and tapped the side, and this one glowed a pale cream like newly churned butter.

Sera nodded and carried on her way. Despite the older girl's indifference, excited chatter resumed behind her and lights flickered off and on as they played with their lanterns. Up the slope Sera trudged, tapping the remaining two lanterns alight to avoid stumbling on any of the litter creeping over the twisty paths.

Ethel waited for her, a dark shawl with a fringed edge wrapped around her bony shoulders. "Is one of them for me?" She gestured to the lanterns.

"Yes. Which colour do you prefer?" Sera held them out, one a buttery yellow, the other a pale blue.

"I'll take the yellow. My thanks." A gnarled hand took the handle.

"I will make more so that every home has at least one. It's just that creating them is rather time-consuming." She berated herself for not being able to do more, quicker. Even once she improved life for this small settlement, there were nearly a million more souls in the greater London area.

Ethel took her hand and squeezed. "That you even try is appreciated. This lot might say nothing, but we see what you do. And we remember."

"Shall we see if this restless spirit will appear for us?" Sera kept hold of Ethel's arm as the old woman picked her way down the rickety steps.

"Lead the way, oh Nyx." Ethel made a sound, half wheeze and half chuckle.

They followed a well-worn path through one side of Bunhill Fields. Once Sera found the main path, the tiny mushrooms guided their way to where the spirit seemed tethered. They stood in the glade, the trees looming over them like giant sentinels, the mausoleums pale shapes at their sides. The aged headstones were harder to perceive in the dim light, their shadows an echo of the spirits on the other side of the veil.

"This is where we saw her last night. She paced from one side of this glade to the other." Sera gestured between the copses of trees.

"Nothing to do but wait. Help an old lady to sit down." Ethel found a raised grave and Sera steadied her as she sat on the corner. Then Sera tucked her cloak underneath her, and sat on the chilled grass at Ethel's feet. In unspoken agreement, both women tapped their lanterns and doused the lights.

Once more, Sera breathed in the night. The rustle behind her a hedgehog, hunting for grubs to fill its belly. A hoot from an owl, calling to a companion. The breeze of unseen wings stirred up the night air to fan her face.

As before, the light began as a floating blob. Over time, it elongated, like a tall person unfolding their legs to touch the ground.

"Not much to her," Ethel whispered.

"I used my magic to hold her in place and help her solidify her form. Would that help again?" Sera sent a trickle to the spirit and spun it around the soul.

"Most definitely. Let's see if she wants to chat." Ethel groaned as she pushed off the tomb and stood.

The spirit turned toward them and drifted over the grass. Sera wound more strands of magic around it and the woman became clearer—long-limbed, her robe billowing out behind her. Her hair floated as though she were underwater. Her features remained vague, though, like a pencil drawing across which the artist had brushed their hand, smudging the lines.

"*Merr... dit,*" she groaned. This time she held out her hands, imploring them.

"Come on, lass, we need more than that if we are to help," Ethel said in a soft, low voice. She murmured to herself, but Sera couldn't make out the words. It was a low, encouraging noise such as you might make to a hesitant child attempting to walk.

"Merr... Mere... Meredith." The spirit managed to form the syllables. Then a shiver rippled through her form from the effort.

"Well done." Ethel nodded approvingly. "Is your name Meredith?"

The woman moaned and shook her head. "Help...Meredith."

"You need us to help Meredith?" Sera asked. She couldn't resist talking to the tormented soul.

The spirit turned to her and a wave of anguish travelled along Sera's magical strands holding the soul together.

"Yes. Help Meredith." The words were clearer now.

"It must be very important to have roused you from your slumber. But there are many people in London. How do we find your Meredith?" Ethel's voice grew weaker, and she dropped to the edge of the tomb to sit.

The spirit let out a wail and became so agitated, she broke free of Sera's magical embrace and resumed flitting back and forth. Strands of silvery light spun from her form, as though she dissolved into mist, each ribbon floating away between the trees.

"Help Meredith!" she screamed so loudly that the birds roosting above their heads took fright. Wings scattered the pearly mist and with one final, ear-piercing howl, the woman dashed at a particular tomb and then disappeared.

"Mark that one. It will be hers." Ethel gestured to where the soul had vanished.

Sera approached with her lantern and examined the old grave marker. This one was unique enough to stick in her memory. Squat and almost square, on top sat an open book. The pages were covered in moss and bird droppings. The worn lettering on the side refused to make itself clear, but she would return in daylight to find the names of the occupants.

"She was a difficult one. Been on the other side a long time, I'd say." Ethel levered herself to her feet and picked up her lantern.

The old woman staggered, as though drunk. Sera took her arm and lent support. "Did it drain you to talk to her?"

Ethel wheezed. "It's like an exchange. Something of mine for a bit of her. She needed my voice and strength to share her message. Not that I was much help to you."

Wings passed overhead with a low and steady thrum. *Something big.* Sera wondered what flying creature hunted near them tonight. It might be the same one that had scratched at Jim.

"You have given me a name and a grave. It should not be too difficult to see who rests in that tomb and find a Meredith in their family."

Sera walked Ethel back to her odd little cottage and left her with both glow lanterns. Then she returned to the dozing horse. Satisfaction flowed through her. Soon she would have a solution. Now that the spirit had passed on her message, she would stop troubling those passing through Bunhill Fields at night.

Perhaps she should ask Lord Ormsby for more nocturnal tasks. Sera rather enjoyed the solitude...and discovering the hidden layers to London only revealed beneath the inky sky.

Once more Sera slept late, ate breakfast in bed and, when she rose, returned to Bunhill Fields. The sexton waved at her as she dismounted from the horse.

"There was a godawful wailing last night. Did you dispatch it, then?" His eyes were bright with curiosity.

Had they? Somehow, she doubted that. "With the assistance of Ethel, the spirit told us I need to help someone called Meredith. I know which grave is hers and I am sure that once I find her family, we will see matters resolved and she will return peacefully to her grave."

"Well, can't say I'm complaining too much. She's scared the grave robbers away. We've had no sign of them since she's been screeching in the dark." His shoulders heaved with silent laughter.

There was an unexpected silver lining. As Sera walked the leaf-littered paths to the small glade, she considered ways to make a sort of spirit scarecrow that would shriek at grave robbers.

In the daylight, the tomb appeared picturesque. The trees behind filtered the light playing over the stone. Fallen leaves softened the edges where they piled up. Atop the piece of stone that covered the grave sat the memorial, the whole waist high and approximately three feet in width. Sera brushed a hand over the open book. The weather had erased much of the text, but it appeared to be a quote of some sort.

On the side of the tomb, names and dates were etched in lead. Time had stolen some letters, others were covered by soft grey-green lichen. Sera whispered to the affected spots, asking them to reveal the details of those who slumbered below.

Her finger caressed the words as she read them. "Lady Imogen Rushbrooke. Born 1628, died 1688."

Apart from the lord and lady, the other names were children who hadn't reached adulthood. The too-short lifespans made her heart ache. None of them was a Meredith. Sera wondered if there were children who had lived long lives, married, and presented Imogen with grandchildren. Could one of those descendants be the Meredith that had roused Imogen from the other side?

"I shall trace your family line and see what I can uncover." Sera patted the granite, when her fingers rubbed over something unusual. Peering closer, she found on the rear of the tomb three lines carved into the stone.

No. Not carved. *Scratched.* As though monstrous claws had raked over the grave marker.

"Now that is interesting," she whispered. A theory wormed into her mind and she knew just the person to ask about the odd marking. Natalie.

On returning home, Sera found the gargoyle in the strip of land behind her house. She couldn't call it a garden, as whatever had once been planted had shrivelled and died of neglect years ago. Natalie wore what Sera would describe as a working mix of women's and men's clothing. Her tweed skirt was both practical and sturdy. In length, it skimmed her boot-clad ankles. Above it she wore a man's cream shirt and a waistcoat. Boning gave the waistcoat more shape and support than a man's garment.

A coat hung over the fence that mimicked the swallow tails and cutaway front worn by men. The gargoyle insisted on making herself useful, and took it upon herself to dig the rill that would form the central part of Sera's plan for the little space. She looked up as she tossed a shovelful of soil to one side.

"You know you do not have to do this." Sera sat on the ground and scooped up a handful of soil.

Nat thrust the spade into a fresh spot. "I like having a task to do, apart from frowning at that silly man from the council. I am an earth creature and working with the soil is almost as pleasing as talking to stone."

Talking to stone. What a poetic way of putting it, as though the object was asked what shape it really wanted to be.

"Well, I appreciate your efforts. I cannot wait to start planting once we have the shape and form completed." The soil would need compost added—luckily, the mews had an endless supply of broken-down manure and straw. "I have another matter that requires your expert opinion, if I could tear you away for an hour or two."

Nat yanked a cloth free from its spot over the fence next to her coat, and wiped her palms and fingers. "Soil or stone?"

"Stone. There is a headstone with unusual scratchings on it, and I wonder if there is a way to identify what caused them." It might be nothing, but Sera would investigate every aspect of her odd task. Kitty and Abigail might know about the Rushbrooke family and their current descendants.

Having cleaned the worst of the dirt from her hands, Nat picked up her coat.

As they walked into the kitchen, Sera found Hugh helping himself to a biscuit fresh from a tray Rosie waved under his nose. A moment of guilt flashed across his face as the delicious-smelling morsel disappeared into his mouth. To save him from trying to swallow it whole and choking, Sera reached for one.

"Are these for all of us, or are you baking for Hugh exclusively?" Sera chose one with caramelised edges and blew on it before taking a nibble.

"He's always hungry, that one. Have you heard how his stomach rumbles? Some days I think it's thunder coming from above my head." Rosie set the tray on the table.

Sera smiled when Hugh blushed. "I think Mr Miles often goes without regular meals when he is tending to his patients. We should not make fun of him for putting their needs above his own."

"Needs a woman, he does, who sees him fed regularly." Rosie tutted under her breath as she moved the biscuits to a cooling rack.

Sera ate the rest of her biscuit to stop the retort percolating inside her. Between Rosie and Kitty, Hugh had no shortage of women ensuring he was fed.

"I have indeed been busy with patients. One of the tenements has whooping cough spreading, but I believe we have it under control now. I wanted to ask if you had discovered what our spirit was trying to say?" Hugh finished his biscuit, but Rosie pushed another into his palm.

"Ethel, the local aftermage, was able to assist her in making her message clear. She wants me to *help Meredith*." Sera wondered what help Meredith needed. From her conversation with Ethel, it seemed most messages were either of undying love or misplaced wills. Perhaps Meredith needed Sera's magical assistance to find lost legal papers.

"Meredith. A woman, then, not a French ocean mystery." The surgeon sounded a little disappointed that there wasn't a sea adventure involved. Or a sea monster.

"Nat is going to lend her advice about a mark on the spirit's tomb, if you have time to join us?" A knot formed in Sera's stomach as she waited for his response.

Hugh grinned, and the knot dissolved into warm, gooey treacle. "I'd be delighted. I have worked long hours the last day and night and could do with a little fresh air."

Nat had washed her hands in the sink and shrugged on her jacket as Hugh finished biscuit number two.

Elliot found them a carriage. Natalie took the seat beside Sera and Hugh sat with his back to the driver. The carriage interior shrank with two large individuals inside it, Sera wedged between them. They might need magic or a shoehorn to get them all out again.

The vehicle rattled over London's streets as a tense atmosphere grew inside the carriage. Sera searched for a topic of conversation. "When I examined the restless soul's tomb, I found curious scratches on it, almost carved into the stone. It is most unusual, and it will be interesting to hear Natalie's opinion of how they were made."

Sera glanced from gargoyle to surgeon. An uneasy air existed between them. She wondered if some argument had taken place during the time she had been unconscious after exhausting her magic, battling as Nyx.

Natalie crossed her arms and glared at Hugh. Hugh tugged at his cravat and shifted on his seat.

After a few minutes of stony silence, Hugh addressed Sera's aunt. "I must enquire, Mrs Delacour—have I done something to offend you? Were you in any way dissatisfied with my care of Lady Winyard during her recent...illness?"

"Hugh took every care of me and my recovery could not have been in better hands, I am sure, Natalie," Sera said.

Natalie huffed and leaned forward. Hugh swallowed, but held his position. Then the imposing woman...sniffed. First his arm, then his chest. She half-rose from her seat to sniff by his ear. "Huh." With this grunt in the back of her throat, she resumed her seat and nodded. "As I suspected."

She crossed her arms and gazed out the window. Sera glanced at Hugh, who shrugged.

"Could you elaborate, please, Natalie? What did you suspect about Mr Miles?" Sera asked.

"He is one of us," Nat answered without turning.

"One of us?" Sera repeated, unsure what it meant. Certainly they could have been related or twins, the gargoyle woman as tall and broad as Hugh. Most people on the street stared slack-jawed at Natalie, as though she were some curious exhibit from a travelling show.

Nat frowned at Sera and waved at Hugh. "He is a gargoyle."

Sera stared at the surgeon. How had he concealed his Unnatural state all this time? How had she never once suspected?

Hugh blustered, his mouth opening and closing in shock before he managed, "You are mistaken. Not that there is anything wrong with being such a creature, but I have no such ability, unfortunately."

Nat leaned forward and tapped Hugh's chest. "In here. I can smell it. There is gargoyle in your blood."

Five

"But—but—I cannot turn into a stone creature as you can." Hugh held up his hands and turned them over, examining them as though he might see pebbles trickling through his veins.

A gravelly laugh rolled off Nat. "You have to be full-blood to do that. You are not as big as one of our men, but you make a delicate gargoyle woman."

Sera sucked on her lips to stop the laughter bubbling up inside her. "You *were* very fetching as Lady Zedlitz, Hugh," she managed to say.

"Are you saying one of my parents was a gargoyle?" He dropped his hands to his knees, and a frown crinkled his forehead.

"You are no half-breed and the trace is faint, but humans live such brief lives. It comes from someone more removed than your mother or father. This is why you are a good doctor. Caring for and protecting people is in our nature." Nat shrugged and returned to the passing scenery.

Sera considered Natalie's pronouncement. Now that she had made the connection between Hugh and the stony Unnaturals, she could see similarities. "It seems you were called to be a surgeon by your blood, just as mine made me a mage. This could also explain your size, Hugh. And perhaps why you were able to touch me without much harm when I coursed with magic."

He rubbed one hand over his jaw. "Physical characteristics do manifest in families. But I am not sure how it helps when your temper is up?"

Sera grinned. It was why she had asked Natalie to act as a chaperone to keep Lord Ormsby at bay. "Being impervious to magic is a gargoyle trait."

"If having such an ancestor means I can aid you when required, despite the sparks flaring over your skin, then I am most indebted to them. Although from the experiments I have conducted, it only gives a slight advantage in such situations. I can attest that your magic shot through me rather effectively that first day at court." Humour sparkled in his eyes.

"I am grateful if the trace of gargoyle in your blood lessened any harm to you. How fascinating that such traits are carried through descendants of Unnaturals, rather like magic in aftermages." How many walked the streets of London while those who passed them were unaware of what lurked under their skin? Then a chill washed over her as she recalled Hugh saying that some who called themselves scientists captured Unnaturals and studied them by performing terrible experiments.

"Perhaps one day, we will study such things openly, and without causing harm to the subjects. I wonder if it makes any difference which parent is the Unnatural as to how offspring are altered?" His gaze went to the roof of the carriage as thoughts flowed through his mind, each casting a different expression across his face. His brows went up, or down, or knitted together. His lips pursed, then broke into a grin, only to be sucked back in again.

Sera studied him as he pondered a study of Unnaturals and warmth settled in her limbs. She appreciated a little more Hugh's solid and dependable presence. Learning that a gargoyle lurked somewhere in his family tree made him all the more intriguing to her. What would it be like to spend a lifetime beside such a man, with his curious and caring nature?

At the cemetery there was no sign of the sexton, and they strolled along the tree-lined paths in companionable silence. Nat stopped now and then to touch a gravestone or caress a mausoleum. Almost as though she greeted an old friend with each type of stone she passed.

In the sheltered glade with its assembled tombs and gravestones, Sera walked to the squat piece of moss-covered stone with its open book on top. "This is the one. Lady Imogen Rushbrooke. But this is what caught my eye." She bent down and gestured to one corner on the back, where three slashes marred the stone.

"This is not recent," Natalie said as she peered closer.

"That is what I thought. The marks have weathered and have dirt and moss in them. I am more curious as to how they were made in the stone." It had to be significant that the restless spirit had come from a tomb with the odd scratches.

"Chisel and hammer." Natalie mimicked holding the tools and chipping out the lines.

"Oh. You think the stonemason made these accidentally?" Disappointment plunged through Sera. Here she'd thought the marks were another layer to the mystery, and it turned out they were simply a mistake made by a careless or inexperienced stonemason. Or perhaps the person who commissioned the tomb thought to play a prank on visitors to the cemetery. How many people had done as she had, and traced the marks and wondered what manner of creature had lashed out at the tomb on its way past?

"Possibly." Nat splayed her fingers and trailed a tip in each line as she drew her palm across it. Her hand didn't match up to the scratches. She curled her hand into a fist and then a soft crackle came as stone wrapped itself around the limb.

Sera gasped as flesh turned to granite before her eyes.

Hugh exclaimed, "I say!"

Natalie extended her gargoyle arm, now longer and thicker than her human one. Each finger ended in a curved claw. She tried again, brushing her hand over the marks, but still her digits didn't easily match. After a long moment of silence staring at rock and limb, she shook her arm, and the stone broke into pebbles that fell away and dissolved to reveal flesh once more. "It was a male."

"A gargoyle did that?" Sera had to confirm the statement.

"Yes. When the tomb was new." Nat laid both hands on the open book and bowed her head.

"Oh. So not relevant to the disturbances happening here at night." Bother. Sera had hoped the mark was significant, given the tomb was the centre of the lights and noises.

Natalie shrugged. "Who knows? One of us passed this way and, for some reason, left his mark on the tomb."

"Could it have been an accident?" If a gargoyle swung their arms, did they slice any rock or stone they touched?

This time, Natalie shook her head. "To leave a sign such as this is deliberate."

"A sign of what, though?" Hugh asked.

"It is normally done as a warning that the territory is protected by a particular clan, to show possession." Natalie stared at the surrounding mausoleums and tombs.

Hugh rubbed his chin. "I believe bears do something similar."

"I have examined the other tombs and headstones here and found nothing similar." Sera considered and discarded several ideas. The most likely being that a hundred years ago, a gargoyle had marked the tomb to say he was in residence in the area. "Are there any London gargoyles we could ask?"

"We are much reduced in numbers. I believe there are a few members of the London clan left. I have not encountered them on this stay, but will see if I can find them." Natalie walked to the front of the tomb and read the inscription.

"There may be some connection to the Rushbrooke family." Sera had to find the descendants of Lady Rushbrooke. First, she would consult her mage genealogy. If any trace of magic flowed in their veins, they would be easy to locate. Then she would ask Kitty and Abigail. One of them would have a copy of *Debrett's Peerage*, which would have information on the current Lord Rushbrooke. He might know of any Meredith connected to the family.

THAT EVENING, Sera stared at her reflection. Tonight's nocturnal adventure required a different outfit, and breeches would most definitely not be allowed. Sera held still as Vicky put the finishing touches to her hair.

"You look perfect, milady." The maid stepped back and surveyed her work with a critical eye.

"Thank you, Vicky. You have a way with hair that is far superior to my magic." Most of her hair was swept up, but Vicky had artfully dangled a few curls around Sera's ears and teased out tendrils to soften her forehead.

While dressing, she realised why the name of the grateful lord who provided Ethel with tea sounded familiar. Lord Thornton was high on Abigail's list of potential suitors. It settled some of her nerves to have one topic to discuss with him—where he sourced his particular blend of tea.

The Crawley family carriage collected her and deposited her outside the address at exactly the expected hour. A sigh heaved through Sera as she glanced up at the mansion's facade. The more she saw of society with its rules and restrictions, the less she wanted to be a part of it. She didn't understand how Abigail could be content with a life confined to a gilded cage. Or was it because a bird that never learned to fly didn't know it possessed wings and could escape?

Sera wanted to have adventures and live by her own rules. To that end, she had set Mr Napier, Kitty's father, to negotiating the purchase of a plot of land out in Westbourne Green. Imagining a sanctuary in the remote location, where she could be whoever she wanted to be, gave her the strength to carry on. It would be her retreat, where she could rest and reflect after an adventure.

Once shown inside the Crawley mansion, she found a small group of no more than eight convened in the drawing room. At least if she broke some unwritten rule of polite company, there would be fewer people to report upon it. Although she was already inclined to view Thornton favourably due to his supplying the old woman with a monthly delivery of tea. What had been in the missing will, she wondered, that he bestowed such a gift on the aftermage?

"Lady Winyard!" Abigail took her arm and leaned in close. "I told you it would be an intimate affair. The earl will not join any company larger than a dozen," she murmured as she led Sera deeper into the room.

They stopped where a trio of men nursed their drinks. Among them was Lord Loburn, who smiled at Sera in recognition. Excellent. She would have one intelligent person to talk to this evening should the earl prove lacking in brains. Conversation halted, and the men turned their attention to Abigail as she and Sera approached.

"Lady Winyard, allow me to present the Earl of Thornton." Abigail gestured to a gentleman of average height, with sandy hair and intense brown eyes flecked with amber that caught the reflection from the gold rims of his spectacles.

"Lord Thornton." Sera managed to conjure a slight smile. The earl's name appeared on two lists—the one prepared by the council and the one prepared by Abigail. Which meant two interested parties to disappoint when she crossed off his name or did something to offend him.

"And this is the Viscount Helensvale." That introduction ended on a breathy note.

Sera schooled her features not to react. Before her stood the trophy her friend had claimed. Her yet-to-be-announced betrothed. The man who would, when his father died, make Abigail a duchess. With dark blond hair and blue eyes, he had the fleshy appearance that would run to fat like his father. At least he was taller than the duke. Sera only hoped he had a better disposition and was worthy of her friend.

Introductions over, they engaged in polite conversation about inconsequential topics until dinner was announced.

"I hope Miss Napier is well?" Lord Loburn enquired as he took Sera's arm to walk through to dinner.

It took no magic to see the marquis was smitten with Kitty. "She is well, thank you. I shall tell her that you enquired after her." *And prod her into hosting an evening you can attend*, Sera added to herself.

Through Abigail's machinations, the earl was seated on Sera's right. Since her friend and the council insisted on thrusting potential suitors at her, Sera decided to interview him for the position. No point in feigning interest only to discover he also shared Lord Kenwood's opinion that she was beneath his notice due to her common birth.

"Tell me, Lord Thornton, what is your position on education for everyone?" Sera asked as the soup was served.

He waited until the footman moved on with the soup tureen before answering. "I believe all children would benefit from being able to read, write, and do simple arithmetic. That is why I pay for the teacher and school in the village near my estate."

"Really? Do you allow both boys and girls to attend school?" Sera could practically hear Kitty's murmured approval in her head at his reply.

"Of course." A frown wrinkled his brow at her question. "A woman cannot run a household properly if she cannot balance her accounts. She should not be reliant upon another to do her sums. Such a creature might find herself taken advantage of by unscrupulous staff, to say nothing of merchants and tradesmen."

So far he had fielded her questions with good grace. Now she would dive into more troublesome areas. "And what of a wife who works and does not have the time to run a household?"

He lowered his spoon and smiled at her. It softened his features; otherwise, his jaw was a little too sharp. "An extraordinary situation, to be sure. But I would rather have a wife who engages her mind and has skills of use to our king. Too many spend their days embroidering handkerchiefs and do little else. I can always hire a trustworthy housekeeper. It is much harder to find a companion with whom I can converse during long winter evenings."

Sera's hand tightened on the soup spoon. The earl's opinions seemed not inconsistent with her own. He was somewhat handsome in a friendly way. His appeal was much enhanced by his talk of possessing a well-stocked library. He might actually be a viable candidate for a husband. If she could stomach the idea of matrimony.

She took a sip of wine for fortification. There had to be some defect in his character or beliefs. Some impediment she could point to later in her hushed conversation with Abigail. Try as she might, she could not find an obvious fault. Nor was he malformed. Blast.

"I have an odd question, if you would humour me."

Warmth and intelligence simmered in his eyes. "Anything, Lady Winyard."

"Where do you source your tea?" Sera leaned back in her chair as the last course was cleared.

"Tea?" He frowned and tilted his head as though he had misheard her.

"Yes, tea." Sera lowered her voice, in case he did not want everyone at the table to know of his association with the crone. "I met an aftermage the other day. An elderly woman called Ethel. We shared a lovely cup of tea, and she told me you deliver a small quantity to her cottage every month."

"Ah." His eyes lit up again. "She did me a great service. A portion of tea seems modest compensation in return. I have shipping interests and specialise in importing tea from China and India. That one is a blend of my own design. I began with pure black tea and then added rose hip, hibiscus, marigold, rose petals, bergamot oil, and a dash of citrus."

Sera blinked. And here she thought she brewed complicated potions. She had no idea so much went into tea. "I did not know one cup of tea held so many different ingredients."

The earl became animated and conversation flowed as he told Sera of his travels to India to see for himself how teas were harvested and blended. He spent as many hours concocting unique blends as Sera did working on spells or potions. Before she knew it, Abigail rose from her seat and announced that the ladies would join the gentlemen for coffee in the drawing room, since they were so few in number.

The earl took Sera's hand and rubbed his thumb over her knuckles. "I have much enjoyed our conversation, Lady Winyard. I look forward to continuing it."

"As do I, Lord Thornton. If you will excuse me, I should like a private word with Lady Abigail." Sera joined her friend, and they stood to one side as the other guests filed into the adjoining drawing room.

Abigail whispered against her ear, "You seem rather engrossed with the earl."

A smile came to Sera's lips. "He is rather passionate about tea, though I admit I find no other fault in him."

Abigail let out a teeny *eek* of excitement. "I *knew* he would be the perfect match for you. Now, let us have our coffee so I can savour my victory."

"Of course."

The perfect match? While Sera agreed that the earl was pleasant on first meeting, the idea of marriage made a wave of sadness crash over her. She would trade her weight in tea for another midnight adventure with Hugh. The surgeon might not own a shipping company or have a title, but he made tingles that had nothing to do with magic race over her skin.

Six

Every night, before she went to bed, Sera pulled out the ensorcelled paper she had found in Lord Branvale's house and hoped for a message from his secret correspondent. Tonight, just as on all the previous nights since she had written the words saying no one would control her, it remained blank.

As she climbed into bed, questions nibbled at her. Should she have started with an introduction? Or asked them straightaway *What or who is Nereus?* rather than venting her frustration at the secrets bound tight around her? She resolved to wait a few more days. Then she would consider a different approach.

A wave of her hand extinguished the light. Dark settled over the room and the shadows deepened. Nyx was unafraid of the dark, but many people thought danger and evil lurked in dim corners. If she were to become a nocturnal creature at the Mage Council's request, she must fully embrace that role. Nyx needed to prowl the streets, both to alleviate the fears of the people and to hunt out anything, or anyone, who meant them harm.

With that idea trickling through her mind, Sera surrendered to sleep.

THE NEXT AFTERNOON, Sera flopped down on a settee in the Napier parlour. She had called together the Kestrels to discuss how to find the Meredith she was supposed to help. "Do you have a copy of Debrett's latest publication? I am trying to find Lord Rushbrooke."

"I believe there will be one in the library." Kitty rose to fetch the book.

Voices from the foyer heralded the arrival of Lady Abigail and Hugh. The surgeon flashed Sera a warm smile in greeting as she rose to kiss Abigail's cheek.

"What has happened to Lieutenant Powers?" she asked. Usually the cavalryman accompanied Hugh, when he was not carrying out quiet investigations for the king. She missed the lieutenant's insights, and he had a dry humour that kept the mood of a room from becoming too serious.

"*Captain* Powers now—his talent is being recognised. Unfortunately, we shall have to tackle this mystery without him. The army has sent him off somewhere on a posting." Hugh waited for the women to be seated and then took the chair opposite Sera.

"I hope he will return to us soon. I do enjoy seeing how he has styled his moustache. I suspect he uses a magical oil to help it keep its shape." Sera relaxed in her seat and Abigail delicately lowered herself beside Sera.

Kitty returned clutching a large book with a distinctive red cover. Two footmen followed, one carrying a tea tray and another a stand of cakes and savouries. Kitty placed the book in Sera's outstretched hands and then directed her staff to set the tray and stand on the low table between the settees.

Abigail pointed to the book and nudged Sera with her shoulder. Mischief glinted in her eyes as she asked, "Why do you need a copy of De Bretts, Seraphina? Looking up the earl already?"

"Oh. No. I'm trying to find Lord Rushbrooke." But now that Abigail mentioned it, she would find the earl's entry afterward. Since she had the book in her hands, of course, not because she had any interest in the size of his endowment.

"What earl would Sera be looking for in there?" Kitty asked as she poured tea and cups were handed around. Sera's was placed on the round side table nestled against the settee.

"The Earl of Thornton. He and Sera were rather taken with each other last night. I always considered him a much better match for her than Lord Kenwood." Abigail smiled over the brim of her teacup.

Hugh's eyes widened. His cup rattled on its saucer. Kitty almost choked on a bite of cake.

"He was pleasant to talk to and open-minded on the subject of education. Lord Loburn was there too, Kitty. He asked after you. Is it not time you hosted your own evening here?" Sera breezed on past the topic of the earl. Discussing marital prospects in front of Hugh made her stomach rebel—as though she walked past a butcher's discard bin on a hot summer's day.

Kitty dropped a spoonful of sugar into her tea and took a sip to banish her fit of coughing. "Indeed! I shall host a salon and only invite intelligent and interesting people. Like Fitzfey and Loburn. And you, Hugh, of course. If this earl can hold up his end of a conversation, he may also attend so I can scrutinise him. In fact, now that I think on people to invite, there is an aftermage painter that Hugh might wish to meet. Apparently, he does extraordinarily lifelike paintings."

"Such an aftermage could certainly bring anatomical illustrations to life, which would aid in teaching when no cadavers are available." Hugh had regained his composure after hearing of Sera's evening with the earl. He carefully plucked a savoury from the three-tiered stand.

"I hear the artist's nudes practically breathe. I shall invite him and ask that he bring one or two to show us." Kitty balanced a plate with a slice of cake on top of the book in Sera's hands.

This time it was Abigail's teacup that rattled. "Really, Katherine. You go too far. Society would never allow a lady to attend such an event. Men clustered around nude paintings? Why, her reputation would be in ruins."

"I am sorry, Abigail. I did not mean to offend. I forget that you and I are on different sides of society. I don't give a fig for what anyone thinks and thanks to my father's situation, I do not need to. Frankly, I don't know how you stand the constant scrutiny you are under without wanting to scream." Kitty reached over and took Abigail's hand.

A slight frown marred Abigail's forehead. "Screaming is most definitely not allowed. As to how, why, it is what I was raised to do from birth. I know my place and I obey the rules stitched into the fabric holding our society together."

Sera squirmed. She couldn't help but think the comment about knowing one's place had been directed at her. "Perhaps you could invite Lady Plimmerton, Kitty? She could act as chaperone for the younger women in attendance?"

"I'm sure Father would appreciate her inclusion.

They have been friends for many years. I shall mull over exactly who to invite." Kitty glanced at Abigail from under lowered lashes, but said no more about exhibiting lifelike nudes.

Sera took a bite of cake before setting the plate to one side. She flipped another page in the book and found the lord related to the cemetery's restless soul. "Ah. Here is Rushbrooke." She scanned the tight lines of dense text, giving the current lord's date of birth, his siblings, his predecessors, and details of the extent of his estate and holdings. "There's no mention of any Meredith among his siblings or children."

"Do you even know this Meredith is a relative?" Kitty asked.

Sera closed the book and tossed it to the table. Then she picked up her teacup. "No. It could be the name of the family dog, for all I know. But given Lady Imogen died a hundred years ago, *something* must have stirred her into activity now."

Abigail nibbled a sliver of cake in such a delicate manner that she reminded Sera of a mouse savouring a morsel of cheese. "Do spirits have an awareness of the passage of time? What if she does not know how long she's been dead and this Meredith is also deceased? It might have been a sister or child of hers who was struck by accident or disease around the time she died, and she thinks assistance might save their life."

Sera hadn't thought of that. She would need to

pay another call on Ethel and ask. "I have no idea. Time might move differently for them, the way it does between the mortal and Fae realms. From the inscription on Imogen's tomb, three children who did not reach adulthood were buried with her, but none was called Meredith. All I can do is start with Lord Rushbrooke. We can expand our enquiries from there."

"You cannot call on Lord Rushbrooke uninvited to go shaking his family tree." Abigail stared at Sera. "I shall ask Mother if we are acquainted, or when he might be found in a setting appropriate to such questions."

Sera managed a smile. If Captain Powers had been assisting, they could call on the lord uninvited. But the king was not directing this investigation. She would simply have to try to work within the confines of what society allowed. A day or two would make no difference when the spirit had slumbered for so many decades. That also gave her time to question Ethel more about departed souls and how they perceived time. "Thank you, Abigail. That would be appreciated."

"Will the earl be calling on you soon?" With one matter sorted, Abigail returned to her favourite topic —marrying off Sera.

"We only dined last night. Give the poor man time to ponder my many faults and make his apologies as to why he never wants to see me again." Sera's gaze darted to Hugh. She would need time alone with him. To reassure him this was no more than a ruse, such as when she had allowed the Austrian diplomat Lord Zedlitz to visit his intended, Inge, at her house.

Then a horrible idea settled in a corner of her mind. What if Lord Ormsby caught wind of her finding one name on his list tolerable? The banns would be read before she could voice any objection.

Kitty laughed. "He's not poor, that one. Quite the contrary. There was a nasty argument brewing between him and his brothers over the estate, the family shipping company, and their tea plantations. While he inherited the title, his siblings claimed the investments had been left to them. Then the will was discovered proving the majority of it went to Thornton."

That would explain Ethel's involvement. "Rich or impoverished, it is a man's mind and actions that matter more to me." She longed to grumble aloud—why couldn't she live a spinster's life with Kitty?—but they had already outraged Abigail enough for one visit.

"You do not want to leave him free to consider his options for too long. Once the matrons hear he is in town, he will be inundated with invitations. I shall do what I can to let it be known you have a pre-existing interest in him," Abigail said.

"Good Lord, Abigail, you make him sound like a piece of property. Next, you will be telling us about his easements." Kitty winked at Sera.

Abigail paled, and Sera's heart ached for her friend. Her life was bound tight by the expectations of her family and society. Her every action was scrutinised, and she carried the weight of having to make a grand match.

"Whatever unfolds with the earl, I could never outshine Abigail. Do we not have a grand wedding to look forward to soon?"

A smile broke over Abigail's face and transformed her worry into stunning beauty. "You do indeed. It has been announced to both our families, and is now official. I will be a duchess one day!" She thrust out her left hand to show off her ring. In an ornate filigree setting, a sapphire in the middle flashed blue fire.

Sera pushed her plate and cup to the table with a waft of magic so she could hug Abigail. Then she admired the ring, which had an enchantment on the stone to make cool fire flicker within its depths. "How exciting! I hope you will allow me to provide some magical entertainment on the day?"

"Oh, yes. Grandfather will be in charge, naturally, but it would be wonderful if the two of you put your heads together. I so wish to marry under a shower of pink rose petals. And they must sparkle like pink diamonds." Abigail sighed and her features softened.

Sera exchanged an arched eyebrow with Kitty. They each had their own peculiar dreams and interests. Sera wanted nothing more than to dirty her hands in an expansive garden. Abigail desired a fairy-tale match blessed by the *ton*. If that was what their friend's heart desired, they would do their best to bring it to life.

Discussing the entertainments for the nuptials would give Sera another reason to visit old Lord Rowan. She wanted to consult with him about the runes on the Fae bracelet and to ask a pointed question about Lord Branvale and the mage genealogy.

They chatted about the forthcoming wedding until Hugh rose to make his apologies.

"If you will excuse me, I still have many more patients to visit today and I do not think I can offer any assistance in tracking down relatives of this Lord Rushbrooke."

"I should also be on my way. Mother and I have many calls to make and we are to discuss my trousseau." Abigail's eyes shone brightly with excitement.

The group was drifting toward the door, when Abigail plucked a scandal sheet from the sideboard and held it between her thumb and forefinger, as though she were disposing of a mouse. Her head tilted as she read the headline. Then, when something caught her curiosity, she held the paper more firmly in both hands. "See here, Seraphina. I told you that your terrifying performance would soon be forgotten in a new scandal."

Sera smothered a grin. She rather liked being labelled *terrifying* and intended to adopt a darker persona to thumb her nose at the council. "I cannot imagine what has occurred to displace my fabulous rendition of Nyx from their pages."

Abigail dropped the paper on the sideboard and tapped it with a folded glove. "They are revelling in the misfortune of Lord Hillborne. Apparently his child has disappeared, and rumours are circulating that his wife is responsible. She is to be brought to London to stand trial. There are whispers that she will hang if she is found guilty."

"It is rather a leap from a missing child to stringing up a mother for murder, is it not?" Kitty picked up the sheet and examined the story. "It says Lady Hillborne was found crying by a lake, clutching the little girl's doll."

A chill washed over Sera. What would drive a mother to commit such a heinous act? "Surely both parties involved deserve our pity, not to be the subject of gossip and speculation."

"Some women fall into a deep state of despair after giving birth and struggle to reclaim their joy in life or their children. If Lady Hillborne was so affected, she should be treated for her condition, not hanged." Hugh took his hat and coat from the footman.

Kitty snorted. "It is no surprise that women are depressed after popping out one child after another. Some women are lashed to that wheel and cannot escape except through the mercy of death."

Abigail sucked in a sharp breath. "Really, Katherine. The joy of motherhood is a noblewoman's finest contribution to society."

"Good Lord, I hope not. I would rather be known for my mind or actions than my ability to push a baby into the world." Kitty fairly bristled as she stared at Abigail.

Abigail's hands tightened on her gloves, and her knuckles turned white.

Sera stepped in to defuse the situation before one woman called out the other. "I'm sure Kitty is concerned for the working-class women, Abigail. Those who do not have nurseries with nannies to care for their offspring. They carry a heavy burden, and their husbands are often away long hours to earn sufficient income to support their families." A bare-breasted duel between them would definitely be front-page fodder for the newspapers, and offer the Hillborne family relief from being dissected by all and sundry.

"Speaking of the health and well-being of lower-class women," Hugh said, "Mr Fleece, the apothecary, is taking on a young woman to train up in such matters. I have agreed to start her education to relieve him of any...embarrassment about the topic. But I would appreciate any input or guidance you could offer?" Hugh turned to Sera as they walked into the foyer.

"I would be happy to help in whatever way I can." Sera embraced both Kitty and Abigail before leaving the house in Hugh's company, discussing potions and remedies that would be most urgently required by women.

She barely noticed how far they had walked until he stopped outside a building where the cries of fractious children squeezed through the gaps in boards and windows.

"I am needed here. But I will call upon you soon, to hear how your investigation progresses." He glanced around at the busy street, then took her hand and placed a kiss in the centre of her palm.

Sera curled her fingers around the kiss as though he had given her an expensive jewel. "I shall endeavour to have something to report."

When he had gone inside she opened her hand. A silver disc shimmered in her grasp.

Her magic had given his kiss a physical form.

SEVEN

The next day, Natalie Delacour sought out Sera in her study. "I have found one of the London clan. Warin has agreed to talk to you." She thrust a piece of paper at Sera with the name of a church scrawled on it, and instructions to meet in the bell tower.

"Thank you, Nat. Will you be coming with me?" Sera rolled the piece of paper between her fingers.

Nat snorted. "I have work to do. I want to finish the trench in the garden." The gargoyle stalked back down the hall.

"I'll go on my own, then," Sera said to an empty room. She finished weighing ingredients for a potion and set them to brew over a cold blue flame.

In the foyer, she flung the grey cloak around her shoulders. "I'm heading out!" she called to Elliot, who emerged from the kitchen stairwell.

The footman waved and turned back to do whatever it was he got up to when she didn't need him. Sera flung open the front door to find her favourite surgeon frozen in time on her doorstep, his hand raised to knock.

His name flew to her lips. "Hugh."

He beamed at her, then a tiny wrinkle appeared on his brow. "I wanted to see you, but it appears I have picked an inopportune moment."

"Not at all. I am about to meet a gargoyle. Do you wish to come with me?" It would give her an opportunity to explain the situation with the earl. Not that she knew what the situation was, exactly. At times, she thought herself an old woman, circumstances forcing her to grow up fast. At other times, she seemed a newborn struggling with new and emerging feelings.

"Of course. Where are we bound?" He crooked his arm and curiosity glimmered in his eyes.

Sera handed him the slip of paper and linked her arm in his. "To find St Barlow's church. But let us find a carriage first. It looks like rain."

Above their heads, storm clouds gathered, their undersides painted in various hues of grey shaded to black. The wind tugged at the hem of her cloak and carried a chill edge. On the main road, Hugh hailed them a hackney, and they clambered in as rain began to fall. Fat, heavy drops dappled the rumps of the horses and pattered against the roof.

A heavy silence settled between them, and Hugh pressed himself to the far side of the seat.

Sera swallowed and tackled the topic brewing in the silence. "I wanted to talk to you about Abigail's statement that Lord Thornton and I are much taken with each other." The words dried up in her throat.

Hugh turned pained eyes in her direction. "I have no claim on you, Sera, and know both king and council will dictate who you are to marry. But…I cannot help how I feel, and only wish you to find happiness."

You! she wanted to scream. *You are the one who makes me happy. You challenge me, protect me, spark magic within me, and I want nothing more than to embark on grand adventures with you beside me.*

But still she held back. Not yet ready to say the words out loud. Not wanting to give him hope when so much was yet unknown. Instead, she nodded and her eyes misted. Blinking away the tears, Sera drew a deep breath. "I think I can keep the council guessing for a while yet. That buys us time, Hugh, to be together. I will find a way to follow my heart, once I determine what it wants."

A sad smile washed over his face. "I do not doubt that you will find a way to outfox them."

She took his hand. "Your friendship is a rare and precious thing to me. Please tell me I have not placed it in jeopardy? I could not bear to lose you." His tender kiss turned corporeal by her magic was a treasure greater than any jewel. She had punched a hole in the uneven piece of silver and wore it on a long chain around her neck.

He leaned over and placed a gentle kiss on her forehead. "I am eternally yours. Nothing will change that."

The mood lightened, and Sera vowed to outwit the council. When she gave her heart fully to Hugh, no one would stand in her way.

On the streets, Londoners pulled hats down low, and clutched coats around them as the rain's intensity built. By the time they arrived at their destination, jumped down from the vehicle, and paid the driver, it was pouring as though the sky had a lake's worth of surplus water to drop in a short amount of time. It tumbled in sheets from overflowing gutters and rivulets criss-crossed through dirt on the pavement.

Sera created a shield above them and Hugh stared up as rain pounded on the invisible roof over their heads and then ran to the edge to plunge to the ground.

"That's very convenient," Hugh said.

Sera grinned. "Yes, my most valuable talents include heating cold tea and repelling rain."

They stared up at a rather derelict old church, the stone blackened by coal soot. One double-height door hung at an angle, creating a permanent gap at the top. The bottom of the door was wedged partly open as the weight of the wood scraped the floor and refused to budge.

Hugh put his shoulder to the wood and heaved to force it open enough to admit his body. He blocked the hole, glancing around before he moved and held out a hand to Sera. Years of accumulated debris littered the interior—dirt blown through the open door, litter dropped from people seeking refuge within, and broken pews strewn across the floor.

"I'm guessing no one attends anymore," Hugh murmured as he paused at the end of the aisle to stare at the stained glass window.

The arched scene depicted a woman surrounded by grazing sheep. A watchful deer stood at her side and she had one hand on its head, as though in blessing. The scene glowed with rich reds, vibrant yellows, and muted greens despite the gloomy day outside.

"Aftermage glass," Sera said, walking closer. "They can infuse it with an internal light source, so light filters through the glass even in the dark."

"At least the vandals have left it alone, although it seems pews have been sacrificed to make a fire." He kicked a charred timber. Several pews were missing from one side and a fire pit had been created in the gap.

"When you have no roof over your head, a church is often the last place of sanctuary." One under construction had sheltered Sera as a baby while her father negotiated with the Mage Council.

"Where are we to meet this gargoyle?" Hugh reached down and righted a pew, setting it back in line with its fellows on either side.

Sera pointed up. "The bell tower. There will be stairs somewhere."

It didn't take them long to find the hidden door.

The panel had been warped by a touch of damp and the wood jutted out from the rest of the wall. Hugh prised it open with both hands and a tickle of magic from Sera. She swallowed her comments that her magic could have moved any impediments. She rather enjoyed watching the muscles in his back bunch as he manhandled the stubborn door. What a shame the day was cold and wet and he wore a cumbersome greatcoat. How magnificent the display would be, if it were a hot summer's day and he wore only a shirt and waistcoat.

When Hugh ducked inside the narrow alcove and placed one foot on the first stair, she intervened. There came a point when, for their own safety, she had to remind him of her abilities. "I think I should go first, as the expected visitor. I would not like to risk your finding an enraged gargoyle in the belfry."

He frowned, but pressed himself to the cold stone to allow her to take the lead. With the door to the alcove pushed shut, there was no source of light and the stairwell resembled a well shaft with only the faint promise of light far above. Sera extracted two glow jars from her satchel and handed one to Hugh.

The narrow stairs wound in a tight spiral. The treads were angled at a steep incline, and Sera placed each foot carefully in case she fell. Although with the surgeon's large form practically wedged in behind her, he acted as a safety net. A fact which probably alleviated some of his concern about letting her go first.

"I'm not sure about this," Hugh muttered.

"Neither of us can fly, so this is the only way to the top." She paused to catch her breath. There were no windows in the thick stone walls enclosing them. The glow lamps emitted their bluish light, adding to the feeling of being in a well and moving through water.

After a few moments of rest, they carried on. Eventually, they reached the solid oak door at the top that opened to the belfry. The square chamber had a soaring and steeply angled ceiling. A brass bell large enough to swallow Hugh hung above them, its rope dangling, waiting for strong hands to tug on it. The pierced openings to allow the sound to carry out to the community didn't start until eight feet above their heads and afforded them protection from the wind buffeting the tall spire.

It also appeared to be empty of anyone else.

"I am Seraphina Winyard and need to talk to Warin of the London clan," she called, unsure how one summoned a gargoyle.

A rustle came from above, and a shadow dropped over them. The gargoyle folded his monstrous wings to fit in the space. In height, he towered over Hugh and was easily twice as broad. Carved veins stood out on his exposed forearms. His stone form was clad in chiselled breeches and an open shirt. His feet were bare, with curling claws in the place of toes. Eyes of slate grey stared at them. Then a frown crackled across his forehead.

His head swung to Hugh, and he took a threatening pace forward. Hugh recoiled, his shoulders hitting the enclosing wall. Sera raised her hands, sparks swirling in her palms as she readied herself to defend her friend.

But instead of dealing a blow, the gargoyle sniffed. Then he grunted in a manner they had seen before. "Delacour was right. Our clan runs deep in your veins."

"Your clan?" Hugh's tight shoulders relaxed when it became clear he wasn't under attack.

"Your blood is laced with that of Tatius, once the leader of the Londinium gargoyles." The gargoyle stalked back to stand under the bell. He crossed his mighty arms.

Hugh grinned as he peeled himself off the wall. "Tatius. If my Latin serves, I believe that is some reference to being honourable."

Only Hugh would be excited to learn the origins of the gargoyle taint in his blood. But it was an infectious enthusiasm and erased Sera's weariness from climbing all those steps. How on earth did the bell-ringers do it numerous times a day? Or was that one reason why the church had fallen into disrepair? She imagined fed-up bell-ringers moving to churches with easier access. Some had the ropes dangling down to ground level.

"Delacour said you wanted to ask about a grave?" The gargoyle's voice had the depth and clarity of a bell.

Apparently, gargoyles didn't engage much in small talk. She had noticed that about Natalie, too. They could almost be taken as rude or blunt, if one did not appreciate their taciturn natures.

"Yes. There is a tomb at Bunhill Fields with a rather distinctive set of claw marks in the stone. Natalie said they were made by a gargoyle, and I wondered if you might know who was responsible, or why it was done." She clasped her hands together to keep them warm.

He turned his back to them and a shiver ran over his mottled wings. Silence was met by the drip of rain against the belfry and moist air circled down to them. They waited so long that Sera's toes tingled in protest at holding one position. Just as she suspected he did not know and could not answer her question, a sigh heaved through his barrel-shaped chest.

"I could not claim her in life. But I did so in death," he rasped.

That sounded like an intrigue worthy of further investigation. Sera recalled the names inscribed on the tomb. A long-ago lord, his wife, and some of their children who had not reached adulthood. She took a guess at *who* and murmured, "Imogen."

The creature reached out and took hold of the bell. A single, gentle note rolled from the brass as the clapper brushed across the mouth. "We were forbidden to marry. Her family forced her to wed Rushbrooke when they discovered...her condition."

Sera stepped forward and laid her hand on a

granite forearm. "I am sorry that neither law nor prejudice allowed you to follow your heart."

He stared at her hand and then plucked it from his arm to cradle it in his huge palm. "I watched. Imogen found much joy in our son. Alexander grew into a robust man who lived to be one hundred years old."

Hugh's eyebrows shot up. "One hundred? That is an extraordinary lifespan for a human. I believe only turtles and elephants reach a similar age. I wonder if it has to do with your tough physique?"

While the tale of Imogen's son was fascinating and rather sad, it didn't solve Sera's problem with restless spirits. "Imogen has awakened and her spirit is uneasy. Do you have any idea why? Is it perhaps some anniversary?"

The name Alexander did not appear on the tomb, and given he had lived an exceptionally long time, perhaps his recent demise had distressed his mother.

"I will visit. That might placate her." The gargoyle stroked a stone finger across the back of Sera's hand, and she wondered how long it had been since someone had touched him. She found his body unexpectedly warm, like stone that had absorbed the heat of the sun. Rather than being coarse or rough, his skin had a velvety texture.

"She managed to say *help Meredith*. Is that someone tied to either of you?" It might be a close friend or valued retainer.

The wind changed direction and drove the rain

through the arches. Sera conjured a barrier over their heads, and as before, droplets dribbled to the edges and fell to the floor.

"Meredith," he repeated, and arched his neck. With his face turned to the bell, he closed his eyes.

Sera assumed he was searching his memory and waited for the gargoyle to share his intelligence. Hugh edged closer and studied the folded wings, his hand reaching out, but not touching, the clawed middle joint.

The wings shook, as though aware they were being scrutinised. "Our line has splintered over the shorter human generations. I believe Meredith is our great-granddaughter. I do not know why she requires help. She does not live in London and is outside my reach."

Not in London? Meredith could be anywhere in England, then, or possibly abroad. "Thank you for what you have told us. At least I know I am searching for the descendant of you and Imogen." Sera would need to visit Lord Rushbrooke after all, and see if he knew the whereabouts of his cousin. She hoped she wouldn't have to shake too many branches on his family tree to find the right twig.

"Do we have to go back down the stairs?" Hugh eyed the narrow door and the black chasm beyond.

"I will take you by a direct route, child of Tatius. What of you, mage?" The gargoyle held out a hand to Sera.

"I shall take the stairs and meet you at the

bottom, Hugh." Theoretically, she could use her magic to float to the ground, but the belfry was so very high and her skill over such a distance untested. While she knew the spell to summon air to cushion her descent, she'd rather practice with a smaller drop first. The tight stairwell presented a different sort of opportunity to use her magic to reach the bottom.

"Race?" Mischief glinted in his eyes.

"Oh, indeed." When would he learn never to bet against a mage?

Sera whispered a spell to the stone stairs, turning the steep treads into a single spiral slide.

Large arms encircled Hugh and picked him up as though he were a child, and he jerked upward as the gargoyle unfurled his wings and jumped to the open ledge.

Sera leapt feet first and created a sled of air under her bottom to aid her journey. As though she tackled an icy hillside, she hurtled down her slide. It took all her magic to keep herself upright as her body corkscrewed around the central post of the stairs. Faster and faster she plummeted to the ground floor —to the point she became certain she'd left her stomach up in the belfry. Sera let out a yell of glee as excitement and sheer terror coursed through her limbs.

She landed at the bottom with a plop, and her legs refused to move. Her breath came in quick gasps as Hugh burst through the little doorway.

"Are you hurt?" His eyes were wide with alarm as

he rushed to her, sprawled on the floor, and crouched down.

"No." She took his hand, and he helped her to stand. Both of them were grinning. "Only winded. How was your flight?"

"I *flew*," he whispered as though it hadn't occurred to him until that moment. "It was incredible, yet terrifying at the same time to be out of control as the ground rushed up to meet us."

Sera shook out her cloak, its folds covered in dust from swiping the walls at speed. "That was how I felt turning those stairs into a slide. I shall concede that you won this challenge, since you had time to rush back inside."

"Perhaps I should claim a prize?" Hugh murmured.

He edged closer, positioning their bodies until Sera leaned against the cool stone. His length pressed against her and he placed his hands flat on either side of her head. She met his warm gaze with a bold stare and parted her lips. The surgeon read her body, lowered his head, and kissed her. As Sera wrapped her arms around his neck, she considered that it didn't matter who had won the race to the ground.

Not with such a victory kiss as this one.

Eight

Abigail's social connections proved invaluable and two days later, Sera received a note advising that she would find Lord Rushbrooke in a jovial mood at the theatre that evening. Apparently, his favourite musical play was being performed. The information contained a sting, however. Sera was to join the Crawley family party in their box, and Lord Thornton was delighted to be included as her escort.

One hand went to the chain at her throat and she tugged on it to pull the silver kiss from under her stays. It warmed in her fingers as she thought of the man who had placed it in her palm. She had at long last admitted to herself that her feelings for Hugh were more than friendship. But love? And if it was love, what then? Neither king nor council would ever allow her to marry a common surgeon. Even one of uncommon skill.

She sighed and pressed the warmed metal to her lips. "Oh, Hugh. What am I to do?"

"What's got you all maudlin?" Elliot appeared in the parlour doorway.

Sera dropped the pendant back down her bodice and waved the letter in her other hand at her footman. "I am to attend the theatre this evening."

He leaned on the doorjamb and crossed his arms. "Opera? 'Cause that would explain the look on your face."

"There will be some songs, but no caterwauling. It's some amusing musical, apparently." Sera dropped the sheet of paper to the desk and mentally perused the gowns hanging in her wardrobe.

"Ah. It'll be the company you're not looking forward to, then. Another suitor who wants a handy mage wife to turn his tin plate into gold?" He waggled his eyebrows at her.

Not having a witty response, Sera stuck out her tongue. The footman chortled and ducked out of the way before she could throw some magical concoction at him.

Sera had a busy week ahead. Once she found Lord Rushbrooke, she had an appointment to visit Lord Rowan, and it was time for her monthly dinner with Contessa Ricci. That, at least, was an evening she looked forward to, because Hugh would be at her side.

The Crown paid Sera's annual stipend, but her funds were further supplemented by the potions and spells she sold to nobles. Buoyed by her success in helping Lady Tinwald conceive, Sera received a steady correspondence from ladies with problems that required the utmost discretion and a touch of magic. This had allowed her to purchase two extra gowns, following the designs drawn by Inge Wassler. She spent a modest amount of coin on books and a plush rug to warm the little parlour. The rest of her funds she left in the capable hands of Mr Napier for investment, and to purchase her plot of land in Westbourne Green.

That evening, she dressed in a new gown of navy silk with silver embroidery. It reminded her of a twilight sky, when the descending sun provided a blush of colour to the approaching night. Vicky fussed with a diamond pin loaned to Sera by Kitty. The spray of gems in their star-shaped settings was the perfect finishing touch to her outfit. The whole was a subtle nod to her Nyx persona and a reminder of the power she wielded.

She made her own way to the theatre and arrived just as the Crawley party exited their carriage. She kissed Abigail's cheek and greeted her mother, Lady Crawley, the origin of Abigail's impeccable manners and deportment. Any grey in her hair was covered by the pale lilac powder that complemented her gown.

Lord Thornton smiled and crooked his arm. "Lady Winyard. I am delighted to accompany you this evening. I was somewhat surprised by your forward invitation, but Lady Abigail said that a woman mage is used to doing things normally reserved only for men."

Sera opened her mouth, but words failed to come out. She glared at her friend, who winked and flicked open her fan as she took the arm of her betrothed.

"Indeed. Lady Abigail has tried for many years to instil in me a proper appreciation for the rules of society. But alas, I fear her efforts were in vain." Sera placed her hand on his arm.

They joined the throng of people surging through the wide entrance of the theatre and up the red-carpeted stairs to the private boxes. The Crawley family had a large box that easily seated their party of six, the women at the front, the men behind them.

Conversation rose from the stalls below. More people clustered at the back, standing and craning over people's heads to see the stage. Sera found watching people as fascinating as the light comedic play. Some were engrossed in the story, and called out encouragement or booed the actors. Others whispered behind fans or bent heads together to discuss assignations or deals while they thought no one noticed.

Sera enjoyed herself. Both the entertainment and conversation were lighthearted. When the actors took their final bows, she still hadn't found a reason to place a wart on the end of Thornton's nose or to turn him into a toad. Nor could she find a valid reason to gently tell Abigail the lord was unacceptable and Sera could never marry him. Blast.

Afterward, people formed clusters in the expansive foyer, chatting and laughing as they discussed the play or perhaps planned their next entertainment for the evening. Lady Crawley steered their party to another group to one side and made the introductions. Apparently she had some tenuous association with Lady Rushbrooke.

"Lady Winyard, may I introduce Lord and Lady Rushbrooke." Then the gracious older woman nodded and swept to one side to gossip with her friends. The rest of their party stood nearby while they waited for Sera.

"Lady Winyard." Lord Rushbrooke bowed, then peered over the top of her head as though he scanned the assembled people for an escape route. Sera tended to have that effect on nobles.

"Lord Rushbrooke, I am delighted to meet you. I am most interested in your family tree and wished to discuss a particular branch with you." Sera wracked her brain for the best approach without shocking everyone around them. People at these events were constantly alert for any hint of gossip to fuel their conversations over breakfast the next day.

"Oh? I didn't think we were of any great interest. Apart from old Lord Rushbrooke, my grandfather, living to such an extraordinary age. Caused a bit of a stir since he almost outlived his heir, my father." The current lord had a genial appearance and the solid build that reminded her of Hugh. Perhaps the trace of gargoyle blood gifted height and girth to the male descendants. That made Sera curious to know if the women of the family resembled Natalie.

"I asked to be introduced to you in my official capacity as one of England's mages. I am tasked with settling a restless soul at Bunhill Fields. The spirit agitating the locals is one of your ancestors, Lady Imogen Rushbrooke." Sera positioned herself between Lord Rushbrooke and whatever had caught his attention across the room. Surely the man could spare her a few minutes without becoming restless.

Lord Thornton hovered near Sera's side, engaged in conversation with Abigail and Lord Helensvale. Twice, older women dragging their daughters tried to catch his attention and Sera swallowed a smile at how he presented his back to them, but edged closer to her. That earned her a number of scowls from the stymied mothers.

Lord Rushbrooke pursed his lips, and his gaze shot up to one corner of the room as he considered the name. "I don't think I recollect her. But we are a steady lot, not given to inciting scandal or lodging in society's memory."

He obviously didn't know about Imogen's true love being a gargoyle and responsible for the heartiness injected into their family line. "Lady Imogen has conveyed a somewhat cryptic message. She asks that I *help Meredith.* I have ascertained she is some descendant. Is she possibly a cousin of yours?"

"Meredith?" A shadow flitted behind his eyes and his jovial mood snuffed out like a candle.

"Yes. I see that name triggers a memory. Is she here tonight?" Sera surveyed the crowd. How convenient if the woman were among them and Sera could fix whatever problem plagued her. Imogen could be satisfied that very night.

"You would speak her name? Here?" He spat the words in a hoarse whisper. His gaze darted around the room, as though fearing someone would overhear them.

Apparently, her task would not be completed by simply finding Meredith at the theatre. "Your very reaction, Lord Rushbrooke, seems to lend weight to Lady Imogen's concerns. What distress is afflicting Meredith?"

He leaned close and lowered his voice. "She is no Rushbrooke, having married Hillborne some years ago, and is excised from this family. You will not speak her name to me again."

Hillborne? Why did that name jump to Sera's mind? She would not be deterred until she had the information she needed. "I will bother you no more, once you tell me where I can find her."

"In jail. They say she...did away with...their child." He murmured the accusation, then nodded and strode away as though to escape even the lingering echo of his words.

"Oh." Sera exhaled the syllable. Now she placed the name—in the scandal sheet Abigail had read at Kitty's a few days previously. A lake. A weeping woman. Meredith had been brought to London to stand trial for her daughter's disappearance. That raised a new question—why had it roused Imogen from her eternal rest? Was Sera supposed to defend Meredith? That seemed hopeless if the woman had done such a horrid thing. She could ask Mr Napier if he were agreeable to representing such a client. Or was there something else about the case that disturbed the ghost?

"All settled?" Abigail returned to her side. "We thought we might take in the evening air with a stroll and perhaps visit a coffeehouse? Thornton doesn't like the noise here, and he's in danger of being swamped by desperate mammas."

"Then let us save him, before they drown him in a sea of silk and brocade." A quieter location suited Sera, as thoughts crammed her mind. She must not ruin the evening by discussing a murderess.

In the wee small hours, Sera returned to her home enveloped in a good mood, which dissipated like morning mist when she remembered what she needed to do. Before seeking her bed, Sera dashed off a note to Kitty on the ensorcelled paper they shared. She asked her friend to enquire of her father for any information about Lady Meredith Hillborne and her impending trial.

She shed her clothing and crawled into bed in her chemise, too tired to find a nightgown. Her last thought as sleep washed over her was not of delightful Lord Thornton, but of steadfast Hugh.

SERA ROSE at midmorning and breakfasted in her room before descending the stairs.

"One night out with the nobles and you're keeping hours like them." Elliot *tsk*ed under his breath.

"The council wants me off the streets during the day, so it is their wish that I become a nocturnal creature." Lord Ormsby probably didn't want her at the theatre, either, but roaming cemeteries and deserted roads instead.

A reply from Kitty waited on her desk.

They have her in Newgate, where Father says her husband has offered her no comfort. She is housed with other female felons. The case against her does not look good.

"Newgate," Sera murmured.

She donned her grey hooded cloak and set out to find a conveyance to take her to the prison. As she passed under its tall outer gate, Sera shivered as magical wards prickled over her skin and her power surged to defend her if required. She shook her shoulders to throw off the sensation once through the main entrance.

A bleak stone office huddled next to the wall. Two guards emerged.

"I am Lady Winyard, here to see Lady Hillborne. On official business for the Mage Council," she added when they stared at her.

"Very well, milady. But I have to warn you, it's not pleasant in there." A guard in a black uniform and with a weighty set of keys dangling by his side stepped forward to accompany her.

"I shall be fine, but thank you for your concern." As a child, Lord Branvale had once set her to empty and clean his chamber pot. She struggled to imagine anything worse.

She was wrong.

The dank walls of the prison sucked warmth, colour, and life from the occupants. Even their clothes turned to grimy brown and drab grey. With less than a hundred female prisoners under its roof, they were housed in their own area. The large cells had windows high up the wall so light filtered in, but no one could look out.

The guard stopped at one set of bars and sorted through his keys. "Get back, you lot!" he yelled as some women shuffled closer. Only when they retreated did he unlock the door and swing it open for Sera.

"Which one is she?" Sera murmured to the guard. Despite herself, her heart ached at the misery. As a titled lady, Meredith ought to have been housed in her own cell, with extra food sent by her household. Was this her punishment from her family, before the king's justice dealt its own?

The wretched creatures all looked so similar. They had lost any hope of escape and stared with blank eyes. He gestured to a woman curled upon herself in a dim corner. "That's her. Do you want me to come in with you?"

"No. I will alert you when I wish to leave." Sera stepped over the threshold and the sharp tang of sweat and urine climbed up her nostrils.

"You could holler, I suppose." He frowned at her.

"Or use magic. I shall ring a bell to let you know when I am done." Sera clicked her fingers, and a bell pealed above the guard's head.

He glanced up. "Right, milady. That will do the trick."

Sera approached Lady Hillborne and crouched on the damp floor before her. The other women gathered around them. One spat at Meredith and growled something unintelligible.

"Lady Hillborne?" Sera asked.

No answer came. Meredith wore only a thin gown; shivers wracked her shoulders and she hugged her knees tightly.

Sera tried again. "Meredith? Your great-grandmother sent me. I am a mage, and she said you needed my unique help."

That made Meredith look up, a frown on her forehead. Her grey eyes were the same drained colour as the surrounding stone. "Who?"

"Imogen Rushbrooke. She passed a hundred years ago, but she has risen because of your situation." Sera's attempts at conversation with the departed soul might have been stilted and cryptic, but Imogen remained adamant that intervention was necessary.

"Another relation demanding my death, I am sure," she murmured, and pulled her knees up close to her chest.

"I only want to discover the truth, Meredith." So far, all Sera had learned from the newspapers was that the child was missing and presumed drowned. A servant had found Meredith collapsed by the lake, clutching her daughter's favourite toy. Despite numerous searches, the little girl had not been found and Meredith refused to disclose what had happened to her other than to say she was gone.

"I am responsible. That is all the court needs to know. He cannot reach her now, and I will die content with that knowledge." She lowered her face to her knees and closed her eyes.

The words dripped cold through Sera. What horrible events had occurred at the estate to drive a mother to such extreme action? Sera wondered if Imogen's concern was not so much for Meredith, but for the family. The idea of the child's body lying undiscovered in a watery grave might have been what pulled her from peaceful rest in the other realm. Perhaps Sera's task was to find the child and ensure she received a proper burial. "Do you not want her body to be recovered, so others can grieve, at least?"

"No!" Her head shot up and her eyes were wild. "Let Hannah be where she is." Meredith reached out and grasped Sera's hand with a surprisingly strong grip. "I beg of you, do not interfere."

There was little to learn here. Sera took Meredith's hand. "I will do what I can to ensure peace for both of you."

Back in her waiting carriage, Sera nestled into a corner and turned her thoughts inward. Meredith had admitted she'd done it, which only left finding the poor child's body. She rubbed her arms, chilled despite her warm cloak. The despair permeating the prison had sunk into her bones. At least she could have a hot bath and scrub it away, unlike any of those poor women.

The direction of her investigation was now altered. Sera needed to find the lake where the girl had gone missing and locate the body. How much easier the job would be if she could call upon the assistance of an undine or rusalka to search the watery depths. Tonight she would call on Ethel and they would reassure Imogen that the child would be retrieved.

After releasing the carriage, Sera trotted up the front steps as Elliot swung open the door and bowed to her. "How did it go at the prison?"

"Cold and horrible. Can you ask Vicky to fill a bath, please? I shall be down shortly." She stripped off her gloves first and then her cloak. Lastly, Sera removed the pin holding her hat to her hair and handed those over to Elliot.

He slammed the front door shut with a foot, since his hands were now full. "Anything else?"

"I'd love a cup of tea and something to eat." The image of the hungry women in the dank cell shimmered before her eyes. There would be no hot cup of tea and warm scone for Meredith.

Elliot hung up her things, saluted, and headed along the hall.

Sera took the stairs up to her bedroom, emotions warring inside her. Sympathy for Meredith battled with indignation. If the woman had indeed taken her child's life, then she did not deserve a decent meal. Prisons were horrible places for a reason—to deter people from committing crimes. No one wanted to end up in such a place.

Only one thing itched in her mind. Why had Imogen said *help Meredith* and not *find Hannah*?

NINE

Sera spent the rest of the afternoon working in her study. There were new potions to brew for her clients and one in particular to complete—the preservative spell for the contessa. The small vial contained a liquid of a deep, glossy red like a ruby, with a faint sparkle. Now that she understood its purpose, she had refined the spell to maintain the viscosity of cattle blood and prevent it from spoiling.

On a whim, Sera dressed in the gown Inge had designed for her battle as Nyx. The black silk swirled around her legs as she paced in the parlour, waiting for Hugh. The surgeon had been unable to attend her first dinner with the vampyre, due to an accident that had required his surgical skills. She hoped nothing would keep him away tonight. Her soul ached with recent events and being pulled in different directions, and she needed his soothing presence.

"He's here." Elliot stuck his head around the door.

She had missed his arrival, her mind occupied with Meredith and the whereabouts of her daughter. Sera batted away Thornton's face when he intruded upon her thoughts. He was an issue to resolve another day.

Elliot held out her cloak and dropped it around her shoulders.

"Don't wait up," she murmured, before stepping out into the chill night.

They journeyed to the contessa's Mayfair home, where the dour butler swung the door open for them as they alighted from the carriage. Hugh practically bounced on his toes like an excited child. His eyes sparkled, and he radiated such a good mood that Sera couldn't help but be swept along with him.

Clad in grey trimmed in silver, the contessa greeted them and kissed Seraphina's cheek with cool lips. "It is a delight to have you in my home." Then she arched an eyebrow at Hugh, who bowed. Laughter bubbled from the vampyre's throat before she looped her arm through Sera's. "Mr Miles looks like a puppy about to be let off the leash at a park, so many questions burn inside him."

Sera glanced behind her and hoped that in his quest for knowledge, Hugh wouldn't be too impertinent with the vampyre. She had questions of her own that needed answers, and didn't want to ruin their friendship before it had fully established itself. "I hope you do not mind. I am sure Mr Miles will respect your privacy."

His jaw dropped a fraction, and his forward progress halted for a second. "I only wish to learn about your unique condition, Contessa, and appreciate this opportunity."

Her lips quirked in a smile, and she nodded. "It has been so long since I made new friends. I shall do my best to indulge your curiosity. I thought we would have dinner in the library. It is more intimate for just the three of us."

In the book-lined room, a small table seating only four was made up close to the fireplace. A crisp white cloth was draped over it and plates of snowy white with a silver edge awaited them. A footman moved on silent feet to serve the first course to Sera and Hugh.

Contessa Ricci did not eat, but sipped from a tall silver goblet, its contents hidden by the solid metal.

Sera wanted to keep her mind clear, and so drank little more than a few sips of a delicious red wine. After discussing the improvements she had made to the required potion, and letting Hugh ask a few questions about vampyre physiology, Sera broached another topic that often lingered in the back of her mind. "Will you reveal Lord Branvale's secrets now that he is dead?"

A smile touched the contessa's lush lips. "I am dead, yet he did not reveal mine."

There was one secret that Sera had ascertained

from examining the mage genealogy. "He was married. But only fleetingly." She guessed that the marriage had been brief, otherwise it might have been known among the mages or wider society. Given that the details had been erased from the master copy of the genealogy made her assume it had been annulled.

A long, pale finger caressed the stem of the silver goblet. "Ah. Yes. A lovely thing. I think losing her was what hardened Branvale's heart."

"But there was something *unusual* about the marriage other than its short duration. He never mentioned it. Indeed, one could say he had it erased from his past." Sera watched the contessa's serene face, hoping for any indication that she had uncovered the truth.

"You know what it is like, Lady Winyard, to be feared simply for what you are. Yet mages alone are treated differently and bound in service to their monarch. Other creatures, such as myself, must hide our true natures and protect ourselves as best we can from discovery." She sipped and then licked a single red droplet from her lips.

Excitement caught in Sera's chest as she recalled her conversation with Warin the gargoyle about his love for Imogen. A puzzle piece fell into place. "Branvale married an Unnatural, but didn't know it." The law forbade such creatures to marry or hold property. That was why the book, or a mage, had erased the entry. "That was the secret you kept for him."

Contessa Ricci sighed. "A fact revealed on his wedding night."

Sera put down her cutlery and leaned back in her chair. The past actions of her late guardian were now cast in a different light.

Hugh spoke and echoed Sera's thoughts. "That was why he sought a cure. Thinking the Unnatural state some sort of condition that could be rectified like a bout of jaundice."

Sera asked, "Do you think desperation made him cruel? His treatment of Jake's mother and sister seemed so callous, as though he did not care whether his so-called cure caused them pain and distress." One answer created more questions, like fish swarming to a piece of bread dropped in water. What sort of Unnatural had Branvale wed, and what had happened to the woman? Had she disappeared into the mists of time, or had something awful occurred?

Hugh said there were men who conducted experiments on Unnaturals and called their perversion *science*. Or had the Repository of Forgotten Things acquired another resident? Sera had much to discuss with Lord Rowan when they met again.

"When love becomes twisted by duty or resentment, it deforms. His prejudices meant he punished himself for loving her, and sought a cure so they could be together. But she rejected him for not loving *all* of her as she was." The contessa grew agitated, speaking with her hands and making grand sweeps through the air.

"Was she born, not made?" Some types of Unnaturals were like gargoyles and Sera. They were born who they were. Others, like vampyres and lycanthropes, were made.

A slight nod. Now Sera itched to know more, but the contessa laughed. "I think I have told you enough, have I not? If she does not wish to be found, her privacy should be respected."

She was still alive, then!

"I am more concerned with whether she is safe. As you pointed out, our world is not kind to those who are different." Sera struggled in full view of everyone to earn their acceptance. If the people could accommodate a woman mage, why could they not accept goblins, vampyres, and other types of creatures?

"You are young and have yet to decide whether you will change to meet the world's expectations, or embrace who you are." The contessa leaned forward, her grey eyes intent on Sera.

Sera blew a strand of hair away from her face. This was a question she pondered in the quiet hours of the night. Her life would be easier if she conformed and did what was expected of her. But to do so would crush part of her soul and kill the very thing that made her unique.

"I am pleased that Branvale's death brought you to my door. You must call me Noemi and we shall be the best of *amiche*." She took Sera's hand and squeezed.

"Only if you will call me Sera." For her part, Sera was fascinated by Noemi. She wanted to ask about all the things she had seen in her long life, and whether vampyres had any enhanced abilities, as gargoyles did. But they had many dinners yet in which to cover such topics.

"You were a divine Nyx. What if your path in this world is to embody the night goddess?" Humour made Noemi's words light and mischievous.

"I will admit, portraying Nyx came easily to me. As though I did not so much play a role, but removed a disguise and showed my true self. I have always thought my gift has a special affinity with Mother Nature." If Sera ignored the council's edicts of how magic was supposed to work, she could embrace however many and whatever goddesses she wanted to. Gaia and Nyx could both be her mentors and guides.

Thinking of the council drew her mind back to more immediate concerns. Sera moved her wine glass and stared at the patterns of light cast on the tablecloth by the cut of the crystal. "The council has set me a task in order to remove me from the public eye during the day. Like Nyx, I haunt the evenings and am investigating the *unquiet dead* at Bunhill Fields."

The contessa laughed, a gentle, tinkling sound. "Am I not also one of the unquiet dead? There are those of us who refuse to lie silent in our graves, but continue with our lives."

"It appears this restless spirit has been awakened by the terrible crime of Lady Meredith Hillborne. She cries out for me to *help Meredith,* but I intend to find the missing child." Sera would have to call upon Abigail and learn where the Hillborne family resided.

"Hillborne? The spirit's troubles are linked to that horrid man?" A sharp tone entered the contessa's voice.

"Lord Hillborne, yes. His wife has been transported to London to stand trial. She is accused of drowning their daughter. From what I read in the newspapers, it is a forgone conclusion that she will hang." Sera glanced at Hugh, who listened intently.

An angry snort burst from the contessa. "It would not surprise me if he did the deed himself."

Sera's thoughts froze, then reformed. *That horrid man.* "Do you know him?"

The contessa stared at her. "Of course. He is Vilma's cousin. When her father died, he is the fiend who wrote to her mother and told them to remove themselves from Mistwood Manor before he arrived with his wife. They were not provided for by the previous Lord Hillborne, and the new one refused them so much as a penny."

Hugh paused in his enjoyment of the excellent meal. "How sad and irresponsible that Vilma's father did not leave them anything to survive on in his will. It would seem, then, that the current Lord Hillborne is no stranger to unkind actions. But to be involved in the death of his child is surely a step beyond what he has done to Vilma."

"Just this week, he wrote to Vilma. He asked her to visit him, claiming he wishes to make amends for his past actions. I suspect he already seeks a compliant woman to father an heir before his wife has even had her neck stretched." Rage bristled over Noemi and her nails rapped on the side of a crystal water bowl, producing short, clear notes.

Sera swallowed a mouthful of trout and let both the food and the contessa's words settle inside her. "You think he means to replace his wife with Vilma?"

Light flashed in the older woman's eyes. "I am certain of it. But he will not have her. He thinks her meek and mild, but that is only due to her illness. Vilma has courage and strength that many under-estimate."

Talk of illness triggered Hugh's curiosity. "Might I enquire as to what troubles her? I could call upon her, if my skills might help?"

With a sad shake of her head, Noemi's shoulders slumped, and she stared into her glass. "None can assist. I have employed the best aftermages to confirm the diagnosis, but there is no hope for my orchid. She has a tumour in her breast."

"It might be possible to remove it. While such surgery is difficult, it is not impossible, with the right aftermage assistance," Hugh said.

Tears misted in the vampyre's eyes and Sera marvelled that such was her love for her *orchid*, that the dead creature could cry.

"The aftermage we consulted says it has spread to her liver and bones. He says no more than a year." Noemi's voice dropped to a raspy whisper. "We can only make her as comfortable as possible for what time remains in her hourglass."

"I wish I could help." Sera curled her hands into fists. Despite all the magic flowing through her veins, she could not cure such a thing. Why did Nature allow her mages to destroy and not heal? There were aftermages gifted in performing feats upon the human body, but such an ability did not exist in mages. She would consult the hidden library. Perhaps if she were powerful enough, she could scrub such terrible afflictions from the earth.

"I treasure each moment with her, and hope is a constant fire within me." Noemi reached out and took Sera's hand.

Her flesh might be chilled, but Sera believed a fierce love burned inside the other woman.

"Could you cure her, Contessa Ricci?" Hugh set down his cutlery. Such was his interest in the conversation that he gave it all his attention.

"Do you mean, can I relieve Vilma's pain by taking her life?" She spoke with a weary tone, as though this were an oft-discussed topic.

Hugh frowned. "Well, yes. It is rather ironic to

ask if you can save a life by taking that same life. But I believe you understand my meaning."

She sipped from her glass, and a brief smile touched her lips. "Yes. But Vilma is not ready, and the decision rests with her. It is no easy thing to stare into the eyes of death and welcome its embrace. Nor to consider spending an eternity with someone."

An image appeared in Sera's mind of three slashes in a granite marker. Some loves endured for centuries. What would it be like to see out the passage of time with a constant companion? She considered Hugh and Lord Thornton. What attributes did she desire in a partner? Kindness and a curiosity about life. And a sense of fun. There would be little point in existing even for decades, let alone hundreds of years, if you couldn't enjoy yourself.

Hugh leaned back as the footman stepped forward to refill his wine glass. "It is honourable that you give her the time to consider her heart."

"It is not the state of Vilma's heart that she ponders. It is mine. She thinks I would grow bored with her, but she is wrong. I know that once vigour returns to her form, she will bloom. I cannot imagine anyone I would rather have at my side for the coming centuries." She raised her glass and toasted her absent companion. "But such talk does not help Sera put her restless spirit back into her grave."

"No. Could I make a proposal for you to consider?" An idea had formed in Sera's mind, but it needed Noemi's assistance.

"Of course." The contessa gestured to another footman, who served a second helping of trout and vegetables onto Hugh's plate. The surgeon commenced second supper.

"I believe that Imogen wishes the body of the little girl to be found before she will return to her grave. I'd like to search the estate, but quietly, without anyone knowing I am a mage. I fear there is more to this case than meets the eye. You said that Lord Hillborne wishes to make amends for his past actions, which drove Vilma into reduced circumstances. It is not uncommon for a noblewoman without a means of support to become a companion. Would it be possible for Vilma to accept Lord Hillborne's invitation, but say that propriety dictates he must invite you? I could insert myself as your maid, if you would allow it." It would be the perfect opportunity for Sera to form her own opinion of the lord, and dig into exactly what had happened on the sad day the little girl disappeared.

A glint of mischief crept into the contessa's grey gaze. "I would relish any opportunity you might find to repay his actions in kind."

Hugh glanced up sharply. "I say, you wouldn't—"

The vampyre shuddered. "I would not foul my body by touching one drop of his blood. If he is behind this crime and not his wife, I will do all I can to help find the evidence. *Si, madonna.* I shall ask Vilma."

"Only if it will not be too taxing for her." Only

too late did Sera consider the displaced noblewoman might not be well enough for the journey.

"I suspect a little adventure might give her a renewed focus and energy." A wistful smile touched the contessa's lips. "With a small garnish of vengeance."

"I can discuss with Sera the best potions to take, to make Vilma more comfortable," Hugh said between mouthfuls of tender trout.

"How did you meet Vilma?" Sera asked as the meal concluded, plates were cleared, and a selection of cheeses and grapes placed on the table.

"She was selling books in Castle Street. Can you imagine the depths of a woman's despair that she could be forced to part with her beloved books?" Noemi gestured for a footman to pour a small measure of port for Hugh.

Sera thought of the many empty shelves in her home. Slowly, she purchased books to fill them. To willingly sell a carefully curated collection seemed near impossible.

"I offered to purchase her a meal, in exchange for talking about the books she carried in her basket. I said I could not bear to see her lose such comforts as she had left. Everyone should have books, both to educate and to entertain." A wistful glint entered the contessa's eyes as she remembered those early days. "Friendship bloomed between us and it became our little ritual. I would pay for a dinner and Vilma would recall a tale or speak with a wistful voice of a place she had discovered in a history or a travel memoir."

Sera met Hugh's gaze across the table. Would they one day tell the tale of how their friendship had grown into something marvellous?

TEN

Home from another entertaining evening, Sera dragged her weary feet up the stairs toward her bed. As was her ritual, she pulled out the ensorcelled paper she'd stolen from under Lord Branvale's bed and glanced at the single sheet. What she saw cleared her mind in an instant. The unknown correspondent had replied at last.

I will await you in Shadowvane
You will be given a key

She knew little of Shadowvane, except that it was a dangerous place in Somerset where the Fae realm overlapped the human one. Normally, one passed between realms through a concealed doorway. Shadowvane was a meadow where beautiful flowers grew and rare butterflies flitted between the blooms. An inattentive traveller, distracted by the marvellous flora and fauna, could wander from one world to the other without realising it. Mages on both sides had cast wards to stop travellers from inadvertently losing years of their lives trapped in the Fae realm. Now, a person needed an item to hold that acted as a key while crossing the meadow.

"Shadowvane," Sera whispered.

Perhaps it was her imagination, but something stirred in the darkened corners of her room as she murmured the name.

Once, she'd worn a Fae constructed bracelet. Branvale had corresponded with someone from that realm. But when she travelled there, would she find friend or foe?

Sadly, Shadowvane would have to wait. First she had to journey to Mistwood Manor and solve that mystery.

"One by one, your secrets will yield to me," she promised the unknown hand that moved against her.

Sera paused on the threshold of Lord Rowan's home and let the wards linger on her skin. With her eyes closed, she tried to distinguish each individual spell.

"Not trying to unravel the spells holding my home together, I hope," his gruff voice said.

"No, my lord." Her eyes flew open.

Lord Rowan stood in the foyer, leaning heavily on an ornate walking stick as he regarded her. Not for him the fashionable attire of a duke—he dressed more like a gardener or a sailor, in brown woollen breeches and a knitted blue jumper. Or perhaps he had reached such an age he could dress for comfort and be damned to what anyone thought.

She rested one hand on the brick by the door and let the protective spell tingle across her palm. "I merely seek to learn how you protect your home, so I can determine where my wards are lacking."

"Are they not the same as those Branvale cast?" He arched one bushy eyebrow.

Sera stepped inside to allow the butler to close the door. "No. But I cannot explain the difference. If I were to compare them to the sound of a bell, the wards here have a deep resonance, whereas what Lord Branvale cast around his home have a lighter tone."

Lord Rowan made a noise in the back of his throat. "Interesting way to compare them. But I am not going to tell you how I secure my home. Mages guard their personal protective wards fiercely. None of us wish to give another the key to our homes. Follow me, Lady Winyard, and I shall listen while you tell me what you think you discerned about my security measures."

He strode off along the hall to his library and Sera followed. She told him what enchantments and elements she had discerned in the dense web cast around his home. In return, he huffed or muttered under his breath, but never told her whether she'd guessed right or wrong.

In the overflowing library, Sera picked her way around perilous stacks of books to a desk the size of a bed. Lord Rowan summoned a chair that knocked over a pile in its path, and it stopped beside his desk. Today a small terrarium sat on one corner. Inside, a tiny tree spread its limbs over diminutive ferns and bright red toadstools. A lime green frog no bigger than her thumbnail sat by a toadstool and watched her.

"What a tiny frog. Is it a rare species?" Sera asked as she took her seat.

"Yes. Grandson," the old mage said with a snort.

She stared at the creature and wondered what he had done to deserve such a prison. She might have misheard, though. "Your grandson's frog?"

"Say hello to Lady Winyard, George." He tapped a finger on the terrarium and the frog croaked. "The lad was, in his mother's words, *being a little toad*. Which gave me the idea. He is spending a few days on my desk to think about his actions."

Sera didn't know if she should be horrified or inspired by the mage's creativity. She was certainly curious. "Might I enquire as to George's crime?"

"My youngest grandchild is something of a Pied Piper to rodents. He finds it amusing to summon mice to terrify his sisters and the staff. Everyone must learn boundaries, and when and where it is appropriate to use one's gifts." He stared at the frog over the gold rims of his spectacles as he spoke the last sentence, as though it was an oft repeated lesson to his offspring.

A pang of sympathy for George rippled through Sera. What an odd aftermage gift, to be able to summon rodents. Certainly not one he could use in polite society, although other lads would find it amusing. Had he been born in the slums, he might have become a rat catcher in high demand. But as the grandson of a powerful mage, his options were limited.

"Let us turn from naughty toads to other, more important matters. Do you have the bracelets?" Lord Rowan settled in his chair.

"No." Sera dug into her reticule and pulled out what had kept her busy in the little free time she found. She had been labouring to find the Fae runes on her bracelet and to understand what they meant. The sheets of paper showed where each rune was placed on the tree and her attempts at sorting the runes into order. Once she understood the spell on that bracelet, she would turn her efforts to the one worn by the late Lady Zedlitz.

"They are dangerous items. I require that you hand them over to me, Lady Winyard." He narrowed his gaze behind the spectacles perched on the end of his nose.

"I have not yet finished my studies, Lord Rowan.

I assure you that once I have found all the runes on both items and translated the spells used to make them work, I shall deposit them in a secure location." She spread out the papers. In the terrarium, little George hopped closer to the glass.

"You are young, unused to protecting your home, and live in a rather dubious area of London. You will deliver them to me this week. One of those bracelets allows a person to control the actions of others. It cannot be allowed to slip from your grasp. It could cause chaos—even bring down a kingdom in the wrong hands. I don't think either of us wants to involve the council and Lord Ormsby. Week's end, Lady Winyard. I expect to find them sitting on the desk beside George." He dragged one sheet closer to him and waved his hand to summon his quill.

Sera bristled. *She* had discovered the bracelets and their magical nature. All she desired was to study how Fae magic differed from their own. The items would be securely stored once she had exhausted her studies, and not before. His caution about her being unused to protecting her home made a tendril of fear crawl up her spine. Would another mage dare try to breach her wards and steal them? She could be away for some weeks with the contessa and Vilma. An alternative arrangement would need to be found to keep the bracelets secure—and it would *not* be with Lord Rowan.

"How did Lord Branvale's marriage come to be erased from the original mage genealogy?" Sera changed the topic. Mr Napier had taught her that the best defence was often an offence.

Lord Rowan froze, apart from a regular blinking of his eyes. His hand was poised over her notes, his long, tapered beard resting on the edge of the desk, about to tumble into his lap. "Pardon?"

"I understood the mage genealogy recorded all our marriages, births, and deaths for seven generations. Yet Lord Branvale's marriage has been expunged from the book. I am curious as to the circumstances that allowed for such a thing." Sera hoped this line of questioning would draw Lord Rowan away from compelling her to deliver the Fae items.

He huffed. "It does. Only exceptional circumstances would allow for an entry to be corrected."

"Such as removing a marriage to an Unnatural?" Given the circumstances that had allowed Sera to live, another idea flitted through her mind. "Perhaps a mage's request to remove the marriage from our records coincided with a pressing need to swear a blood oath to a gargoyle?"

Lord Rowan barked a loud laugh that startled the tiny frog, who leapt into the cover of the ferns in the glass cage. The old mage waggled a finger at her and chortled. "Told them you would be an exceptional mage. What a mind that head must contain. You are correct. Branvale's marriage was annulled, given it was never legal to begin with, yet the stubborn book retained its details. This happened around the time you were born, so I doubt many of us noticed the addition to his page. I couldn't let those gargoyles take you who knew where for who knew how long. Branvale refused to swear the oath without some sort of payment in kind."

"You removed the entry in return for his promise to my father and the gargoyles." Another piece of Sera's history now made sense. This was what had made Branvale her reluctant guardian and bound him to her life by his blood and magic. No wonder he had resented her.

"However did you discover it? I thought I had done an exceptional job. I drained myself to alter the genealogy. Damn book fought hard to keep it. I was unconscious for three days afterward." He stared up at the rotating globe that illuminated their work.

"The day I received my edition, I happened to have it in strong sunlight. The correction is invisible except when the sun hits the page at a certain angle." Discovering the faint erasure had brought her to a better understanding of why Branvale had behaved as he did. And she had discovered a link to her father and two gargoyles who had protected her fiercely. Now her life possessed a symmetry with her discovery that a faint trace of gargoyle blood flowed through Hugh's veins. The one man she trusted to protect her should the need arise.

"That's why it's supposed to be kept out of direct light." Lord Rowan opened the lid to the terrarium and rubbed his thumb and forefingers together while muttering under his breath. A trio of tiny flies, no larger than pinheads, dropped into the jar and flew around the tree. George jumped after them, trying to catch them with a thin pink tongue no larger than a needle.

"Are there other entries that have been quietly erased over the years?" Could a mage marry, like Lord Branvale, and have it kept from anyone else's knowledge? Or could a child be spirited away with no one the wiser?

Lord Rowan snorted. "If there are, I doubt that over the centuries there could be more than a handful. The book holds tight to its knowledge. No mage would risk their life and exhaust their magic simply to cover up a bad decision."

"Yet you risked both to save me. Why did *you* not raise me? Why was I given to Branvale?" How different her life would have been if she had been brought here and lived with someone who wanted her. Plus, she would have had the companionship of Abigail.

But not Kitty.

Changing anything in the past created ripples. To follow a path where the old mage was her mentor meant she would never have met the sharp-witted and fiercely loyal Katherine Napier. Nor would she have received instruction from Mr Napier on worldly matters and finance.

Considering what she would have to give up, if Sera stood at a crossroads and was asked to decide for her five-year-old self, she would willingly choose Branvale to keep Kitty's friendship. In making the choice for herself, her anger at how Branvale had treated her evaporated like morning mist under the gaze of a rising sun.

Lord Rowan shuffled the papers and laid them out in a grid. "I had Tomlin still with me at the time. Pendlebury sought to be your guardian, but Branvale said he was too young to raise a mage, let alone a girl. The blood oath no doubt compelled him to take you on." He took a quill from the silver desk set, and began marking her work in red ink.

"Lord Pendlebury?" Sera calculated the mage's age. He would only have been in his mid twenties when he'd offered to become mentor to the young Sera. She would thank him, next time they met at the tower. So many moments in her life could have gone in a different direction, but a certainty flowed through her that some force navigated the true path for her.

Sera left Lord Rowan with a handful of notes covered in red ink. He was an exacting teacher and her rudimentary translation of the Fae runes had not met his standards. To be fair, the language was entirely new to her. It would be weeks, if not months, before she could fluently translate the spell that had suppressed her magic.

Needing to clear her head, Sera walked most of the way home, only hopping onto the back of a cart as the light dimmed.

"Supper's nearly ready," Elliot said as she walked up the stairs. "Popping out for witchy business tonight?"

"Yes, I will be. Could you fetch me a horse after supper, please?" She shrugged off her cloak and headed to her study to leave her notes.

After enjoying a meal with her cobbled-together family, Sera trotted up the stairs to her bedroom to change into her men's attire. Brown leather boots were laced over wool stockings and she tugged on breeches and a coat. Then she packed more luminescent lamps into her satchel, wedged a cloth cap on her head, and strode out to the snoozing horse.

Sera breathed in the night air as she rode toward Bunhill Fields. As her eyes adjusted, she spotted a fox rushing through the grass beside her. Overhead, a crow circled twice before heading off at an angle. A grey owl darted by like a moon thrown by a child.

Soft lights glowed from the cottages. Music came from one home and a clear voice sang a poignant ballad. Sera tied the horse to a tree nearby and then left a magical lamp on the doorstep of a house lit only by a flickering lantern. She carried on up the hill to find Ethel seated on the porch of her crooked little cottage, a pipe clutched between her lips and a mug in her hand. "Shall we go a-visiting, milady?"

Sera leaned on the corner post of the porch and caught her breath. "If you have time. I'd like to talk to Imogen again, if possible."

Ethel rose to her feet and tied the ends of her

shawl around her middle. With her pipe in one hand, she took up a gnarled walking stick in the other. In silence, the two women wandered the shadowy paths. Ethel stopped beside a pile of recent earth and cocked her head. Sera let tendrils of magic drift over the grave and a shape took form, hovering above the pile. A murmured conversation took place, but Sera couldn't make out any words. After a few minutes, Ethel coughed, spat a gob of phlegm to the ground, and stepped around the grave.

"He's worried about his dog. Wants his wife to bring it to see him." Ethel gestured for them to continue on their way.

"Does it ever stop, hearing them? Or do you need to open yourself to their messages?" Sera wondered how the old woman heard the spirits tugging for her attention.

"Oh, they are always there—talking, laughing, or screaming. Heard 'em ever since I was a babe. It's like people standing on the other side of a wall. Sometimes one opens a door and shouts, or I can poke my head through if I need to concentrate on one or the other." She pushed away a branch that had snapped and sagged over the path.

"How do you find their family to pass on a message, like the man who wants to see his dog?" His grave had been so new it had no headstone, only a plain white cross with a number marking the burial site.

Ethel shrugged. "I cannot help them all. I'm not

getting any younger and can't run around London looking for people or dogs. If it's obvious, I do what I can. It's far easier to work the other way around and let their families come to me. Most come for money, not so many for love anymore."

Sera thought of Lord Thornton and his search for his father's will. Financial gain would motivate many to try to contact departed relatives or business associates. How sad that people did not want the comfort of knowing their loved one was at peace. They only wanted to find a contract or a lost piece of jewellery.

What Sera considered Imogen's corner was cloaked in black velvet. The moon hid its face, and they relied on the blue glow from the jars and the golden light of the little mushrooms to find their way. The distressed soul floated near her tomb, as though she had been waiting for them.

"Meredith!" Imogen moaned as she drifted across the grass toward them.

"What of Hannah?" Sera asked.

The soul stopped in the middle of the glade. Without clear features, Sera couldn't tell if she had confused the dead woman or if she was waiting for her to say more.

"I will find Hannah so her father can bury her." Sera held her glow lamp by her side. As Imogen became animated, she emitted more light than the jar.

"No! Help Meredith!" Imogen spread her arms and swooped at Sera like a large owl.

"We will do as you ask, but you must give us time." Ethel stepped between Sera and the angry spirit.

A low moan came from the insubstantial shape. Imogen's edges blurred and bits broke off to drift free as fireflies. Then she turned and floated back to her tomb.

"Hurry. Time runs out," she rasped and then sank into the open book and folded herself onto its stone pages.

With Imogen's light extinguished, the dark deepened. Sera picked up her lamp, wondering why both ghost and mother didn't want Hannah found. Time was certainly running fast through Meredith's hourglass. If she were found guilty, she might be taken directly from the courtroom to the gallows.

"Will Imogen return?" Sera asked Ethel.

The old woman rested her palms on the carved book. "You have a few days. Then she'll be back hollering the same thing."

"I must go to Mistwood Manor, and find Hannah," Sera whispered.

The answer had to lie with the missing child—but why did neither Imogen nor her mother want her found?

Eleven

The next day, a steady flow of correspondence required Sera's attention. Lord Ormsby demanded to know why Imogen was still howling at night and disturbing passersby at Bunhill Fields. Sera considered her response, then wrote that the spirit had agreed to bide her time while Sera went to Mistwood Manor to locate her descendant's body, so the family could bury the little girl. Only once the child was found would the spirit permanently return to the other side and no longer disturb the locals.

Her reply wasn't entirely accurate, since Imogen insisted that it was Meredith who required help. But surely Lord Ormsby's rotund form held some trace of sympathy for the bereaved family, and would allow Sera time to fully investigate. It also meant she would be removed from London for some weeks, which probably appealed to the Speaker.

Contessa Ricci sent a letter to inform Sera that Vilma had agreed to accept Lord Hillborne's invitation. The group would leave in two days' time, once they had packed and prepared for the long journey. That gave Sera time to consider what brews or spells might ease Vilma's condition and give her a respite from the pain and fatigue of her disease.

A smile warmed Sera's insides. She would consult with Hugh. Once she better understood Vilma's condition and how the tumour affected her, she could make a more effective tonic. She knew exactly where to find the surgeon that evening. The invitation sat on her desk among all the other correspondence. Kitty was to host her first soirée and only the witty and intelligent were invited. Even the infamous artist would be present.

Lady Abigail had refused to attend and warned Sera of dire consequences to her reputation if she went. That only made the night more appealing.

She summoned Vicky and flung open her wardrobe. "What to wear to an intellectual salon?" she asked herself, the wardrobe, her maid, and her aunt Nat perched on the windowsill. It had been a surprise to discover the large gargoyle could shift into a small rainspout ornament if she wanted to sleep on a roof.

"The blue silk, milady. It's so beautiful." Vicky lifted the gown from the wardrobe.

Inge had left the drawing, and a local modiste had constructed the dress. Made of navy silk, a silver thread ran through it that reminded Sera of raindrops tricking down a window. The fabric fell in simple folds from an elevated waistline under the bust. It looked very Grecian, and while lovely, utterly disregarded the current fashion. Perhaps she would start a new trend. Doubtful, but you never knew.

Sera whispered a spell into her palms, rubbed them together, and then finger combed it through her hair. This changed her locks from dark brown to blue black. Then Vicky gathered it up loosely and secured it with silver pins.

Elliot wrapped her favourite grey cloak around her shoulders and held the door open. "I'll be waiting when you come home. I want to know the look on the surgeon's face when he sees you," he murmured as she passed.

The Napier family carriage waited for her in the street and the footman helped her in. At times, Sera had to pinch herself to realise this was her life. The former kitchen maid, now wearing a fairytale gown and sitting in a fancy carriage on her way to a party. But she had no interest in a prince or living in a castle. Each time Hugh took her hand, Sera's certainty grew that she would much prefer a modest life in a home surrounded by trees, with a man who could both challenge her mind and send tingles along her skin.

When she arrived, the butler opened the door. "Miss Katherine and her guests are in the drawing room, Lady Winyard." He gestured to a footman to take her cloak.

Sera paused in the doorway to the richly decorated drawing room. Deep red was offset by brass and copper tones. Her friend was engrossed in conversation with Arwyn Fiztfey on one side and Lord Loburn on the other. Hugh turned as though he had sensed Sera's approach, whereupon his jaw dropped and his drink froze halfway to his lips. Then he grinned and toasted her, before tossing back the contents of his glass in one shot.

Good humour warmed Sera's limbs as she approached the group. Kitty rested one hand on Arwyn's arm and Sera wondered if she had even noticed the presence of the marquis. A protective urge flared through her body, and she curled her hands into fists. If the handsome Fae bastard ever hurt her friend, he would have an angry mage ruining more than his delectable face.

"Sera!" Kitty cried, and thrust out her hands to her friend—actions that would have earned her a scowl from Abigail. No polite bobs and curtseys here. Sera enjoyed the informality of a salon intended to thumb its nose at society.

"We are talking about schools and I have decided to support one. Where do you think would be the best location?" Kitty asked.

"By best, I assume you mean worst and in most need?" Sera lifted a glass from the tray offered by a footman.

Hugh's fingers grazed her palm as he moved to stand beside her. "Whitechapel is full of struggling people. Perhaps you could also provide a nourishing lunch for the students? For many, it might be the only meal they receive that day."

"An excellent suggestion. The site needs sufficient room for a kitchen." Kitty's eyes sparkled as the conversation flowed.

Arwyn stated that more than education should be freely given. He called for property to be redistributed to those most in need. Saying that the landed gentry should not hold excessively more than required to provide for their families. That caused a few awkward moments, but thankfully dinner was announced.

As there were only ten of them present, they ate in the smaller dining room, where everyone could converse across the table. Kitty took her mother's seat at the end of the table opposite her father. Arwyn and Lord Loburn were seated on either side of her. Sera sat next to the marquis with Hugh on her other side. Sera assumed the man in red velvet with an orange waistcoat must be the artist. Their numbers were rounded out by a poet (who must be the individual with floppy lace covering his hands and who kept sighing dramatically) and a politician who was as passionate about workers' rights as Kitty.

There were only three ladies in attendance. Kitty had invited her mother's old friend Lady Plimmerton to chaperone the two younger women. She sat next to

Mr Napier. In her forties, age had sprinkled silver in her hair and added lines around her eyes. She had a graceful, serene look that reflected a happy life, rather than one spent in misery. The widow kept a trim figure and Kitty whispered that she looked fetching on her father's arm.

"How wonderful to hear lively conversation over supper again. I do miss Francesca sitting at the foot of the table." Lady Plimmerton glanced at Mr Napier and then dropped her attention to her plate.

"Her presence is missed every day, but Kitty would say life goes on." Mr Napier toasted his dinner partner.

"I do not believe Mother would have expected you to live your life alone, Father. You have not entirely lost either your mind or appearance to old age yet. I believe you still have much to offer, if you choose to seek out another companion," Kitty said.

"Indeed. Some men become enhanced as they age, rather like a fine wine. I'm sure there are many women who would be honoured to see out their remaining years at your side." Perhaps realising she had said too much, Lady Plimmerton blushed in a becoming fashion.

Mr Napier stared at Lady Plimmerton as though he was seeing her for the first time in his life. He opened his mouth, but for a lawyer skilled with words, he was strangely silent. Then he gulped a large mouthful of wine.

Swallowing, he turned to Sera. "You will be

relieved to hear, Sera, that we finally have the numbers to defeat the amendment to the Mage Act when it is put to the vote next week. Indeed, the House is keen to rush it through so they can argue over the Regency. The lords are busy trying to snatch that prize from each other."

"At least the Regency is one fight mages can stay out of. I understand lines are drawn between politicians and physicians on the matter." Sera glanced at Hugh, wondering if he had been consulted about the king's visibly deteriorating state.

Hugh set down his cutlery for a moment. "Lord Viner has attended the king, as does Doctor Warren. The queen is deeply suspicious of Doctor Warren and believes him to be in the pocket of the Prince of Wales. There are even rumours he seeks to make the king's state worse. Queen Charlotte leans more heavily on Doctor Viner's opinion."

"Yet the Prince of Wales is not the king's eldest son. There are rumours that the king seeks a way to change the succession. Some whisper that since Arwyn is the child of a human king and a Fae princess, with a foot in both kingdoms, he ought to take precedence over entirely human offspring. Whether he is legitimate or not. Is it true, Fitzfey?" Kitty turned to the half-Fae seated at her side.

The king's bastard smiled upon Kitty and plucked his wine glass from the table. With his other hand he grasped Kitty's. "I enjoy discussing matters that affect this nation with my royal father, and am allowed to sit at the table during meetings of the Privy Council. But I would never claim the throne for myself, even if he offered it to me. Nor do I think anyone should sit upon it. The people should govern themselves."

Sera narrowed her gaze at their linked hands. A private conversation with her friend appeared to be in order. "Have any of the attending physicians been able to identify what is causing the king's decline?" She must change the subject from revolution and establishing a republic before talk became too heated.

"Lord Viner says it is most perplexing. Some hold his condition is not a medical one at all, but magical." Hugh glanced at Sera as he said the last two words.

Dread plunged through her. "No doubt that burden will be deposited at my door. How convenient for the council if the king descends into madness at the same time as a woman mage appears at court. A woman who trails darkness behind her." Would she never be able to prove her worth?

"Oh, I'm sure Fitzfey's mother must shoulder some of that blame. Some believe it was gazing upon the loveliness of Princess Deryn's form *au naturel* that affected his mind." Kitty nudged her companion with her elbow.

"It is said that a human eye cannot look upon a Fae without being forever altered. Certainly the court is littered with fainting bodies that I must attend when Lord Fitzfey passes among them, and he is only half-Fae," Hugh said, and laughter erupted around the table.

After a delightful supper, they adjourned to the drawing room, where the artist, a Mr Benjamin Lapwing, amazed them with his painted nudes. One portrait winked. Another crooked a finger in invitation to Hugh. The poet recited some of his works and they were so moving, one of the painted nudes burst into tears and nearly ruined its canvas.

Kitty sat next to Lady Plimmerton. "I wonder if I might prevail on you, Lady Plimmerton, to have a care for Father in the coming weeks while I am away?"

Mr Napier turned from his spot by the fireplace and stared at his daughter, worry written all over his features. "What is this? We have not discussed your going away."

"Sera is off on an investigation and I intend to accompany her. As much as it pains me to leave you, Father, I cannot let my friend go alone." Kitty grinned at Sera.

Sera sipped her coffee and kept her silence. She had already had this argument with Kitty. And lost. Her friend wished to assist and was adamant that it was time she had a share in the adventure. Besides, Sera would appreciate Kitty's keen mind to discuss whatever she uncovered in the countryside. The contessa had been delighted to include Kitty in their party, and had muttered that Lord Hillborne wouldn't know what struck him, with such a contingent of fierce women descending upon him to unearth the truth.

A smile transformed Lady Plimmerton's face into gentle loveliness, and kindness shone in her blue eyes. "I shall be delighted to look in on Mr Napier. We will dine together at least once a week—and perhaps I might even lure him out of his offices to accompany me to Hyde Park in the afternoons?"

"Of course I will accompany you, Lady Plimmerton. I enjoy our conversations. But you have never left me before, Kitty." Mr Napier's fingers curled around the stem of his port glass.

Sera and Kitty exchanged a look. When they tested their wings and sought independence, that impacted Mr Napier. His days would be as lonely as his nights when Kitty left. Under normal circumstances, a daughter would remain under her father's roof until she married. But Kitty would no more follow convention than Sera would, and they both intended to see something of the world.

"Your daughter is eighteen and a most charming woman. Such is the way of things, that our children leave our nests to embark on their own journeys through life. Why, my daughter has been married these five years and is about to become a mother herself." Pride sparkled in Lady Plimmerton's eyes. Sera had contributed to that happy event and Lady Tinwald had been generous in showing her appreciation.

Kitty reached out and took her father's hand. "I will return, Father, with a tale to entertain you. And we will leave you in the capable hands of Lady Plimmerton."

"As long as you come back to me, Kitty. I could not bear to be without you, too." He toasted his daughter and sipped his port.

One by one, the guests took their leave until only Kitty, Sera, Hugh, and Mr Napier remained. She had asked Hugh to stay behind, as there were matters to discuss before she left London. They gathered in Mr Napier's study. Kitty dropped into a leather armchair opposite her father. Hugh remained standing.

Sera stood by the fire and regarded the two men most important to her. "I need to ask the assistance of you both, gentlemen, while Kitty and I are away."

"Oh? I am intrigued that you require both a solicitor and a surgeon. You're not planning to stab someone, are you?" Mr Napier tilted his head as though already considering defences for such an attack.

"I need you to delay the trial of Lady Meredith Hillborne. She stands accused of murdering her daughter. I need time to try to find the girl. Not only that, there is something about her husband's actions that strikes me as odd."

Mr Napier walked to his desk and opened a drawer. Pulling out a fresh sheet of paper, he seated himself and began to take notes. "What evidence is there?"

"Very little, from what I understand. The girl's

body has not been recovered. Meredith was found clutching a toy on the shores of a lake and muttering *she is gone*. There is also the matter of her confession." The mother's own words would be used to condemn her.

The quill scratched over the paper, and then Mr Napier looked up. "Ah. A confession makes this problematic if I am to stay proceedings. Do you know what she said?"

"I visited her in Newgate, as you know. She said to me, *I am responsible. He cannot reach her now, and I will die content with that knowledge*. It seems rather clear cut, does it not?" Sera twisted her hands together. All she needed was a few days to satisfy herself that Meredith deserved such a fate.

"Ah. Now that is interesting." Mr Napier gestured to her with the pen. "*I am responsible*. That does not mean *I did it*. It could be she feels that her actions led to her daughter drowning. A moment of inattention, perhaps, while her child played by the water's edge? Or entrusting her to a servant who proved unreliable. That gives me room to manoeuvre."

This was why Sera admired Mr Napier. Only a lawyer would pounce on the words used and angle them to show a different meaning.

Mr Napier caught Hugh's gaze. "Mr Miles, I will require you to ascertain Lady Hillborne's mental state. I will build a defence around possible scenarios where she might have been inattentive and inadvertently contributed to her daughter's demise. We shall also build a counter to the prosecution's charge, by suggesting that even if she did commit this terrible act, she was not in a fit mental state."

"Of course. I am not sure claiming insanity will help her case, though. Bedlam is a worse place to end up than Newgate," Hugh said.

"Thank you, gentlemen. We will send you what evidence I discover." Sera retrieved a plain box from Mr Napier's desk and drew Hugh to a shadowy corner while father and daughter conferred. "I have something else I would ask of you that is dangerous but important."

"Anything. You have only to ask," he murmured.

Sera opened the box to reveal a package wrapped in oiled green cloth. Since the Fae bracelets did not give off any magical resonance, she was reluctant to bind them with magic. The oiled cloth kept their creeping silver threads imprisoned as effectively as any spell—unless someone opened up the parcel. "This bundle contains the Fae bracelets. The box is a temporary measure only. It will only open to your touch, but any mage could force the lock. Plus, the spell on the box will attract anyone looking for a magical item. I need you to hide the bracelets somewhere no mage would think to look, away from the box. I am concerned that someone might try to find them in my home while I am away."

He closed the lid and took the box from her. "I

shall ensure they are concealed, and no one will disturb them until you wish them returned."

Sera kissed his cheek. "Thank you." That was at least one concern lifted from her mind. Now she could concentrate on a more immediate concern—her role as lady's maid.

TWELVE

The next morning, Elliot found Sera with an old carpetbag open on her bed as she packed into it the plain gowns she'd worn while under Branvale's roof.

"Giving those to charity?" he asked, his dark gaze curious.

"No. I am leaving you to seek employment as a lady's maid." She packed only what a maid would possess, in case anyone decided to search her belongings. The tonics for Vilma were safe in a small wooden box to go among the contessa's luggage.

Elliot snorted. "Give over. What is this trip really about?"

She had told her staff she would be away for a week or two, but skimmed over the details. "I believe Imogen—that's the restless spirit plaguing Bunhill Fields—won't retire to her grave until I find her descendant. I don't want the lord of the manor to know I am a mage. Not yet, anyway. So I am playing the role of the contessa's maid."

"You're terrible at doing hair." He chuckled under his breath.

"Then it is lucky I can do magic, isn't it?" Sera packed the last item and buckled the bag shut.

A serious look dropped over Elliot's handsome features. "I'll guard the fort, don't you worry. Me and her." He gestured to Nat, snoozing outside in the sun after finishing the rill in the garden. Her granite claws dug into the stone at the corner of the house.

Sera never doubted Elliot's loyalty. "Keep your eyes peeled. I am expecting to be given a key by someone, but it might not be a literal key. It could be anything."

"Weird magey stuff?" One dark eyebrow arched.

She flashed him a smile. "Something like that. There is also a risk that other mages might test the strength of the wards I have protecting this house. If someone does break in, don't be a hero. Anything here can be replaced except for you, Rosie, and Vicky. I find I have grown rather used to your annoying ways."

He nodded. "If anything happens, I'll send my crow friend to tell you."

The crow was another entry on Sera's list of things to figure out. "Are you going to tell me what she really is?"

He shrugged. "She really is a crow. Anything more than that isn't my secret to tell."

Sera blew out a sigh. That was the problem with fierce loyalty. She could not simultaneously expect it for herself, but want it broken for others.

Elliot carried the bag downstairs while Sera fetched the potions. At midmorning, Contessa Ricci's large travelling coach stopped outside her home. She embraced Rosie and Vicky. She'd not left them for any length of time before, nor had Sera journeyed much beyond the outskirts of London. Elliot handed her carpetbag to the coachman, who wedged it among the multiple trunks and hat boxes stored atop the carriage. The small box of potions went inside the coach with Sera.

Ordinarily, a lady's maid would travel on the seat at the rear of the carriage next to a footman, but Sera wasn't taking the pretence that far.

"Don't go getting into too much trouble," Elliot said as he handed her up.

Sera kept hold of his hand and met his gaze. "Keep watch for anything unusual and tell your crow friend that when I return, I am going to have a long conversation with her."

In the cosy interior, Sera took the seat facing backward next to an excited Kitty, who wore a marvellous travelling outfit of tawny wool.

"Will anyone recognise you?" Vilma asked. She wore a blue velvet cloak with fur trim around her neck, despite the late warmth outside. Her complexion was pale, but with a flush of pink to it and excitement in her eyes.

"I will alter my features when we stop tonight and at Mistwood Manor. But I don't think anyone will be looking for a mage among the staff." She took Kitty's hand and squeezed, grateful to have her friend at her side for whatever they encountered.

The contessa wore deep grey edged in blood red. Her hat sat at an angle and she wore dark-lensed spectacles that obscured her eyes. The blind was pulled halfway down on the window beside her. Since no breath filled her lungs, Sera had no idea if she was awake or asleep. Then she rapped on the ceiling with a walking cane and the carriage lurched forward.

"Are you able to travel in the daylight without distress?" Sera knew little about vampyres. Would the older woman spontaneously combust and set fire to the seat?

Lush red lips quirked in a brief smile. "I will not burn or dissolve into a pile of ash, but I am a nocturnal creature. The light hurts my eyes and a weariness attacks my limbs at being outside at such an hour."

"Noemi is a grumpy morning person, liable to snap off heads if disturbed before four in the afternoon," Vilma teased. Then she mitigated her words by taking Noemi's hand and gazing at her protector with adoration in her eyes.

Noemi raised Vilma's hand and kissed her knuckles. "After two hundred and fifty years, I have learned that nothing interesting ever happens early in the morning. So why force myself from bed at such an hour?"

"Leaving London is thrilling to me, but then, I lead a rather dull life," Kitty said.

A quiet laugh came from the corner. "No woman who hosts a salon that includes a half-Fae royal bastard and an artist with weeping paintings could possibly be called dull. I am delighted to include you in our party, and hope you will reciprocate by inviting me to your next evening."

"That is a bargain I will happily strike!" Excitement blazed in Kitty's eyes.

The monotony of their journey soon made them all quiet. Silence settled over them, and Sera pulled a book from her satchel. As the sun rose higher in the sky, the scenery outside the window changed from the grey sky and bleak buildings of city life to cleaner skies and rolling pastures.

After three hours, they stopped so the women might stretch their legs and relieve themselves.

"How are you faring?" Sera enquired of Vilma.

"Today is a good day," Vilma replied. "I believe the prospect of seeing my old home again has invigorated me. Besides, an adventure is always a marvellous tonic, is it not?"

The footman helped them back into the coach, and they continued on their way. Noemi became more animated as the sky dimmed outside the window. Night had fallen by the time they reached the coaching inn.

Noemi pulled Sera to one side as they crossed the yard. "You and I are more used to protecting ourselves. I ask you, as a mage, to have a care for Vilma during this trip."

Sera easily gave her assurances. "Of course. We are four women alone. I suspect some will think we are easy targets to prey upon."

Noemi grinned. "It will be fun, will it not, if they try?"

They took two rooms, Noemi and Vilma sharing one, Kitty and Sera in the other. While weary from the hours in the swaying coach, the two friends whispered long into the night until exhaustion silenced them.

They set out early the next day, determined to make their destination by nightfall. The contessa seemed to doze in the corner and the others attempted to play cards to keep themselves entertained.

As the conversation turned to the missing child at her former home, Vilma clasped her cards to her chest, and whispered, "Did you see her in prison?"

Sera drew a breath and collapsed her hand of cards as though she folded a fan. "Yes. She was a miserable sight, huddled on the ground in a cold and damp cell."

Vilma swallowed and glanced down. "Did she proclaim her innocence?"

That was the bit that weighed on Sera's mind, despite Mr Napier's casting the words in a different light. "No. Meredith said she was responsible, and that she was content to die."

Vilma let out a small cry that stirred Noemi into movement. "How horrid. How could a mother do such a thing?"

The idea plagued Sera. "That is one of many questions I seek to answer."

"My father will delay proceedings to give us time to find out exactly what happened and, we pray, to find little Hannah." Kitty gathered up the cards, the game abandoned.

"Something about this entire affair itches at the back of my skull. Meredith said that Hannah is beyond his reach and she begged me to leave her where she is." Sera met the gaze of the contessa. Sera might lack years, but her brain absorbed knowledge like a sponge, acquired both from life below stairs, and from the world view imparted by Mr Napier.

Noemi sucked air into her dead lungs and swore.

Vilma frowned and looked at her companion. "Death makes the child unreachable. Is that what she means?"

"Si, cara mia." Noemi patted Vilma's gloved hand, but she shared a knowing look with Sera.

Why would a mother forfeit her own life to place her child beyond a husband's grasp? The few answers presenting themselves to Sera made her blood run cold.

They reached Mistwood Manor that evening. Excitement fluttered through Sera, tempered by the sad circumstances. This was her first secret mission. The idea had been inspired when she had adopted the appearance of a maid to prowl the palace's hidden corridors. They decided to say that Kitty was under the care of the contessa, placed in the older woman's hands by her father, who wanted the heiress to see something of England before being married off.

"There it is!" Vilma exclaimed, pointing.

The house was sheltered by a tree-covered hill at its back and a forest to one side. The dark stone building resembled something from a twisty fairy tale, with pointed turrets and high walks. Before it, a lake stretched to wooded shores. The water shimmered like quicksilver in the setting sun.

"Its name comes from the mist that rises from the water in the mornings and drifts through the surrounding forest. As a child, I imagined fairies and unicorns hiding in such a magical place." Vilma leaned forward, her eyes clear and alive.

Sera stared at the lake, wondering if the chill water embraced the body of a child. That would be her first task—to search its depths—once she ascertained whether the groundsmen had dragged it.

Lord Hillborne greeted their carriage as two footmen helped unload their luggage. The new viscount stood slightly taller than average, and filled out his clothes like a man used to physical entertainments such as riding, fencing, or boxing. His dark hair was tied back at his nape. Unfortunately, he possessed dark, bushy eyebrows that slanted toward his nose, giving him a perpetual look of annoyance. The contessa stepped down first, followed by Kitty.

"Vilma! My cousin, how delighted I am to finally meet you." He rushed at Kitty and kissed her cheek.

"You are mistaken, Lord Hillborne. I am Miss Napier, a friend of Contessa Ricci." Kitty arched an eyebrow at the lord and leaned away from his embrace.

"Miss Napier is under my care. Here is your cousin, Miss Winters." Noemi tilted her head toward Vilma, whose alabaster skin was even paler in the descending light and strands of her hair turned to spun gold.

Lord Hillborne huffed and looked from the robustly healthy Kitty to the ethereal Vilma. "Cousin. Charmed." He took the slender woman in an awkward embrace and kissed her cheek with a familiarity that earned him a scowl from Noemi. "And the delightful Contessa Ricci and Miss Napier. You are all most welcome to Mistwood Manor." He bowed.

"We are sorry it is under such terrible circumstances, but I hope our presence brings you a little comfort in these times." Vilma extricated herself from his grasp, but rested a hand on his arm.

Lord Hillborne placed his hand atop her gloved one. "I have come to realise how important family is. I hope you will forgive my previous actions. Only now do I realise how abominable they were. I wish to make amends."

Noemi snorted under her breath, and Sera

silently shared her sentiment. The viscount's words, it appeared, did not ring true to either of them.

"Will there be a service for your little girl?" Kitty asked.

A twitch pulled at one side of Lord Hillborne's lips. "Nothing is planned at this point. I still keep hope alive that Hannah may yet be found. But come inside and have something to warm up. Night falls quickly here and you don't want to be outside after dark. My footmen will show your maid to your rooms." He waved a dismissive hand at Sera.

Kitty smiled and wriggled her little finger with the mage silver ring Sera had crafted. She would signal if Sera was needed. The ring would also give Sera a way to find her friend in the rambling house.

She followed the footmen who carried the trunks and bags. The pair would need to make a number of return trips to cart all their luggage into the sprawling house and up the main stairs. They took a turn along a corridor with dark panelled wood and a deep blue runner on the floor. Sera imagined she was being swallowed by a whale, the panelling somewhat like enclosing ribs.

One man shouldered open a door and walked into a spacious, light-filled room positioned at the front of the house. He dropped the trunk on the floor and its companion soon joined it. "This is the contessa's room. Miss Winters is through there." He gestured to a door beside the fireplace, its trim picked out in yellow. "Miss Napier is across the hall."

"Thank you." Sera stripped off her gloves, untied her bonnet, and removed her cloak while the footmen delivered the right luggage to each room. She walked to the window seat and stared out at the lake—now a mirror reflecting the stars appearing above.

A soft tread behind her made her turn to find a young maid of perhaps only twelve or thirteen. Her apron was covered in dusty smudges and she carried a bucket. "Excuse me, miss, I've come to light the fires."

"Hello, I'm Sera, the contessa's maid," Sera said. The fire would soon take the chill off the room, as would a magical gush of warm air once she was alone.

"I'm Truby," the girl replied with a shy whisper as she knelt before the wood laid in the grate. She rubbed her hands together and then clicked her fingers. A small flame appeared at the end of the girl's index finger.

"Trudy?" Sera repeated, thinking she had misheard as she watched the aftermage summon the flame.

The maid used her finger to light the tinder and then curled her hand into a fist to extinguish its flame. "Truby. It's my last name. We don't use Christian names here. His lordship doesn't like familiarity."

"Oh. Well, in that case, I am Jones. I wouldn't want to get anyone in trouble." Sera had decided to adopt Jones as her name for the trip. The married name of her late mother, but one which had never been bestowed upon her.

With nothing else to do, Sera opened the trunks and unpacked the contessa's clothing. Gowns were hung in the scented cedar-lined armoire, smaller items tucked away in the drawers. By the time the women sought their rooms to change for dinner, Sera had everything sorted.

"I did not think you would unpack for me," Noemi said as she ran a hand down a gown.

"I am your maid, milady. It's what we do." Sera winked at her co-conspirator. At least her placement below stairs in Branvale's household meant she had experience to draw upon. The only difference between that house and this one was its size and the number of staff.

"I am famished. Travelling gives one ever such an appetite." Kitty stood before the fire and held out her hands to warm her chilled flesh.

"How did you find Lord Hillborne?" Sera asked.

Vilma lowered herself into a chair, her complexion turning grey as exhaustion from the last two days depleted her. "My cousin was most solicitous about the state of my mother's affairs."

"Are you sure, *cara mia*, that this is not too much for you?" Noemi knelt before Vilma and took hold of her hands.

"Do not send me back to London, I beg of you. It means so much to me to be here once more. Besides, I think if we throw the young and innocent heiress at my cousin, he will lose all interest in me." A soft laugh came from Vilma's delicate throat.

Kitty snorted. "He was rather interested in how many men were vying for my hand, to say nothing of the extent of my fortune."

Sera tucked Kitty's words away. Why would a married man want to know that?

"If it becomes too much, you have only to say." Noemi kissed Vilma's hand before rising.

Vilma smiled at her lover. "I thought that before we change for dinner, I would show Sera to the kitchens. I wish to see if any of the staff from my parents' household remain."

The contessa arched an eyebrow at Sera. She nodded in understanding and held out her arm to Vilma. "Come along, then. You lot are going to have a fancy meal and I want to see what is on the table in the servants' hall."

Vilma set a slow but certain pace through the house. At times, she paused to touch a familiar object or to sigh over one lost. At length they descended a dark panelled staircase into the bustling heart of the manor. Footmen and maids scurried to make ready for dinner, and Vilma and Sera had to step out of their way more than once. Yet when Sera paused to watch, there weren't as many staff as she imagined a house the size of Mistwood required. The few there were moved faster, as though each tried to do the work of two or three.

"Perhaps this was a bad idea. They will be ever so busy without us intruding," she murmured.

"Miss Winters?" a woman called out.

Vilma turned, and a huge smile broke over her face. "Mrs Pymm!"

Her tiredness forgotten, Vilma rushed to the woman with a willowy build and greying hair. The chatelaine hanging at the waistband of the woman's plaid gown announced that she was the housekeeper. They hugged and then the housekeeper set Vilma at arm's-length to examine her.

Mrs Pymm touched a strand of Vilma's golden hair. "I always knew you would grow into a beautiful young woman. How it warms my heart to see your face, but it aches with wishing that your father was still lord here."

That piqued Sera's interest. Perhaps a private chat with the housekeeper would reveal much about the differences between the two holders of the title.

Thirteen

"I am so glad to find you are still here, Mrs Pymm. Has much changed?" Vilma peered around the housekeeper and into the kitchen.

"There are a few old and wrinkled ones left who fondly remember you and your parents." The housekeeper let go of Vilma and turned a critical eye upon Sera. "Would this be your maid?"

"No. This is Jones, Contessa Ricci's maid." Vilma made the introductions.

Sera bobbed a curtsey. "Pleased to meet you, ma'am." She remembered the maid's caution about familiarity.

"We are busy preparing for supper, Miss Winters. But do say you will return and have a quiet cup of tea with me? I'd so love to hear how Lady Hillborne is these days." The housekeeper's hand fell to the silver chatelaine at her waist, a plain oval with multiple chains dangling below as though they sprouted from the main part. Each chain held some useful item in the housekeeper's daily life. Keys, scissors, needle holder, notebook...some women crammed so much onto the devices that Sera wondered they didn't walk at an angle to compensate for the weight.

"I have a letter from my mother for you, Mrs Pymm. She entrusted it to me should I find you still here. I shall bring it to you tomorrow morning, if that would suit?" Vilma said.

"Oh, I shall look forward to it. Now Jones, I will show you to your room and where we take our supper. Then you must return upstairs to tend to your mistress. They will want to change for dinner, I am sure." The housekeeper nodded to Vilma and shooed Sera through an open doorway.

Mrs Pymm pointed out the servants' hall with its long table, where they took their meals and gathered. Along another corridor, she pushed open a door. "This will be your room. There is a bell outside your door to let you know when your mistress requires you." Her task done, the housekeeper bustled away to supervise the preparation of the upstairs meal.

Sera stepped inside the small room with a single window high on one wall. The walls were unadorned. A pitcher and ewer sat atop a plain dresser with four drawers. Her bag had been deposited on a narrow cot with a flat-looking pillow. A wool blanket was folded at the foot of the cot. She lingered long enough to whisper a spell to protect her privacy and to fix the room's location in her mind. Then she hurried upstairs to help Noemi change out of her travelling clothes.

Twice on her trip back upstairs, she became lost in the rambling twists and turns of the corridors, and had to stop and focus on Kitty's mage silver ring to orient herself. By the time she found the contessa's room, her companions had already changed. Vilma sat by the fire and watched as Noemi twirled Kitty's locks and pinned them atop her head. Having a vampyre with over two hundred years of experience with such things was proving invaluable.

"How are you feeling?" Sera asked Vilma, kneeling on the rug before her.

A sad smile graced her lips. "Pain is a constant friend. I struggle to remember a time before, and what it is like to be without it."

"I will fetch the potion. You do not have to suffer when there is a remedy at hand." Sera found the carefully stowed vials in their box and poured a small measure of brown syrup into a glass for Vilma. Then she added a splash of wine to mask the sharp taste.

A little colour returned to Vilma's cheeks after she drank the medicine. Sera fetched her a shawl to protect her exposed shoulders from any chill. They didn't need any other illness reaching for the delicate woman.

Then she pulled Kitty aside and took her friend's hands. "Remember, stick as close to the truth as possible. You are an eligible young heiress enjoying the countryside with an old family friend. The fewer outright lies we tell, the easier it will be to keep track of them."

Kitty beamed at her friend and mischief gleamed in her eyes. "Do not worry. Father taught me well. I shall evaluate the witness and the available evidence and report back to you with my findings and a suggested plan of how to advance."

The excitement of their adventure brushed up against their true purpose. A missing child, presumed deceased, and a distraught woman huddled in a cold prison cell. "We are here to find Hannah, but Meredith's words are still in my mind. I would understand what drove her to commit such a crime."

"And I want to know why Lord Hillborne invited Vilma here now, at such a time. He has had some years to apologise for the callous way he treated her and her mother." The contessa took Vilma's arm and tucked her companion close as they left the room.

"How marvellous it is to be here again. How I love old Mistwood. Her walls and grounds are soaked in history and stories." Vilma trailed a finger along the wainscoting as they walked.

"You speak of the house as though it were a person," Sera said. She and Kitty walked behind Noemi and Vilma, since the former resident knew her way around the labyrinthine structure.

Vilma half-turned as she spoke to Sera, with a lightness in her tone and the sparkle returned to her blue eyes. "Can a house not have a soul? For two centuries it has stood here, and sheltered families and staff alike as we have laughed, cried, and loved. Surely so many lives brushing against its walls must leave an impression over time. Besides, I always thought this place was magical. Please do not shatter my childish illusions."

Sera glanced at the dark hall stretching before them. While it presented as gloomy if one were alone, in the company of Vilma it seemed more like an embrace. Could the very essence of a person seep into their home? What an intriguing idea. "Now you have made me curious. Mistwood certainly has a presence. I rather like the idea of a house possessing a mind of its own. Imagine a house unhappy with its residents sporting leaks and drafts as a means of communicating its displeasure."

"Perhaps, just as only a few mages possess magic, only a very few special estates have a soul," Noemi said.

"Oh, do you truly think so, Noemi?" Vilma paused and gazed at her protector. "How I would love to travel the world and discover other old homes like Mistwood."

"We could, if you so desired." Noemi stroked Vilma's pale cheek.

As they neared the drawing room, Sera fell behind, as expected of a servant. How she wished she could join the other women beyond the door, to listen in on the conversation and observe how Lord Hillborne behaved. It occurred to her that she could use her magic to seek out a willing mouse to sit under a sideboard and be her ears, but she couldn't risk someone coming upon her while in the trance state needed to perform the spell.

"I shall wait for you to ring, milady, when you require me." Sera curtseyed to Contessa Ricci as a footman flung open the door to admit them to the warm room. She glimpsed only a deep green and blue colour scheme and the viscount standing by a black marble fireplace.

With nothing more to do, she followed a maid back to the kitchens. Laden trays were carried out by footmen, other dishes were stacked into a dumb waiter to rise to the dining room. Not wanting to be underfoot, Sera retreated to her room. She stood on tiptoe to squint out her window, but there was little to see in the gloom. The moon hid behind the clouds and she caught only the rough glimpse of cobbles and something that resembled a barn or stables and other outbuildings.

From her bag, Sera extracted a notebook that fitted neatly into her palm. She had ensorcelled a companion one for Hugh. A small notebook was easier to tuck about one's person and harder to lose than a larger sheet of paper. There was also less risk he would use it to write instructions on to a patient or the apothecary. A space in the spine accommodated a pencil no longer than her finger.

Flipping open the diminutive book, she found a message from Hugh. Mr Napier had appeared before the court and succeeded in having proceedings delayed. He had argued that Lady Hillborne was not of fit mind to stand trial and needed to be assessed by physicians. The court had ordered that Meredith be moved to Bedlam for that purpose. However, Hugh cautioned, she now faced horrid conditions in the cramped asylum. He feared the effect it would have on her mind if she remained there for more than a week or two.

Sera blew out a sigh. Meredith most likely wouldn't linger for long. English justice could be very swift, and delivery of a guilty sentence was often followed promptly by an execution. Some prisoners were taken directly from the courtroom to the gallows. The poor woman might live only an hour or two once convicted of her child's death. While Lady Hillborne's fate saddened Sera, there didn't seem to be much they could do to avert it.

Another worry gnawed at her. Should they even try? Justice should be done for the child, and prolonging the mother's life seemed a cruelty. How could any mother live with the blood of their only child staining their hands? Was that what Meredith meant by being content to meet her fate?

In response to Hugh, Sera wrote they had arrived at Mistwood Manor and that Vilma seemed much revived to be back in her childhood home. After summarising her first impressions, her hand hovered over the page. Her missive seemed...incomplete.

On impulse, after a gap of a line or so, Sera wrote, *I miss you.*

There was little more to do until Noemi rang for her. The staff would not eat until the master and his guests had finished. Pondering Vilma's belief in Mistwood having a sort of soul, Sera gathered her skirts about her and sat on the striped rug on the floor. With legs crossed and eyes closed, she let her magic drift through the house like the mist across the lake.

Tendrils filtered through brick, wood, and plaster. Then, like a tide washing over the sands of a beach, Sera's consciousness searched the old manor for something other than the expected. Just as she grew bored and her buttocks numb, she encountered an answering touch. Dark, yet warm and old. It shivered against Sera's magic and, while it offered no words, it conveyed an impression of shrinking upon itself. Like a light-sensitive plant would curl a leaf away from the sun. Not sure what else to do, Sera pushed a sense of reassurance to whatever inhabited the house, promising to do what she could to alleviate whatever distressed it. Then it retreated, leaving only a faint trace of sadness.

The sound of a bell drew her back to her physical form. Some hours had elapsed—it was the bell to Noemi's room that clanged above Sera's door. Her joints protested the time on the cold floor as she climbed to her feet and hurried to hear how the evening had gone for her friends.

When Sera entered the bedchamber, Noemi was

wrapping Vilma in a warm velvet robe, her gown tossed over the back of a chair.

"There is little to tell. Lord Hillborne avoided the subject of either his missing child or imprisoned wife. He mainly wanted to know about the latest entertainments in London and the composition of my fortune." Kitty rolled her eyes as she plucked pins from her hair.

"That in itself tells us much about him. Hardly a man consumed by grief for his situation." Sera took the hairpins and returned them to the dressing table.

"He asked pointed questions of Vilma about how her father had afforded the upkeep of Mistwood, what investments he used to manage, and what her mother had taught her about the running of the manor," Noemi spat out the words.

Sera stared at Kitty with widened eyes and a silent question.

"Vilma once lived here and is familiar with the house and surrounding community. We did suspect he might be assessing Vilma as a replacement spouse," Kitty replied.

The contessa growled, but a soft laugh came from Vilma. "He will be sadly disappointed, will he not? Even if my heart was not already given to another."

Kitty yanked her gown off her shoulders. "There is also the slight impediment that he already has a wife living."

"But for how long?" Sera murmured as she held out a dressing robe for her friend. It was beyond callous to consider a replacement for Lady Hillborne when the current one still breathed.

"What is the plan of attack for tomorrow?" Kitty asked as she donned the robe and tied the belt around her waist.

"The most obvious—I will search the lake for the child." That would be a chilly task, but a necessary one. Sera hugged Kitty's still-warm dress to her chest.

"Lord Hillborne had his men row out into the lake and drag it. But they found nothing apart from an old boot, apparently." Vilma's voice was fading as the day took its toll and stole her strength.

Sera fetched the potion that would allow Vilma to sleep undisturbed by the tumours pressing inside her. "We shall see whether I can discover anything by magical means."

Once the women were prepared for bed, Sera returned below stairs in time for her supper. In the servants' hall, a pine table stretched nearly twelve feet long. Plain wooden chairs were crammed along its length. The table was capable of seating twenty, but only half the seats were occupied. Sera counted ten, including herself. A small number for such a large house.

The butler sat at one end, the opposite chair for his equal—the housekeeper.

Sera paused, not wanting to upset the pecking order. Conversation hushed as everyone stared at her, assessing both her appearance and her position in the servants' social structure.

"This is Jones, lady's maid to the contessa. Sit here, Jones." Mrs Pymm pointed to a chair on her right.

With everyone seated, conversation hushed as the butler cleared his throat and led the staff in prayer. The noise level rose afterward as platters were passed around and the staff resumed talking. The food was plain but hearty, and Sera had no complaints. She let the chatter wash over her and only spoke up when addressed.

You could tell much about a lord from his staff. From the quality of food they ate, the tidiness of their uniforms, to general demeanour and how they spoke of him. While there were one or two outbursts of quickly swallowed laughter, overall the tone of the room was subdued. The household suffered under the weight of two losses—Lady Hillborne and her daughter.

"I am very sorry to hear of the tragedy that struck this household," Sera said at length. No one had mentioned the topic directly, but she found it in the gaps in conversation. The sudden stops and the hushed whispers when someone veered close to the subject.

"Poor wee mite. Miss Hannah was a lovely and kind little girl," the maid next to Sera said.

"It is a terrible thing indeed, but God will judge Lady Hillborne for what she did, whatever her reasons." The housekeeper's expression left Sera in no doubt the subject was not up for general discussion.

Not that one woman's disapproval would stop Sera from enquiring. It made her all the more determined to get to the bottom of things.

After a satisfying meal, she returned to her room and shrugged off her gown. Once she had climbed under her blankets, Sera pulled the notebook from under her pillow and flipped the pages. Hugh had replied.

I dream of you every night.

Sera closed the book and held it to her heart. How did you know if you were truly in love, and that it would last?

Pondering that puzzle led her into a deep sleep.

Fourteen

Sera awoke early the next morning, despite the lack of light creeping through her tiny window. She wanted to search the lake before the rest of the household roused and asked awkward questions. Washed and dressed, she ate a hearty breakfast with the few other staff who were required to start before dawn. Truby, the young housemaid, attacked a bowl of porridge. Her waif-like form had shed childhood but hadn't yet claimed adolescence. She had coal-black hair tucked up under her cap and long, dark lashes that framed her eyes.

"You're up early. I'm sure that lot will sleep late. His lordship was snoring when I crept in at five this morning to lay his fire." Truby shuddered as she gestured to the ceiling with her spoon.

"I wanted to have a walk by the lake, if that's allowed." Sera finished her bowl of porridge and washed it down with a mug of tea. The brew lacked any of the flavour of the tea mixed by Lord Thornton. Thinking of the earl made her meal churn inside her.

The young maid glanced around and lowered her voice to a whisper. "Yes, but be careful. There's a vengeful spirit lives in the lake. I think it's what took little Miss Hannah."

That piqued Sera's interest. "A vengeful spirit? Like a rusalka?"

Truby frowned. "I don't know what that is."

"It's the spirit of a woman who has drowned, usually as the result of being unhappy in love. She then haunts the place where she died, to lure men into her cold embrace. It would be unusual for one to snatch a child, but anything is possible." Sera gazed at the ceiling without seeing it as she recollected a book on Unnaturals that inhabited waterways and the ocean that she had found in the locked library. A rusalka sought to replace her unfaithful bridegroom, but what if Mistwood's lake had one wanting to start her own family?

The maid's eyes grew wide and her mouth made an O. "That could be her. One of the lads reckons he saw her and all, just before Miss Hannah disappeared. All dressed in black, he said, like that witch in London."

Sera paused. Should she be angry that people still thought of her as a witch, or pleased that her reputation had spread as far as secluded Mistwood? She decided to be pleased. No one was talking about Tomlin's performance.

Her thoughts returned to the rusalka. If a vengeful one had indeed taken the child, that would explain Imogen's night-time wailing. But why would the watery demon take a child when she could have lured a robust gardener into the lake? "I'll be careful. If I do encounter her, I will ask for Miss Hannah to be returned."

"Do you think that is possible? Lady Hillborne loved her little girl. I don't believe them that say she did it. No one that nice would do such a thing. She used to...well, doesn't matter now..." Truby's voice trailed away, and she stared into her mug.

Sera wondered what Lady Hillborne used to do for the staff. Small acts of kindness, most likely. Or perhaps simply treating them like living, feeling creatures rather than pieces of furniture. Whatever it was, Sera shared Truby's opinion and found it difficult to believe Meredith had committed the heinous act. But if a rusalka had grabbed the girl, why not say so? Was that why she felt responsible? Had she not noticed the vengeful spirit creeping up on her child until too late?

A distraught mother might not want to live without her child. For those of strong faith, allowing the courts to find her guilty and send her to the gallows was a way around certain restrictions on entering Heaven.

"I shall go see if I can find this watery demon." Sera smiled at Truby and took her dishes through to the kitchen. She wrapped her shawl around her shoulders. Leaving the kitchens, she walked across the cobbled yard that led to the archway out to the grounds.

"You there! Where do you think you're going?" a sharp male voice called.

A tall man with a frock coat swinging around his knees emerged from the gloom of the stables, leading an equally tall and leggy horse. The equine's breath condensed on the air as it snorted.

Sera eyed the man, dressed in a plain and workmanlike manner, with stubble clinging to his jaw. Given he led a saddled horse, she assumed he was a groom. Who was he to question her movements? She gestured through the archway to the lake. "The lake is ever so pretty. I wanted to go for a walk and enjoy it, before my mistress will need me."

"You shouldn't be wandering around on your own." His hand tightened on the reins as he scowled.

"Because of the rusalka?" Sera tilted her head. No one was chasing her off with a foul look.

He narrowed his eyes. "Who told you that nonsense, then?"

Sera pulled her shawl tighter, the damp air chilling her flesh. "A child is missing and people talk. I don't think it is nonsense if there is a spirit haunting the waterway that might have been responsible."

"People should leave well alone what they don't understand." He flicked the reins over the horse's head and placed one hand on the pommel of the saddle.

Sera had no intention of letting a grumpy man deter her from searching the lake. "Some people shouldn't make judgements about what others understand. They might be wrong."

He swung up into the saddle and stared at her. "Only people with no sense aren't afraid of what's lurking in the shadows of Mistwood."

"Perhaps things in the shadows should be afraid of me." With that, she turned on her heel and stalked off toward the mist-shrouded lake.

The gravel of the drive crunched underfoot and seemed overly loud in the stillness. Still, the lake was beautiful in the early morning. Mist rose from the water and drifted among the trees, obscuring their trunks, only the very tops jutting out like logs in a river. A jetty ran out into the water, where a rowboat was tied up. Nearby were stone benches, positioned to look out over the lake.

A crow called from a nearby willow, its boughs draping the water. Sera glanced up at the creature, part of her certain it looked like the one in London. "There is more to you than meets the eye, my friend." Sera released a tendril of magic and let it curl around the crow. If it were a shifter or some other form of Unnatural, she would peel back its disguise and see who lay underneath.

The bird flapped its wings as the tendril wound around it. Another beat of its wings and Sera's magic...broke apart and dissolved.

Sera's mouth fell open. Impossible. A crow could not repel her magic.

With a *haw-haw-haw* that sounded distinctly like a laugh, it took flight.

She shielded her eyes to track the bird until it disappeared into the sky. "Oh, I will find out what you are. You have only made me more determined. But today, I have a different mission."

Sera sat on a bench at the water's edge and let the silence wash over her. She considered how she might summon a rusalka. Why did Lord Branvale not teach her such things? Since a rusalka was a type of spirit, rather like the restless Imogen, then a similar method of communication might work—if there was indeed a watery soul inhabiting Lord Hillborne's lake. She closed her eyes and sent out tendrils of magic, letting it entwine with the mist.

"Talk to me," Sera whispered, sending her message skimming over the still water.

"Do you mind if I join you?" The quiet voice didn't sound at all like a vengeful spirit trapped in a lake.

Opening her eyes, she saw Vilma standing in the grass nearby, dressed in a gown of deep pink that complemented her pale skin and blonde hair. A cloak in bright cerise wrapped around her shoulders and the deep hood was pulled up over her head.

"Of course not." Sera patted the seat next to her. Not whom she'd expected to summon, but she was growing fond of Vilma's gentle presence. Rather like sitting beside a river, being near her had a way of lifting and washing away your worries.

A tired smile crossed Vilma's face, and lines tugged at her eyes. "You are awake very early. I am sure you didn't get to bed until long after we did."

"I have a mission and want to search the lake before anyone else is around to question me. Shouldn't you be resting?" The stone of the bench was chill under Sera, even through the layers of her gown and petticoats.

Vilma chuckled. "There will be plenty of time for rest soon. I find that as my end nears, I cannot sleep. As though my body knows it will soon draw its last breath and I must be alert to savour every one. I loved this spot as a girl and swam in the lake often—much to my mother's horror." She tugged her cloak more tightly about her shoulders.

Sera whispered a spell to create a weather orb around them filled with warm air. It was a small enough thing she could do to ease the other woman's condition.

"Do you think there is any chance of recovering little Hannah's body?" An involuntary shiver ran through Vilma at the horrible fate of the child.

A group of ducks climbed onto the bank after a morning swim, and the mother settled in the long grass with her offspring clustered around her.

"I intend to try." Sera had given the problem much thought overnight. Men in boats had dragged the lake with no success. The water had not surrendered the child. Instead of searching from its surface, Sera would look from its depths. "When you lived here, did you ever hear whispers of any creatures living in the lake?"

"You mean like a freshwater mermaid?" Vilma chuckled at the idea.

"Or a water spirit, ready to grab the unwary." Sera would need to be alert, in case a rusalka dived at her from behind.

Vilma slid her hood off her hair. "No. Never. Only the manor house ever gives people the sensation of being watched when there is no one around."

"On that count, I can confirm you are correct in your belief that Mistwood has something like a soul or heart." Sera recalled the *otherness* she had brushed up against when she sent her magic to filter through the house.

"Oh, really?" Excitement gleamed in Vilma's eyes.

"Yes, I found something deep in Mistwood's core that skimmed across my magic. It felt far older than the house and was tinged with sadness." She glanced back to the structure, wrapped in its misty shroud.

A sigh from Vilma stirred the mist trying to gain entry to their warm cocoon. "Given recent events, that is understandable, is it not?"

"Perhaps finding Hannah's body will give everyone a chance to grieve and then heal." Rising, Sera shed her outer layers. Coat, boots, and stockings were all removed and folded before being placed next to Vilma on the bench. Then her dress and stays, until Sera stood in only her chemise.

"You will freeze. The water is very deep and cold." Concern edged the other woman's voice.

"I am sure I can think of something to keep me warm. I am a mage, after all." Sera winked. She walked to the edge, dipped a foot into the water, and gasped. The chill shot up her leg, and she curled her toes.

"Do be careful, please. The bottom drops away quickly and we cannot afford to lose you, too," Vilma called.

Sera wriggled her toes on the silty ground between water and grass. She whispered to Mother Nature to protect her daughter and let her magic coat the surface of her skin in a protective layer, as though she wore some form-fitting suit that would insulate her body. A touch rippled over her limbs and across her torso. Trying again, Sera immersed her foot in the chilly water. This time it didn't bite with cold, but registered more like tepid bathwater.

"This will work," she murmured and waded deeper. Her chemise tangled around her legs and when she tugged on it, the fabric floated up around her like seaweed. There was no point in keeping it on and getting it soaked when it would only impede her. Sera stripped the cotton garment off over her head and gave it a magical push so that it draped itself over the back of the bench.

Naked, she closed her eyes and welcomed the

water's embrace. She might be unable to swim, but she trusted in her magic and nature. Before her face went under, Sera formed a bubble of air around her head to breathe. Then she dived under the surface. A moment of panic gripped her, but she made her body relax until it passed. Immersed, she let her body sink, using her hands for direction.

As Vilma had cautioned, the bed of the lake dropped away sharply not far from the bank, and only darkness rose up to nibble at Sera's feet. She called the water to her body and asked it to support her weight. That enabled her to remain suspended beneath the surface while she took stock of her surroundings. A few curious fish congregated in a loose school, and watched her.

"Show me Hannah," Sera asked the lake.

The current tugged her body first one way and then another. Light rippled through the water and played over the fish hiding in the shadows. Back and forth she searched, reaching into thick bracts of weed. Time ticked by. The shafts of sunlight became brighter and played over rocks and plants. When the air in her bubble turned stale, Sera still hadn't found the child. No longer able to breathe the rancid air around her head, she commanded the water to return her to the shore.

A gentle push propelled her back to the shallows, where she got her feet under her. Rising from the water, Sera popped the bubble and breathed in gulps of cool, fresh air.

Vilma, Kitty, and Noemi watched her from the bench. The vampyre, dressed in red and grey, held a parasol to shade herself from the morning sun. Noemi angled her head to regard Sera over her dark spectacles and gave her an appreciative grin.

"You have been gone two hours. I roused Noemi, worried that the lake had claimed you, too," Vilma said.

"I do not have to breathe. I could have walked out to find you," Noemi murmured.

Why hadn't Sera thought of that? Two of them could search the lake quicker than one.

Kitty passed a towel to Sera, and she wiped her face before wrapping the fabric around her body and rubbing briskly at her chilled flesh. Then she pulled the now dry chemise over her head.

"I assume you didn't find her?" Kitty asked.

"No. I couldn't stay under any longer. I shall try again if Noemi does not mind joining me." Sera squeezed the ends of her hair in another towel. "I found no evidence of a vengeful spirit hiding in there, snatching innocent lives."

"Is it possible she is not in the lake? Her maid found Meredith kneeling by the water, clutching the girl's favourite doll. Did anyone actually see her fall in?" Vilma voiced the nagging doubt in the back of Sera's mind.

"Anything is possible. I only know that Meredith claims she is responsible and awaits her death." What had driven the woman to snatch her daughter's life in a moment of madness, then meet her fate so calmly?

Sera turned to stare at the manor house. What had happened under its roof that culminated in that day?

Kitty stood. "The house is awake and we are expected at breakfast. We shall all continue to ask questions about what happened and whether anyone saw Meredith and Hannah." Now that Sera was fully dressed, she shoved the damp towels at her friend.

They headed back across the lawn. Sera fell into step beside the others. "I will see what I can learn below stairs. Vilma, could you gently enquire with Mrs Pymm about what happened the day Hannah disappeared?"

"Of course. I am having tea with her later this morning, to deliver the letter from my mother." Vilma slipped her hand into the crook of Noemi's arm.

The contessa moved her parasol to protect the fair skin of her companion. "I shall pick at Lord Hillborne. His wife may have given some hint of her intentions beforehand."

When the vampyre said she would *pick* at the viscount, Sera couldn't help conjuring to her mind the way a cat tormented a mouse with a sharp claw.

"We can reconvene before luncheon and discuss our progress," Kitty said.

With their plans laid, Sera left the women. They returned to Mistwood through the front door, while Sera crept back past the stables to find a laundry hamper for the wet towels. As she passed the open barn door, she wondered about the grumpy man. How odd. He hadn't warned her specifically about any danger from the lake, but from what was lurking in the shadows of Mistwood.

She glanced up at the dark stone and empty windows, and a chill ran down her spine. As though something looked back at her.

Fifteen

Once the others had breakfasted, Sera retrieved a blank journal from Vilma's room and joined the others on the pretence of acting as secretary to her mistress. They sat in the restful drawing room, its colours inspired by a peacock's feather with deep blues, muted greens, and touches of bronze. Vilma read a book in the window seat overlooking the lake. Noemi and Kitty played chess. Sera sat beside the contessa and pretended to read aloud correspondence about her London affairs and take notes about business she wanted done while away.

Lord Hillborne was sitting in his armchair, the newspaper open, when his voice drifted from behind the paper shield. "Vilma, could you please consult with Mrs Pymm over the menu for tonight? I have no idea of the dietary requirements of fashionable women. Nor is it my role to sort such things."

"Of course, cousin. I would be delighted to assist in any way I can." Vilma set aside the novel in her hands. "I intend to see Mrs Pymm later this morning, so I shall discuss the week's menus while I am with her."

Hillborne snapped the newspaper and peered over a corner. "Good. While you are below stairs, there is also some dispute with the butcher that you might sort out."

Vilma paused, a tiny wrinkle marring her pale brow. "Is the butcher still Mr Hankin?"

"How would I know? Ask Pymm. Meredith was no good at dealing with tradespeople. She was elevated beyond her natural station when I became viscount and struggled to run the household. Just another of her many failings, sadly." His voice drifted over the top of the paper.

Sera bristled and shared a look with Kitty. Lord Hillborne's words were all too similar to an insult hurled at Sera by Lord Kenwood. Women were capable of much, whatever the circumstances of their birth. All they needed was the opportunity and perhaps a little guidance.

"I hope it is not a financial matter? I understood my father left Mistwood in excellent condition." A rare sharp note had entered Vilma's tone.

Hillborne huffed and folded the newspaper. Then he rose and tucked it under his arm. "It might have appeared that way to you, in youthful ignorance.

But I have had to make a number of economies since taking over here. I cannot fathom how your father paid the number of staff he kept. Many of them had to be let go. The estate simply does not generate sufficient income for the excessive lifestyle you once knew." He bowed to the noblewomen and took his leave.

"Was the estate really in financial difficulty when your father died?" Kitty fixed Vilma with her piercing gaze once the door snicked shut.

"No. Not as far as I am aware. Mother always said that Father managed the land and his investments very well. Indeed, I seem to recollect him saying that Mistwood would look after us once he was gone. Sadly, he was wrong." A frown wrinkled Vilma's brow.

"Then this is most odd. Given he knew the estate was entailed, he should have ensured his will contained a stipend or annuity for you to live on if he predeceased your mother. Perhaps there were unknown debts that needed to be settled upon his death and they swallowed up any surplus funds." Kitty rose and paced before the window. Sera could see the cogs spinning in her friend's mind.

"Father did not leave a will," Vilma whispered. "The entire estate went to my cousin, which must have included all Father's investments."

The contessa snorted. "Odious man. He could have looked after you both if he had wanted to. I do not find it in any way a burden to support you and your mother. Your mother maintains excellent accounts and is a frugal housekeeper."

"Was it a happy marriage between your parents?" Kitty rounded on Vilma, questioning her witness.

"Yes. My parents were a love match, and that did not change over the years. Father was a devoted parent to me." Vilma worried at a corner of the book cover with a fingertip.

"But that simply does not make any sense. If he was so devoted to you and your mother, why would he not ensure you were cared for after his death?" Kitty stared at the ceiling as she gathered her thoughts.

Vilma rose from the window seat. "Perhaps Father thought he had more time. He was taken from us quickly when his heart gave out. By the time we summoned help from the village, it was too late."

Sera bowed her head for a moment, thinking of a life snuffed out too soon. Like little Hannah. Like the cancer that would soon snatch Vilma. Yet others, like the current Lord Hillborne, exhibited rude good health despite their bitter natures. Life was not fair.

Or was it death who refused to play an honourable game?

Kitty pursed her lips. "Putting aside Hillborne's comment about making economies, a man such as your father, who took care of his estate and family, would do nothing so irresponsible as to fail to make a will, or to provide for you in it. Especially if he claimed Mistwood would look after you. Did you search his study afterward?"

Vilma's eyes widened as she moved deeper into the room. "My mother did, of course. But we found nothing among his correspondence or in his desk."

"Such a document is not normally kept in a drawer where it would be easily seen. What about at his solicitor's offices?"

A shuddering breath drew through Vilma. "They did not have a will, either. Mr Morgan said he had asked Father about one some years ago, and he replied that it was taken care of."

"In the safe, then?" Kitty persisted.

"The safe?" Vilma froze, and her hands tightened on the book.

"Every lord has a safe for valuables, deeds, and important documents. I am sure a home like Mistwood has one hidden away behind a picture or a moving bookcase." Kitty stepped toward Vilma, reaching for the other woman as though she thought Vilma might faint.

Vilma dropped to the settee with a gentle *oomph*. She stared at Noemi with wide eyes. "There was a metal lock box on Father's desk. When we opened that, it contained only a small quantity of coin, some letters, and a diamond stock pin. We never found a safe. Mother assumed that Father kept all his important documents with his solicitor."

Kitty positively burst with excitement. She reached down and took Vilma's hands. "I am certain your father left a will bequeathing something for you and your mother. We have only to find it." She spun to face Sera, her eyes gleaming. "You will help, won't you?"

Sera wondered what they could do. Surely over the intervening years Lord Hillborne most likely would have found, and destroyed, any such document. It seemed a futile quest. "Of course. But I cannot see Lord Hillborne taking it with good grace if we wish to find a will that eats into his inheritance. Especially when it appears funds are running out at Mistwood. That's assuming one even exists."

Noemi cackled. "Oh, what fun! But Sera is right. Surely Hillborne would have removed anything of import from a safe by now?"

A moment of doubt made Kitty's grin droop, but it rallied. "If Vilma did not know such a hiding place existed, and she grew up here, can we be sure Lord Hillborne, a stranger to the property, found it?"

"It is worth trying, is it not? It would ease my mind to know Mother had something of her own, to provide her with comfort in her old age when I am no longer here." Vilma sat up, her spine a little more straight with determination.

The contessa scowled. "You know I will always look after the dowager Lady Hillborne. She is as much my family as yours. And you, *cara mia*, are not leaving me just yet."

"This will be an adventure inside an adventure, will it not? Like those little dolls that open to reveal another much smaller doll." Vilma smiled and excitement rippled over all of them. A sad purpose had drawn them to Mistwood, but perhaps in laying the child to rest, two more lives might be saved.

Noemi took Vilma's hand and held it between hers.

Kitty perched on the edge of a straight-backed chair. "We need to find a time when he is not around and the staff will not notice what we are doing."

"He said at supper last night that he rides the grounds every morning. That would give us an opportunity," Vilma said.

"I can craft a spell so that the servants do not notice us slipping into and out of his study," Sera contributed.

"Then it is decided. Tomorrow, when Lord Hillborne goes out for a ride, we shall search for a hidden safe and a missing will." Kitty rubbed her hands together.

Worry etched itself into Vilma's face again. "Does the passage of time make any difference? My father died seven years ago. The estate is long settled."

"Wills endure, so long as they are properly drafted and witnessed. There might be issues if property has been disposed of in the intervening time, but we will worry about that once we find something." Kitty patted Vilma's shoulder.

Sera thought the search would prove a diversion from the sad cloud hanging over Mistwood. But with the estate entailed and from the sounds of it, in some financial difficulty, there would be very little left for either Vilma or her mother.

All that remained was the principle of the thing.

With that sorted, Vilma asked Sera to fetch the letter for Mrs Pymm, and then the two women headed below stairs. The housekeeper sat at the kitchen table, a large ledger open before her. The stern face smoothed into a wide smile on seeing the former daughter of the house.

"Miss Winters, lovely timing. Shall we take tea in my parlour?" She closed the account book and rose.

"I can bring it through, if that helps?" Sera offered. The kitchen staff were all busy either chopping vegetables, covered in flour, or scrubbing breakfast dishes.

Vilma looked mortified that Sera, a mage and duchess, would serve a tea tray. Mrs Pymm pursed her lips.

"I started in a kitchen, ma'am. Not one as grand as this, but I'm sure I can muddle through and provide what you need." Sera put a bright smile on her face to reassure Vilma that she didn't mind.

"I'll help Jones, Mrs Pymm. I know where the tea things are kept and I have a bit of spare time," Truby spoke up. The young maid had returned from emptying her bucket of ash, and put it away in a corner until needed again.

"Very well." The housekeeper led Vilma through to her private sitting room.

"Thank you, Truby. Let's start with a tray, a teapot, and two cups." Sera surveyed the large kitchen.

They made a game of it, dodging out of the way of the busy kitchen maids. The cook waved with a knife toward what they needed or could have. When they finished, two slices of cake sat on a plate and steam curled from the spout of the pretty pot.

Sera picked up the tray once everything looked to their satisfaction. "Lead the way, Truby."

Her accomplice slipped from the kitchen and a short way along the corridor, stopped at an open door. Within, Sera found a tiny parlour with a single window overlooking the kitchen garden, and a desk pushed up underneath it. Mrs Pymm and Vilma sat in two armchairs positioned before the fire, where they caught the morning sun streaming through the window. Sera waited to be told to enter, then deposited the tray on the round table between the armchairs.

Vilma whispered her thanks, then Sera left with Truby on her heels. Since the opportunity had presented itself, she decided to see what the house-maid knew of the day Hannah had disappeared.

"What say we sit out in the sun for a little while, before we are both dragged back to work?" Sera said with a wink.

"I suppose I could have a wee break, but I don't want to get into trouble." Truby followed Sera through the kitchen door and out into the yard.

Two benches were positioned against the stone walls of Mistwood, one bathed in sunlight. Sera sat down and turned her face to the sun, relishing the faint warmth of the day.

"Have you worked at Mistwood long?" she asked without opening her eyes.

"Since I was eight years old. Lady Hillborne found me in the village. My ma didn't know what to do with a child with a candle flame for a finger." Truby spoke in a matter-of-fact manner, as if it were common for young children to be taken from their parents and entered into service.

Curiosity nibbled at Sera. The maid had a watered-down gift, and she guessed the girl was one of the last generations of a long-ago mage. "Do you know what generation you are?"

"Seven. All I have is this pathetic little flame. I can't even produce a fire big enough to roast a chicken. Least it's more useful than my brothers'. One knows when it will rain and the other can tell when a pig is about to farrow." She laughed at some old joke only she knew.

"But your gift brought you here, and who knows what you will become one day? Perhaps head cook, housekeeper, or a lady's maid." Sera opened her eyes and gazed at her young companion. A girl who worked hard could advance through the ranks.

"I'd do anything rather than have to light the fire in his bedchamber in the morning. Especially now with Lady Hillborne gone..." Truby's voice trailed off, and she curled her hands into fists.

"Why, Truby? Is he not usually asleep when you creep into his room?" Dread cascaded over Sera, as though thrown from a window above them.

"Sometimes he's awake, and he watches me. Once—" The words caught in the maid's throat and tears misted in her eyes. Then she rolled forward with a sob, her head touching her knees.

"Truby, has he ever done something he shouldn't?" Sera rubbed the maid's back as an old wound ruptured.

"He tried," she rasped. "Lady Hillborne heard me cry out and rushed in. She hit him over the head with a vase to make him let go. But what will happen now she's not here?" Truby's shoulders heaved as she sobbed.

"I am here, and I promise it will be resolved by the time I leave." Sera didn't know how, but she would make sure the lord didn't abuse any of his staff. *Or family.*

The idea became a shadow looming over everything in her mind. How did such a husband treat his wife? There was one person who would know—Lady Hillborne's maid.

"But you're only a maid, too. What can you do?" Truby wiped her eyes and sat up again.

Sera blew out a snort. She couldn't very well say, *Actually, I'm a mage in disguise and I'll put a hex on him to protect you. Like the black witch you think I am*. "You will have to trust me, that is all I can say. But I give you my word he will never hurt you again. Now, did Lady Hillborne have a lady's maid?"

"Oh, yes. Gibson. His lordship made her leave when they took Lady Hillborne away. I don't know what happened to her, though. I'd better be getting back to work. The kitchen fires have to be kept going for luncheon." Truby jumped to her feet, and was swallowed by the shadows of Mistwood.

Closing her eyes again and leaning against the warmed stone, Sera let her magic filter through the house. She drifted through the walls to find the housekeeper's parlour. There were no mice or spiders to lend their ears. Instead, she found a finch perched in an apple tree in the kitchen garden outside the window. She didn't need to overhear, but wanted to catch Vilma as she left without having to lurk in the hall.

When Mrs Pymm placed the used tea things back on the tray and the ill woman rose from her chair, Sera shook loose from the finch and walked back through the kitchens.

Vilma brightened on spotting her on her way through the narrow halls. "Ah, Jones. Are you able to drive a gig?"

"Yes." Sera had some experience. Abigail had seen to it she could ride and take the reins of a lady-like vehicle if required.

"Excellent. I'd like to go into the village to talk to the butcher, but Mrs Pymm tells me Lord Hillborne is unlikely to let me use his carriage, and the contessa's travelling coach is far too large and cumbersome for such a short journey. But a gig will do, if you have time to join me?" Vilma leaned on Sera's arm as she spoke, but her eyes seemed clear, with no hint of pain. It appeared that having a purpose was an amazing tonic in itself.

"Of course. I will find someone to harness a horse for us." Perfect. After Vilma discussed unpaid invoices with the butcher, Sera could find Gibson and ask about Lady Hillborne's relationship with her husband.

Sixteen

Sera retraced her steps out to the cobbled yard and entered the sun-dappled stables. There were six stalls, three on either side of a wide aisle. Most were empty; only two held horses. The contessa's horses had been turned out in the pasture until their return journey. In one stall, the tall, leggy beast she'd seen the other morning slumbered in a corner, its head lowered. In the other, she found the foul-tempered man brushing a bright chestnut, its coat the colour of burnished copper. He crooned under his breath as he worked.

"You there. Miss Winters requires a gig and horse." Sera paused outside the stall. Then, as an afterthought, added, "If you'd be so good as to harness one, please."

He patted the horse and glanced at Sera from under his raised arm. "And who will drive it, then? I have work to do here and can't go gallivanting around the neighbourhood."

Sera rolled her eyes behind his back. She'd never asked him to take the reins, which implied they had that part in hand. "I will drive Miss Winters into the village."

He grunted and muttered under his breath to the horse. After some moments, the equine appeared to whinny in response. "Blossom here says she'll take you. But mind you go easy on her mouth. She's a gentle one."

The retort that flew to her lips withered on her tongue when the horse turned a soft brown eye to her. Sera swore that Blossom winked at her, as though to apologise for the groom's rudeness. "Of course I shall take care of Blossom. Just as I shall ensure Miss Winters does not overexert herself."

He turned then and scrutinised Sera with a hard stare. The horse nudged his shoulder with a large head and his shoulders relaxed. "I'll jump to it now. Shouldn't take too long."

"Thank you." That gave Sera time to do a few more things before they departed.

Back into Mistwood she went and along the hall to the housekeeper's parlour. The door was now partially cracked. She rapped softly and waited.

Mrs Pymm looked up from the papers on her little desk pushed under the window. "Jones. What can I do for you?"

"There is someone I wish to find, who I understand has left this household." She chose her words carefully, even though Vilma had vouched for the forthright housekeeper.

The pen kept tallying numbers in a column. "Who? Spit it out."

"Gibson. Lady Hillborne's maid. I understand Lord Hillborne dismissed her the same day they took Lady Hillborne away." Sera had a name for the woman, but knowing where to look would make her task easier.

The paper in Mrs Pymm's hand shook, and she set it down on the desk. "Her services were no longer needed."

Her maid would have been privy to Lady Hillborne's mood in the days before the disappearance. "Where might I find her?"

Mrs Pymm turned in her chair and fixed Sera with an icy stare. "What business do you have with her?"

Sera considered saying that a distant ancestor of Meredith's was causing a ruckus at the cemetery, and so she was investigating what had really happened to Hannah at the behest of a ghost. Or would it be better to say she wanted tips on styling hair? "I wish to speak to her, lady's maid to lady's maid."

"About her mistress, no doubt." When Sera opened her mouth to protest, Mrs Pymm waved a hand at her. "Miss Winters said you want to bring peace to this household. She mentioned that you had some aftermage skill that might locate little Hannah.

I pray she is right. Poor wee mite deserves a decent burial and not a watery grave. They kept it quiet, but Gibson married his lordship's groom three years ago and has retreated to their cottage in the village." Mrs Pymm gave Sera directions to their home on the outskirts of the village.

Once she had retrieved a shawl and bonnet, she joined Vilma in the drive, where the groom helped the pale woman into the gig. Then he arched an eyebrow at Sera.

"I can manage. Thank you." When she was settled on the wooden seat, Sera took up the reins and released the brake. Catching herself before she flicked the reins against Blossom's rump, she instead clucked her tongue and murmured a polite, "Walk on, if you please, Blossom."

The groom chuckled, a smile flashing on his lips before he turned and stalked back to the stables.

The mare was an obliging sort, and it took little encouragement from Sera to have her trot along the packed dirt road toward the village. The trees lining the track had turned with the chill of autumn and presented a glorious display of rich reds and bright orange, with the occasional evergreen among them.

"I am going to find Lady Hillborne's maid after we have taken care of the business with the butcher. I am hoping she can tell me about Meredith's behaviour in the days before Hannah was taken from this realm." Saying the child might have been murdered stuck in Sera's throat. The idea was too horrible to voice aloud. Better to say *gone* or *missing* than face the harsh reality of the girl's fate.

"It seems Mistwood Manor is no longer a happy home." Vilma kept one hand on her broad straw hat, as though she didn't trust the light scarf securing it under her chin. "Mrs Pymm said there were many arguments between Lord and Lady Hillborne. He was dissatisfied with the dowry she brought to the relationship and that she had not provided an heir. There are also businesses in the village who have not been paid for some months. Staff are let go if they complain about too much work, or late wages."

Sera recalled the groom's words the day she'd encountered him in the yard, about not being safe on her own. At the time, she'd thought he meant because of some malevolent spirit in the lake that might grab her. Now she wondered if he referred to a far more corporeal hand that might seize an unwary woman. That was a topic she would discuss with Kitty and Noemi after Vilma fell into her bed. No need to distress the woman any more than necessary.

"Money causes many arguments. I wonder if that is why my guardian, Lord Branvale, did not marry. He was fond of keeping his money all to himself." Except Sera now knew that wasn't true. He had married, and spurned his wife on their wedding night when he discovered she was an Unnatural.

"Mrs Pymm said Lady Hillborne took a tumble down the stairs a few years back, and lost the babe she carried at the time. She has not conceived since, and suffered a melancholy from that day." Vilma reached out, snatched a maple leaf from a low-hanging branch, and laid it over her palm. The leaf enjoyed a moment of brilliance before she crumpled it into dust.

"I shall tell Hugh. It is possible they can work that into her defence." To move away from such sad topics, Sera asked Vilma about her childhood at Mistwood.

The other woman shook off her sadness and spun tales about the secret passageways she'd found hidden in the walls, and the rooms with no other access. Soon, cottages with thatched roofs came into view and they met other people on the road. Horses and carts carried goods to and from the village. Two men shepherded their flock to a new pasture. A rider cantered by on urgent business.

Sera halted Blossom outside the butcher's premises and she hopped down first to provide a steadying hand for Vilma. The shop had a barn attached, and Sera wrinkled her nose at the smell emanating from it that reminded her of unblocking drains in London.

"I'll not be too long, I hope." Vilma held her skirts out of the dirt as she made her way to the open door.

Sera stood by Blossom's head and scratched the mare behind the ears. Part of her wanted to install drains for the butcher, sweep the streets, and string glow lamps between buildings to create a magical atmosphere at night. But to do any of that would be to give away that a mage had passed through. Instead, she watched the locals go about their day and used her magic to make unseen repairs to holes in boots or pockets.

Vilma exited the shop, a large barrel-shaped man with a bald head following her out to wave.

"I have smoothed the waters somewhat, but Mr Hankin is not the only man not being paid by Lord Hillborne. I am at a loss to explain it. Mr Hankin confirmed that Father was never late with his monthly accounts. Is it possible that, as my cousin said, we lived an excessive lifestyle that exhausted the living at Mistwood, and my cousin inherited empty coffers?"

An impossible question to answer without a full accounting. Sera helped her back into the gig. "It would take Kitty delving into the account books to figure out why the situation deteriorated so quickly once Mistwood passed to your cousin."

"Perhaps she could look while we search the study, when my cousin is out?" Vilma clasped her hands in her lap.

"I will ask her. But before we return, I need to talk to Meredith's maid. I have brought your pain tonic if you require it." Blossom moved off and, recalling Mrs Pymm's directions, Sera followed the river out east of the village to find the Gibson cottage.

"The maid might be more talkative without me lurking at your side. I shall wait by the river." Vilma pointed to a stand of willows, their boughs trailing in the slow-moving water.

Sera left Blossom tied under the dappled light cast by a tree. The mare happily munched on willow leaves. They found a blanket tucked under the seat of the gig and spread it on the grass. Vilma sat, content to watch the swirls and eddies in the water with the steady equine as her guard.

At the Gibson cottage, a riotous garden spilled over the front path. Flowers had gone to seed and provided an autumn feast for the birds. Sera knocked on the door and waited. When it opened, a woman clutched at the latch and stared. In her thirties, with lines radiating from the corners of her eyes, she had tawny hair pulled back into a neat bun at her nape. She wore an apron over her sage-green gown. A frown dug across her brow. "Can I help you? Are you lost?"

"Mrs Gibson? I am Sera Jones, a friend of Lady Hillborne's. I need to talk to you." Describing herself as a friend was a stretch, but Sera needed to get her foot inside the door.

Her hand tightened on the door, and she glanced up and down the cobbled lane. "You had better come in. Best not to talk of her out in the open."

Sera entered a clean and tidy parlour with a cheerful fire throwing out a companionable heat at one end of the room. The long sofa with its carved wooden back and arms looked large enough to accommodate a sleeping child or short adult for a comfortable snooze. At the other end of the room was the kitchen, with a square table, a long work table with a washing basin under the window, and tall cupboards on either side.

"You don't look like a noble, to be a friend of Lady Hillborne." She gestured to a chair with a padded seat before the fire and perched on the edge of the sofa.

Sera sat and considered how much to say. Most of the truth seemed safest. "I'm not. I am maid to Contessa Ricci who, along with her companion Miss Winters and a friend, Miss Napier, has been invited to stay at Mistwood Manor by Lord Hillborne."

"Then how do you know her?" Mrs Gibson clasped her hands in her lap and her demeanour bristled.

A lady's maid knew the intimate details of a noblewoman's life and, in many instances, a deep bond of friendship and loyalty formed between them. If Sera didn't win the woman's confidence, she would be thrown out without so much as a cup of tea to wet her throat. "On behalf of someone who is worried about her fate, I visited her. In Newgate."

Mrs Gibson gasped and concern flashed behind her eyes. "How is she?"

"It is a pitiful place, and she is lost within it. I understand she is to be transferred soon to Bedlam." Sera stared into the fire. Even criminals did not deserve the cold, filthy cages they were kept in. A humane society should provide everyone with the basics needed to exist—whether young or old, sick or criminal. A warm and dry roof over their heads and at least one decent meal a day in their bellies shouldn't be so difficult to supply.

"Bless my soul. Bedlam." The former maid chose a side in some internal conflict and rose to her feet. "Let me put the kettle on and you can tell me why you were at Newgate."

Sera narrated her tale while Mrs Gibson spooned tea leaves into a pot and waited for the kettle to whistle over the flames. "An old spirit has awakened at a cemetery in London. She is an ancestor of Lady Hillborne's and when I spoke to her, she cried out, *Help Meredith*. I discovered that *Meredith* is Lady Hillborne, which is why I spoke to her in prison and, by chance, came to be at Mistwood."

"You can talk to spirits?" Mrs Gibson wrapped her hand in a cloth to remove the kettle from its hook over the fire and poured steaming water over the tea leaves.

"Yes. After a fashion. They are tricky to converse with." So far, Sera had spoken the truth. She wanted the other woman's trust and would not deceive her with falsehoods about the reason for her questions.

"My Georgie can talk to the horses. Not a proper conversation, like you and I are having now. He says it's more pictures in his mind. Feelings." She fetched two large pewter mugs from a cupboard and placed them on the table by the kettle.

"Would he be the stern-looking man in the

stables?" Being able to communicate with the horses under your care would be convenient indeed.

Mrs Gibson chuckled. "That's him. Loves horses more than people, he does. He says horses never lie and they're excellent judges of character. They show him who uses too much whip or pulls on their mouths." She poured tea and held up the sugar bowl.

Sera gestured for one lump. "What do the horses think of Lord Hillborne?" she asked in a low tone.

Mrs Gibson's hand stilled. "You're staying at Mistwood and must have encountered him. What is your opinion?"

"From what I have seen, I think he should keep his hands to himself." Sera took the mug of tea and leaned back to sip the sweetened brew.

Mrs Gibson took her tea to the sofa and regarded Sera with a curious look over the rim of her mug. "The horses don't like him. Like you say, too rough with his hands."

The conversation with Truby ran through Sera's mind. If he was rough with the horses and tried to take advantage of the maids, how had he treated his family? Sera sided with the horses. The lord was a man to be avoided if possible.

"The spirit urged me to help Meredith, and I wonder if she may not be responsible for the horrible crime she is accused of. But I need something that can be used to defend her." The more time Sera spent at Mistwood, the more she believed that, just like the brooding house, much lay under the surface of Meredith's actions.

Silence fell for a long minute. Then the former lady's maid spoke. "It isn't just the horses he handles roughly. I was her maid. I dressed her every morning and saw the bruises on her body." Her gaze drifted off. Lost in memories and seeing things she had been powerless to do anything about. "Once, he blackened her eye and told everyone she had walked into a door. We all knew the truth, but what can you say against a viscount?" She sagged against the back of the sofa.

Conversations with Kitty filled Sera's mind. Her friend advocated for women to have rights, especially when they were trapped in unhappy, and sometimes violent, marriages. A noblewoman without independent means relied on her husband to support her. Any children they had belonged to their father. If a woman wished to escape a miserable marriage, she would have to leave everything behind. Even a beloved daughter.

"Mrs Pymm says she never recovered from losing the baby when she fell down the stairs." Sera crossed her fingers that the terrible suspicion in her mind was wrong.

Mrs Gibson snorted. "She only lost her balance because he shoved her."

Vilma said Mistwood had been a happy place when her father was lord. But his death had brought a cancer to the manor that devoured its soul, the way the one in Vilma's breast would steal her life.

"He needs an heir and was angry that Lady Hillborne had Hannah first. Then she quickened with child again and we all hoped it would be a little boy. I don't know what drove her to say it. Perhaps she wanted to hurt him as deeply as he hurt her with all his taunts that she wasn't good enough. He said he'd never take her to London because she would embarrass him. It was such a terrible argument that afternoon." She held her tea in both hands and stared into the steam wafting off the surface.

"What did she say?" Not that any words justified what he'd done.

A sip of tea allowed the tale to spill forth. "A lie. She told him she had consulted an aftermage in the village. One who can tell if a babe is a boy or a girl, and if the child is growing as it should. She shouted that she carried another girl and she would never give him his heir."

Images appeared in Sera's mind. Meredith hurling the words at her husband as they argued at the top of the stairs.

"He told her he would not support another useless girl. That she was a parasite taking up room that belonged to his son, and had to be removed. She laughed and turned to walk away when he grabbed her arm. He said if she would not do it, then he would. Then he flung her down the stairs..." Mrs Gibson's words trailed away as tears trickled down her face.

"He could have killed her." Cold rage flowed

through Sera. Whatever the outcome from her stay in Mistwood, she vowed one thing with certainty—Lord Hillborne would never hurt anyone else.

"He nearly did. She bled so much. The after-mage surgeon worked through the night to save her life, but Lord Hillborne had killed her spirit. The poor wee babe. He was perfect in every way, except he never drew breath." She pressed one hand to her forehead and rubbed, as though to ease the pain the memory brought with it.

"A son." Lord Hillborne had killed his own heir that day. Sera hoped that guilt tormented him at night.

SEVENTEEN

Mrs Gibson cupped her mug in two hands. Once she began to talk, the tightly held secrets tumbled out in a rush. "That was four years ago, and she hasn't quickened since. He calls her useless and barren. Said he needed to be rid of her to start anew with a younger, and richer, bride. He blamed her for their mounting debt, as she brought him only a small dowry. Said that if he was stuck with her, she was stuck with him. He once yelled that she would never leave."

Sera leapt on those last hurried words. "She wanted to leave him?" *Needed to be rid of her*. If Meredith had left him, Lord Hillborne would never have his legitimate heir. How convenient if she were hanged for the missing child instead. "There are two people I trust, a solicitor and a doctor, working to craft Lady Hillborne's defence. If there is anything at all you know that might help, please tell me."

The other woman sipped her tea. "She used to cry when I brushed her hair at night. Said all she wanted to do was escape, but she couldn't take Hannah. It's wrong that a husband controls his wife and children. She would never have left Hannah behind. So she stayed and protected us as well as she could."

A chill seeped into Sera's bones. "Like she protected young Truby."

"Yes. That's why I don't believe what others say. Lady Hillborne would never harm Hannah. You must believe me. She loved that girl something fierce." She placed the mug back on the table to reach out and take Sera's hand. Her eyes were pained and the lines were tight around them.

"You think he did it. Meredith will hang, and that leaves him free to remarry." And they had provided him with two potential replacements. Vilma, if he believed her easily manipulated, although penniless. Or Kitty, if he wanted a fortune to revive his finances.

Sera couldn't shake Meredith's words. *I am responsible*. Yet now she cast them in a different light.

What if the mother, wracked by guilt, believed that her words thrown during an argument had festered inside her husband and led him to do away with their daughter?

Mrs Gibson swallowed a lump in her throat and whispered, "Yes. He'll get what he wants, won't he?"

If Hillborne had done it, Sera refused to believe he was clever enough to get away with it. He would have made a mistake or left a witness somewhere. "What happened the morning Hannah disappeared? Did he have the opportunity to take her somewhere?"

"I don't know. They were both up early that morning. He set off on his ride, and Georgie says the horse came back with a bleeding side from his spur, and covered in sweat. I went in search of Lady Hillborne and found her kneeling by the lake in her dressing robe. In her hands, she clutched Hannah's favourite doll—the one with the red dress. There were crows in the trees that called out before they took flight. She sobbed that they had taken her girl. I thought it was an odd thing to say. So odd that I've never spoken of it until now."

Sadness flowed through Sera. "Crows are believed to take a spirit to the next realm. It must have been her way of saying Hannah had died." That meant there was no possibility of Hannah's being found alive. But still her mind baulked at admitting the mother had deliberately drowned her daughter.

What would Captain Powers do if he were there? Review all the facts before making a decision.

"Is it possible Lord Hillborne took Hannah from the nursery early in the morning and—" Sera's voice faltered as she struggled to say the words. "—placed her in the lake? Or might he have left her doll by the water to give that impression, and ridden off with Hannah somewhere else?"

"Georgie asked his horse, and it carried only Lord Hillborne away that morning. But if he did it, how do we prove it? If Lady Hillborne saw him, why does she not say so?" A fevered light burned in the other woman's eyes as she leapt at a possible course of action.

A lord's word carried more weight in such matters. Meredith was already suffering from her time in Newgate. What if, as Hugh feared, she deteriorated further once she was moved to Bedlam?

"No one believes a madwoman," Sera whispered.

"But you will try, will you not? You must do anything to help her, and find Hannah." A determined tone entered the other woman's voice. Her unwavering loyalty to her mistress.

Already Sera could hear Mr Napier's voice in her head. If they could throw enough doubt on who had stolen the child's life, it might yet save Meredith from the hangman's noose. Who had the greater motive—a loving mother trapped in a violent marriage, or a lord desperate for an heir? A man who would do anything, no matter how foul, to rid himself of a troublesome wife? But why harm his daughter with such a horrid plan, when all he had to do was poison Meredith? With the entail, the girl could never inherit Mistwood.

An answer burst into her head, and it spoke to the true brutish nature of Lord Hillborne's character. Taking Hannah away would hurt Meredith more than any raised fist or tumble down a flight of stairs.

"I will do what I can. I have searched the lake, but have failed to find Hannah's body. There might be some clue about her that we could use to save Lady Hillborne." If only she could write to Captain Powers and ask for his direction. Or if Hugh were here when they found the child, he might discern something about her physical remains. Without all her Kestrels, she struggled. But Sera would persevere. Hugh and Mr Napier had important roles to play in London. She would trust that all their efforts would come together to solve the mystery.

"What you need is something to condemn Lord Hillborne." A hard light entered Mrs Gibson's eyes.

Whether or not they found enough proof to convict him in a court of law, Sera would ensure justice was done. Such a man was poison in a well, affecting the lives of all who tasted of him. Let him discover that not all women were powerless.

"Thank you, Mrs Gibson. You have given me much to think upon and a new direction for my efforts." Sera left the neat cottage and returned to Vilma.

"Did you learn anything that might help?" Vilma asked as they folded the blanket and stowed it under the seat of the gig.

"Possibly. Both Lord and Lady Hillborne were up early the morning Hannah disappeared. We do not know for certain which of them saw the child last." Sera took up the reins and turned Blossom back to Mistwood.

On the return journey, Vilma spoke of the village and the changes she observed since she'd left the area.

As they halted outside the manor, Georgie Gibson, the groom, appeared to take charge of Blossom. Sera scratched the mare's nose and thanked her as a footman helped Vilma down.

"I hope Blossom gives a good report of my conduct," Sera said.

Georgie took the reins and arched one eyebrow. "She likes you. Bet you bribed her with apples."

Once upstairs, Vilma took a little more of her pain tonic and retired to her room to rest.

Sera sat with Kitty and Noemi in the window seat overlooking the mirror-like lake and told them of her visit with Lady Hillborne's maid. "He tried to assault the young maid who starts the fires, and Lady Hillborne stopped him. I wonder if that was not the first maid he laid hands on. Certainly not the first woman. Gibson said Lady Hillborne often had bruises on her body. She wanted out of the marriage, but would not leave her child behind."

Noemi snorted. "A horrible man who abuses women in many different ways. Financially with Vilma, physically with his wife and staff. He should be paraded naked through the streets and shamed for his behaviour."

"In some men's clubs, he would be applauded for disciplining his wife. Remember, the law allows it, so long as the switch is no thicker than his thumb." Kitty thumped her fist into the palm of her other hand. "Men place the blame on us for how they lash out, rather than examine their own flaws and weaknesses.

The situation will continue until we rise up and demand our due as equals."

"Let us solve this crime first, Kitty, before we march for equal rights and throw off the shackles of domestic servitude." Sera loved her friend's fiery spirit, but they had to tackle one thing at a time. "Some four years ago, Lady Hillborne miscarried a son after Hillborne pushed her down the stairs. In his quest for an heir, Lord Hillborne told his wife that if she did not provide one, then he would find another who could."

Sera had cast a silence spell around them to protect their conversation from other ears. Yet they still spoke in hushed tones. The topic demanded reverence. Nor did they want to disturb Vilma with the content of the discussion.

"An heir needs to be legitimate to inherit. For him to try with another, he would need to be either divorced or widowed." Noemi played with a lock of jet-black hair as she thought out loud.

"Divorce is terribly difficult to push through Parliament. Not to mention expensive, and it can drag on for years." Kitty jumped to her feet and paced between the window and the four-poster bed. Sera observed that her friend thought better when her feet were moving.

"Much easier and quicker to be widowed. Do you think he planned to do away with her?" Noemi asked.

Sera pursed her lips. "Who knows? After the

attempt on the stairs failed, perhaps he tried again and was foiled by the staff. I believe there is a chance he committed this terrible crime himself, to torture his wife and be rid of her."

Kitty crossed her arms. "He is a thoroughly repugnant man. Please tell me you will place some horrible pox upon him? His exterior should at least reflect how rotten he is on the inside."

"I know an untraceable poison that would give him a heart attack over dinner," the contessa murmured.

Despite an age difference of well over two hundred years, Kitty and Noemi had fallen into an easy friendship. The two women shared similar views about the hardships women endured and were pragmatic about dealing with problems. Sera hoped Kitty wasn't as keen to poison a *problem* as the contessa, who had learned her skill at the side of Catherine de' Medici.

They couldn't solve one murder by committing another. Besides, Sera could just imagine the outcry in the next council meeting if Lord Ormsby found out a viscount had died unexpectedly while she stayed under his roof. "No one is slipping poison into his dinner. Even an untraceable one. We may yet find proof against him. Somewhere out there is little Hannah, and a clue might be found with her."

"The child could still be alive. He might have placed her with someone, or have a hunting lodge in the forest." Noemi stared out at the dense forest encircling the lake.

While they all hoped Hannah still drew breath, Sera doubted it. *The crows took her away.* In her grief, had Meredith glimpsed her child's soul being pulled from the water by a crow? "His horse said he was alone that morning. He did not have Hannah with him."

"His horse is now a witness for the prosecution?" Kitty stared at Sera with a wrinkled brow.

That made Sera wonder...if the horse had carried Hannah away that day, could the equine be called to give evidence in court as to his master's guilt? "His groom is an aftermage who can converse with the horses. Whatever happens, I don't think Hillborne deserves an easy death, do you? If he thought to torture his wife by doing away with their daughter, I think I can devise something to twist the blade in his gut a little."

Kitty emitted a satisfied huff, content that Sera would turn her mind to any punishment meted out to Lord Hillborne. "I look forward to searching his study as soon as he rides out. We might find more than a will. He might already be courting potential replacements, which will prove the crime was premeditated."

There was little they could do until then. Sera would continue to keep her ears open below stairs as to the slim possibility of a cottage or lodge hidden in the forest, or someone who might have taken charge of the girl and spirited her away. Perhaps a maid who had left abruptly? "Vilma's discussion with the butcher confirmed there are financial problems. We might also uncover what has consumed the money her father left."

"Slow racehorses and fast women are the usual ways to fritter away a fortune," Kitty said.

"Yet he hides away here and does not often go to London," the contessa pointed out.

"Mrs Gibson said he refused to take Lady Hillborne to London. He said she would embarrass him due to her lowly origins." The words stuck in Sera's throat. "I wonder why he did not go alone and leave her here?"

"Most likely because if he did, she would have taken the child and disappeared," Kitty said.

The next morning, Sera glanced out into the courtyard before hurrying under the archway and toward the lake. Today, Vilma was already seated at a bench, a blanket draped over her knees. She coughed as Sera approached and her cheeks were flushed despite the chilly temperature.

"You shouldn't be out here." Sera hastily erected the warm ball of air around them.

Vilma drew a breath that rasped through her

lungs. "Noemi would say that despite my gentle temperament, I can be somewhat stubborn. I do not know how many more sunrises I will see, and I do not want to miss even one."

Sera sat close to the other woman, lending her body heat against her side. If only she could let her magic scurry through Vilma the way it did through the manor, and seek out what destroyed her health.

"As a girl, I imagined all the amazing things I might do with my magic one day. To raise up forests from the ground, or create sparkling buildings. But I would trade it all for the ability to work magic on something the size of a cherry. I am sorry I cannot remove the tumours. I wonder why we are gifted such magic when we are unable to heal those who need it most?" The more fond she became of Vilma, the more her inability to do anything gnawed at her and stole her peace of mind in quiet moments. Why did Mother Nature allow some to suffer?

"Perhaps it is to remind us of the fragility of life. We appreciate things that are precious and break easily, like delicate vases." Vilma's shivers eased as she relaxed in the warmed enclosure.

"But why allow one good person to suffer, when a horrible person may dance through life with no afflictions at all?" Anger built inside Sera, aimed at whatever power or entity allowed such things to happen.

"Because life isn't fair," Vilma said in a sad whisper. She picked up Sera's hand and held it between her gloved ones. "I am loved, and that is a rare treasure."

"Will you allow Noemi to...alter you?" While Sera knew little of the habits and ways of vampyres, it didn't seem such a terrible transformation when compared to the end Vilma currently faced. Although once undead, there was a slight risk of being beheaded or burned on a pyre by ignorant people.

"I don't know. I fear she will grow bored with me. Imagine the pain of spending an eternity watching someone you love, but cannot be with." Vilma watched the family of ducks swim by, all in a row behind their mother. The ducklings were moving into awkward adolescence as their feathers came in. Soon they would fly away to live separate lives.

"I don't think true love works like that." The mist from the water thickened as the sun rose behind the trees.

"Oh?" Vilma turned with a smile gracing her lips. It transformed her face to such ethereal beauty, Sera wondered if any Fae blood might flow in her veins.

"I met a gargoyle recently." Sera recalled the raw grief in Warin's voice at being forced apart from Imogen and spending his long span of years alone. He watched their descendants from the shadows. After a hundred years of mourning her death, he still choked up saying her name.

"Those horrid things that squat on the corners of buildings? I thought they only existed in fairy tales."

A soft laugh of disbelief rippled from the other woman.

Sera had once thought vampyres were only contained in books...until she followed her curiosity about a thick, red potion her guardian used to brew for the contessa. "Warin said his kind can live for a thousand years and if they are lucky, they find a true love who walks beside them through that many centuries."

Vilma let out a sigh. "How do they not argue and fall out with one another?"

"They do. But isn't that the way of all relationships? There are disagreements and times of change. But the core of love endures and is what allows you to come back together again and continue on. Warin said that, for gargoyles, having someone by their side to share the experience of shifting times is what grounds them through the centuries. A constant love in an ever-changing world is like a star in the sky by which to navigate your path."

Her own words resonated through Sera and a puzzle piece fell into place deep inside her.

"Worries plague my mind. What if our love does not endure? Sometimes fairy-tale endings only ever occur in books. They are stories we tell to give ourselves false hope." Her fingers plucked at the blanket as she spoke.

Sera shook her head and met Vilma's gaze. "But what if your love endured for centuries? Isn't it worth the risk to find out? I think our fears will come up with a thousand reasons not to do something, when all we need is one reason to do it."

"It is a way of protecting ourselves. We hold a piece of ourselves back, so we don't risk everything. Because we cannot withstand the pain of losing someone." Vilma's eyes filled with tears.

Sera couldn't fathom the pain Vilma experienced every day with the cancer growing inside her, yet it was the thought of losing Noemi's love that caused her the most agony.

In the way that, for a mother, the pain of a lost child was worse than death.

Eighteen

Is that why I hold back from Hugh—to protect myself from heartbreak one day?

Sera wrenched her thoughts away from that gloomy rabbit hole. What was a more hopeful topic of conversation, one far removed from death and pain? "What would you do if you had hundreds of years before you?" Sera asked.

Vilma sighed. "You would laugh at my silly dream."

Sera adjusted the blanket over Vilma's knees as the air in their little bubble grew warmer around them. "I would never laugh at another person's dreams."

Vilma turned and gazed at the manor with its turrets and dark stone. A structure that only turned beautiful at night, when caressed by the silver moon. "I would write novels, set in a house with a soul such as Mistwood. Where an innocent heroine would prise apart the secrets held within its walls, and lay to rest the demons that torture the handsome but brooding lord. My books would be dark in tone, but there would always be the bright spark of hope and love at the end. To make the pain and suffering they had endured worthwhile."

Sera stared at the other woman. Never would she have guessed that delicate and sheltered Vilma Winters harboured the desire to write gothic novels about tortured love, populated with ghosts and demons. "Ah, but you have centuries. Surely it would not take more than a decade or two to write your Mistwood novel. What would you do afterward?"

"I would explore the world with Noemi and seek out other places like Mistwood. Oh, to be blessed with hundreds of years. To settle in a new land and immerse myself in its people and culture. To learn a new language, taste new foods, and sing new songs. Then I would write a tale about *their* Mistwood, flavoured with everything that makes that place and people unique." Vilma spoke with longing and passion.

Sera nudged her with a gentle touch. "You must promise to send me each completed novel. I shall keep a world map in my study, and place pins where each is set to track your travels."

Vilma drew a wheezy breath, and when she turned to Sera, she smiled and blinked away her tears. "I think the stories are true—you are a rare kind of witch. Your magic has helped me peer into my heart and see the truth hidden there. For a young person, you have a rare wisdom."

At times, Sera forgot she had only walked the earth for eighteen years. Part of her was connected to something ancient. She considered herself a daughter of Mother Nature, or Gaia, depending on which book you read. "When a mage dies, his magic is transferred to a new body. For generations, the power in my veins has coursed through the bodies of others. I think of it like a family treasure. A silver bowl or a sideboard, perhaps, passed from parent to child. Each generation uses it a bit differently. Some honour it, some do not. Some embrace it and make it a pivotal part of their lives. Others don't want to use it, and hide it away. Each hand alters it somewhat before it passes to the next. While I have not lived for long, part of me is a thousand years old. Or older." A realisation burst into Sera's mind. "Now I understand what you meant about Mistwood. We are both affected by what dwells inside us."

Vilma's smile widened. "It seems we have helped each other this morning."

Voices carried through the mist and then figures appeared, turning into two men, one pushing a barrow and the other carrying a rake and spade. Sera recognised them as the footmen who served dinner in the evening. Lord Hillborne economised by making his few staff perform the work of many. Their chatter dropped away, and the men touched the brims of their hats as they made for a flowerbed surrounded by a low privet hedge.

"Shall we go back inside? I will see if the contessa is ready to rise for breakfast." That made Sera pause. How was the vampyre sustaining herself? "Is Noemi...umm..." How did one politely ask if one woman drank from the other? The exchange was made all the more unfair given Vilma's condition. Did the vampyre's feeding weaken her further and hasten her demise?

Vilma leaned on Sera's arm and murmured in a low tone, so the men would not overhear, "She brought bottles of what she requires. Do not be concerned for me. Noemi only takes a small measure, perhaps less than you would pour into a sherry glass to savour of an evening. And I do not mind. Her touch is—" Colour rose in Vilma's pale cheeks. "Pleasant. It drives away the pain as effectively as any potion, and warms my bones for some hours."

Upstairs, Sera assisted the contessa to dress. Kitty was already awake, dressed, seated at a desk and doing her correspondence. A letter to her father, Sera thought. Or did she write to a certain royal bastard?

Kitty rose and tucked her papers into a satchel when she saw them. "Will you be joining us for breakfast?"

"Yes. Let us continue the deception we started." Noemi picked up a journal and thrust it at Sera. "What would I do without you? You are such a versatile creature, performing secretarial duties when not helping with my toilette."

"Lord Hillborne will appreciate that. His footmen do grounds work when not required inside to serve at the table." Sera found a pencil and clutched it against the spine of the book.

With that settled, they walked down to the breakfast room. The large windows overlooking a side garden were unable to counter the creeping gloom that clung to the lake and swept over the house. The contessa had waved a hand at Sera and told Lord Hillborne that urgent business necessitated her maid's presence. He merely nodded and returned his attention to his plate. Sera perched on an uncomfortable chair behind Noemi and scribbled notes as her mistress gave instructions to be relayed to her modiste for new winter clothing.

Murmured conversation took place between Kitty and Vilma. They shared a love of literature and Vilma enthused about the last book she had read. They were halfway through their meal when Lord Hillborne finished his and turned his attention to a stack of correspondence the butler had left by his plate. He opened one letter, scanned the contents, and let out an oath.

He slammed a fist on the table. "This is ridiculous!"

"Bad news about an investment?" Noemi purred.

He stared at her, his cheeks flushed. "What? No.

This is from my man in London. Apparently my wife has been moved from the prison."

"Is she to be released?" Kitty asked.

Sera held her silence. They already knew Lady Hillborne was to be moved, since Mr Napier and Hugh had worked to delay the trial.

"No. She has been taken to Bedlam. Some *lawyer* —" He tinged the word with distaste. "—has taken up her cause and is arguing she is not of sound mind."

Kitty feigned a wide-eyed look. "That is excellent news, is it not? If Lady Hillborne is ill, then she might receive the care she needs to recover. Perhaps after the passage of many years, she might even be deemed fit enough to return here to Mistwood, to comfort you in your old age."

Sera stared at the notebook in her lap to stop the laughter bubbling up.

Lord Hillborne looked like he might burst a blood vessel as the veins popped up in his temples. "This is not acceptable. I need an *heir*, Miss Napier, not a madwoman bashing her head against the walls of a cell. I shall write to the prosecutor at once. This charade must be put to an end. Swiftly."

The way he said *swiftly* conjured an image in Sera's mind of the guillotine slicing off Meredith's head. Her eyelids would still be fluttering as Lord Hillborne rushed a replacement wife to the altar.

Kitty grinned and then, perhaps belatedly remembering she had a part to play, schooled her features in a frown. "I recall my father saying that the legal system never does anything with haste. Especially with a gently bred woman such as Lady Hillborne. I am sure it should not take more than five years for the physicians to determine her state of mind, and for the courts to rule on her fate."

Lord Hillborne's mouth opened and closed, but no words emerged as he stared at the noblewomen seated around his table. Then he crumpled the letter in his fist and leapt to his feet. "Tell Gibson to ready my horse!" he shouted at the butler before striding from the room.

"Do not be concerned for us, cousin. I am sure we can entertain ourselves this morning in your absence," Vilma called out in a surprisingly strong voice. A good night's sleep, and the ministrations of her friends, had put the sparkle back into her eyes.

They finished their breakfast, while Sera tried not to fidget. They had to ensure he was gone before they rushed his study, and she would need to lay spells to keep the servants away and alert them should Lord Hillborne return unexpectedly. It was only when he cantered past the window and around the curve of the lake that they rose. Sera spared a thought for the poor horse, who would bear the brunt of his lordship's anger.

Vilma led the way, Sera walking at the rear of the group and brushing spells against the walls to keep the servants away. Then she anchored one to the yard, to alert them when the viscount rode back to the stables.

The former resident of Mistwood stopped at a tall, broad door and rattled the latch. "It is locked."

"Locks will not stop us." Kitty pulled Vilma to one side and gestured Sera forward.

She liked locks. Whispering to such tiny mechanisms and gently coaxing them aside challenged her magic. It took skill and patience to cast in such a precise manner. Sera rubbed her thumb over the brass and murmured under her breath in an arcane tongue. After a soft *click*, she tugged on the latch and pushed the door open, allowing Vilma to enter first.

"Where shall we begin?" Vilma asked as they stood in the middle of the darkened room.

"Why don't you search the correspondence on his desk, *cara mia*? That might reveal his plans. We will search for a hidden safe." Noemi took Vilma's arm and escorted her to the expansive desk. Made of walnut, the solid front piece was carved with twisted brambles bearing tiny wooden thorns.

Vilma caressed the wood as she took a seat. "As a child, I used to hide under this desk and pretend I was a princess in a castle, trapped by a wall of poisonous vines. Waiting for a prince to rescue me."

Noemi kissed her cheek. "We do not require princes. All a woman needs is other women, and we would rescue you. Sera would fly down on a broomstick, I would poison the vines so they withered, and Katherine would organise a rebellion among the servants."

While Vilma read through the correspondence,

the rest of them took a wall each. Sera ran her hands along the wallpaper, painting the surface with magic and hoping to detect the safe behind the flocked covering. But after two fruitless hours, Sera's alarm spell warned that Lord Hillborne had returned.

"We cannot stay any longer. He has ridden into the courtyard," she told the others.

"Blast!" Kitty stood with hands on her hips and surveyed the room. Its walls still held fast any secret they contained.

"Even with my magic, I cannot detect a safe concealed in here." Sera rubbed her knuckles, the skin tingling from the constant trickle of magic she'd kept up while touching every surface she could reach.

"Did you find anything of interest, Vilma?" Noemi approached the desk as Vilma tidied the papers back to where she found them.

"Somewhat. He complains to his solicitor in London that my mother stole investments due to him, and asking how to force us to hand them over. That would explain his questions. He thinks we absconded with part of his inheritance." She patted the desk, as though bidding farewell to an old friend. "Other letters are to his associates, stating Meredith...took their child's life and how he looks forward to starting afresh once she is hanged. He must have asked for recommendations, as some have written with the names of eligible young women of their acquaintance."

Sera held the door open until they all exited and then coaxed the lock to click shut once more.

"Nothing that we can use to prove his guilt or cast doubt on Meredith's actions," Kitty said. "Nor any sign of a safe. Yet I am certain your father must have left a will here. Somewhere."

"Perhaps it is simply a dream we pursue to distract us from the ugly truth of what happened here," Vilma murmured.

Noemi glanced at Sera. "Is there nothing we can do?"

She had one idea. There was one *entity* who might know if a safe or lock box was concealed within the walls of the house. "Yes. We ask Mistwood. But I will need Vilma's assistance."

Sera proposed they try later that day, to give Vilma time to rest and recover some strength. They would reach out to Mistwood while Kitty and Noemi stood watch.

"Perhaps you could fetch a tea tray and we will adjourn to the drawing room?" Noemi suggested.

Sera left the women and found an entrance to the world below stairs. However, with other thoughts pressing on her mind, she soon became lost in the narrow, dim maze of corridors squeezed between the walls for the servants' use. As though she had stumbled into a rabbit warren, she found herself unable to pick the correct direction at each fork in the path. At last, a glimmer of light hinted at a larger space beyond, and she pushed on the panel. It gave way with a soft *pop* and she stood in a wide hall. Life-sized portraits hung on both sides and stared down at those who passed by.

She didn't recognise the space, but it must lead somewhere. While she had anchored a finding spell to her room below and it tugged at her, it did so in a direct line. She couldn't simply open up the floor and create a slide like she had in the abandoned church, but had to navigate the twists and turns of Mistwood's arteries.

Footsteps sounded up ahead and Lord Hillborne rounded the corner, clad in mud-splashed boots and breeches and with a red flush to his face. It appeared his ride had done little to ease his anger at Meredith's being moved to Bedlam. His eyes narrowed further on seeing her. "What are you doing here?"

"I am sorry, my lord, I became lost. The manor is ever so large." She infused innocence and a hint of being overwhelmed into her words.

He grunted and stepped closer, the reek of spirits on his breath. Not yet midday and already he was well into his cups. "Not exactly pretty, are you?"

A million retorts flowed to her tongue. First among them being, *Who are you to cast aspersions about appearances?* But no maid would challenge a lord, so she bit her tongue instead.

He shoved her, and Sera stumbled. Her back hit the wall. Magic flared along her skin and she curled her hands into fists. Breathing slowly through her nose, she controlled her temper. She wanted to believe it was a drunken accident.

"Not that looks matter with your face to the wall. All cats are grey in the dark, as they say." He took hold of her shoulder with one hand, and spun her body to face the portrait of a sour-looking woman in a tall riding hat. The scent of century-old varnish and dust went up her nose.

Sera struggled and tried to wrench herself free. "Let me go, Lord Hillborne!"

He laughed and backhanded her across the face.

Heat bloomed over Sera's cheek and the metallic tang of blood burst over her tongue from contact with the signet ring on his pinkie. Rage heated her limbs. Magic sparked in her palms, ready to be used in her defence.

He pushed one elbow into her back and used his weight to keep her imprisoned against the panelling. With his other hand, he fumbled at her skirts, dragging them up her leg. He leaned his torso against her and worked his knee between her legs.

Lord Hillborne thought his position and size gave him free rein to abuse those beneath him. That, as viscount, he could take what he wanted from any woman.

Today, he'd learn he was wrong.

Nineteen

Sera had spent the last few days considering how to ensure the viscount never harmed another woman under his roof, so that she could keep her promise to Truby. She was no executioner and would never cast a spell to kill him. Besides, that would raise too many complications with the Mage Council.

Lord Hillborne used his physical and social advantages to dominate others. Sera couldn't do anything about his title, but she could do something about his strength. With no access to the mage library and the tomes it housed, instead she had used her time in the still of the night to call upon Mother Nature to aid her in crafting a spell to sap the viscount's vitality. Like a leaf that changed with the advent of autumn, so he would curl upon himself as his vigour drained into the earth, until a permanent winter descended upon him and he became a withered shell of his former self.

All Sera had needed was the opportunity to unleash her spell, as it required contact for her to drive it deep into his body. Her curse would embed itself in his bones and then, over a period of days, dissolve to seep through his body. It would become a part of his tissue and blood, and, since it was based in nature itself, would be untraceable by any aftermage or mage he consulted to relieve his mystery ailment.

As his lordship struggled with her skirts and the fall of his breeches, Sera turned her magic inward, letting the words of her casting pour through her veins. When she bubbled with the potent hex, she sent it pooling by her knee. It swarmed and solidified until it became a seed. The incantation poised beneath her skin, ready to be unleashed. With her hands flat on the wainscoting, Sera sent a trickle of magic downward through Mistwood, to connect herself with both house and Mother Nature.

When manor and earth answered, she spun and struck out, unleashing the curse as she jerked a bent leg upward. Her knee connected with Lord Hillborne's groin with such enhanced force that it flung him backward. He lay sprawled on the floor, curled around his nether regions. Tears dribbled down one side of his face as he drew wheezy breaths, gasping for air.

"You wench! You'll pay for that!" he stuttered in a much higher pitch.

"I look forward to seeing you try." Sera bent over him, one hand outstretched as though she feared to touch him. Magic rippled along her palm. Her hex had shot through him and burrowed into his pelvis. Now, Nature would take her course throughout his body.

Turning on her heel, she ran to the hidden door and yanked it open. Leaning on the closed panel, she imagined the kitchen and sent a trail of magic to find the way. A pale silver line appeared at her feet and she followed it along the narrow hall and down the steep steps. She burst into the kitchen with anger still fizzing under her skin, muttering under her breath.

"Whatever happened?" Mrs Pymm asked, looking up from where she was writing in a notebook. "Good lord, you'll need something for that lip."

"Lord Hillborne just tried to lift my skirts in the hall!" Sera spat. Only now did she remember he had struck her, too. She ran a tentative finger along the cut to her lip.

Silence dropped over the kitchen. Behind her, someone's breath hitched in their throat.

"What did you do?" Cook turned, a bowl cradled against her side, her hand still on the spoon.

She had cursed him to become weak, to wane, to rely on the staff he abused. But best to keep that to herself. "I kneed him and left him curled on the floor clutching the family jewels."

A slow grin spread over the cook's face. "Good on you, lass. Let us hope he learns a valuable lesson."

Truby placed a bowl of warm water and a cloth at Sera's elbow. "Does it hurt?" She pointed to Sera's face.

"Not as much as he is hurting, I'll wager." She winked and dropped the cloth into the bowl.

The housekeeper laid down her pencil and laced her fingers above her notebook. "It is heartening that you stood up for yourself, but mind you don't go making a bigger problem for us. You will leave when your mistress does. We have to live here."

They would be safe from his unwanted advances once her spell took effect. More and more, she wondered at Meredith's choice of words in the prison. *He cannot reach her now, and I will die content with that knowledge.*

A chill froze Sera's blood in her veins as she became certain that Lord Hillborne had struck or abused his own daughter. What would a mother do to protect her child from such a horror? Even had she taken Hannah and fled, if ever they were found, both of them would have been returned to Mistwood.

Oh, Meredith. What did you do?

Sadness swept through Sera and brushed away the last traces of her anger. A certainty that the girl no longer walked this earth dug deep into her bones. Meredith had said she'd seen a crow take her child. It had plucked Hannah's soul from the lake and ferried it to the next realm. There was nothing more she could do here, but at least she could tell Imogen she had tried.

Late that afternoon, Contessa Ricci summoned Sera. She entered the drawing room and curtseyed to her employer, who perched on the edge of a settee.

"You sent for me, milady?"

Kitty and Vilma sat in the window seat. Lord Hillborne sat in an armchair, a large glass of brandy in his hand and a pained look on his face.

"Yes, Jones. Lord Hillborne says you assaulted him. This is a serious charge." The contessa regarded Sera with a speculative gleam in her eye, noting the swollen lip and redness to her cheek.

"No, ma'am. That is not true. His lordship pushed me up against a wall, struck me, and lifted my skirts. I was having none of that. I'm not a loose woman." Sera glared at Hillborne.

Lord Hillborne spluttered and waved his glass, the liquid slurping up the side of the crystal. "She lies. The girl thrust herself at me, and got upset when I rejected her."

"How do you account for the cut to her lip and bruise on her cheek?" Noemi arched one ebony brow.

"I pushed her away. Clumsy thing fell against the wall." He squirmed in his chair.

The same way Lady Hillborne tumbled down the stairs and lost your heir.

"I do not believe you. This girl speaks the truth. Do not touch my maid again, or I shall not be responsible for the outcome." Noemi dismissed her with a wave and a wink. Sera left the room before Hillborne saw her grinning.

She retreated to Noemi's bedchamber and waited for the others, certain they would not be far behind.

Sure enough, Kitty burst into the room some fifteen minutes later. "The nerve of him to lay hands on you!"

"I am fine. I let him throw his punch before I threw mine." Sera waved away their concern.

"I noticed him walking rather oddly." Noemi chuckled.

Vilma stood by the window, a deep sadness in her eyes. "Such terrible events taking place within Mistwood's walls. No wonder the house is sad."

"Let us see if we can conjure one small measure of cheer, since we are all assembled." Sera gestured for Vilma to join her on the rug in front of the fire.

"What do I need to do?" Vilma asked as she settled herself.

Sera took the other woman's hands. "I think you will strengthen the connection to Mistwood. Close your eyes and call to mind happy memories and how much this house means to you."

When Vilma nodded that she was ready, once again Sera let her magic flow from her and throughout the walls and floors. This time, she carried Vilma with her as she sought the old manor's heart. Whatever dwelt beneath the floors shook itself and rose to brush against the essence of Vilma. It reminded Sera of an old hound that only stirred when a beloved owner came near.

Help us, Sera asked. *What is hidden within your walls, left by the previous Viscount Hillborne?*

The spirit of Mistwood gathered them to it in a gentle embrace. They wandered the sprawling structure, passing through its walls like ghosts. Locked doors revealed rooms picked clean of furnishings, or containing only abandoned armoires too large to fit through the doors. One part of the manor possessed a picture gallery. The long space had mullioned windows all along one side overlooking the lake. It stretched so far that three fireplaces were dotted along its length, where ladies could stroll back and forth in inclement weather.

Then they were shown to the library, a room little used, judging by the dust on the shelves and coating the tops of books. The ceiling soared so high it disappeared above them like a starless sky. The shutters were closed and only shafts of light broke through the slats and cast shadows like prison bars across the floor. A fireplace the height of a man sat all dark and gloomy on one side of the room. Across from it was a carving of barbed vines that seemed to represent the inhospitality of the library.

Mistwood released Sera and Vilma with a push, and retreated back to its core. Sera opened her eyes and let out a frustrated sigh. All they had received was a tour. While interesting, it didn't answer the question of whether the previous Lord Hillborne had hidden papers anywhere.

Vilma wiped away a tear. "Thank you. That was

an experience I will always treasure. How amazing to touch the soul of Mistwood. Now more than ever I want to put pen to paper and give it a voice."

Sera stood and helped Vilma to her feet. "I am glad it inspired you, but sadly, I do not feel it was helpful. I wonder if the house knows nothing of anything so mundane as a safe or lost papers?"

Vilma frowned. "But Mistwood showed us where to look. The panel in the library matches the one that forms the desk. With the thorny brambles climbing over it."

"Of course! The place where you loved to hide." Excitement surged through Sera. What would they find behind it?

"Do you feel up to a search now?" Noemi took Vilma's arm and studied the grey cast to her skin.

"You cannot expect me to go down to supper without knowing what is behind the panel. And I promise I will not overexert myself." Vilma gazed up at her protector.

"Why don't we change for dinner first and Vilma can have some of her tonic. Then we can see what we find in the library. If there is anything, Sera can spirit it up here for us to examine later." Kitty laid out the best plan.

Sera fetched the pain tonic for Vilma while the others decided on what gowns they wanted to wear. When they left their rooms an hour later, there was a pallor about Vilma that caused concerned glances among the women.

The library was situated close to the drawing room, where Lord Hillborne sat and stared into the fire.

"Kitty, you must distract Lord Hillborne for us," Sera whispered.

Kitty blew out a pained snort. "I hope you realise what a sacrifice I am making. I shall seek his advice on where to invest my fortune. That will keep him talking for some time."

"I will join you. I do not think any woman should be alone in his company." Noemi linked arms with Kitty, and the two entered the drawing room.

Sera and Vilma continued on to the library. The door protested being opened. Once inside, Sera created a glowing orb to show the way as they crept over the carpet. Dust stirred up under their feet and motes danced around the light. With the fireplace at their backs, they faced the ornate panel that mirrored the one forming part of the desk in the study.

"What do we do now?" Vilma asked as she laid a hand on a carved vine.

"There will be a hidden catch. We just have to find it." Sera began pushing on vines, careful to avoid the thorns, which were as sharp as splinters. At the same time, she let magic trickle over the wood, hoping to trigger the catch.

They worked in silence, alert for any footsteps in the corridor. Vilma traced one particular limb from where it sprouted from the bottom of the panel. She reached out to a bramble and her palm fitted a smooth spot. Then she leaned her slight weight against the carving. A faint *click* came from under her palm and a hidden panel popped open a fraction of an inch. The edges were hidden due to their following the contours of the carved plant.

"He was your father. I think you should look first," Sera murmured.

Using her nails, Vilma eased the door open and thrust a hand into the dark beyond. Her eyes widened. "I feel something." After a little scuffling, she pulled out a folder tied with red ribbon, the two halves formed of deep green hardened leather. She pushed the folder to Sera. "I must join the others for dinner. Please keep it safe until we can all join you."

An easy promise to keep. If whatever the folder contained scraped away a little from Lord Hillborne and redistributed it to Vilma and her mother, then Sera would defend it to her last wisp of magic. She nodded and kissed Vilma's cheek.

In the bedchamber upstairs, Sera paced, unable to settle. Her stomach churned as part of her leapt with excitement at what the documents might reveal. Another part of her mourned the passing of little Hannah. Her failure at being unable to locate the child in the lake weighed her down. They had no direction or clue as to what had happened to her.

Perhaps some things are best left unknown.

Once back in her little room later that night, she would write to Hugh and tell him there was no hope for Meredith. Which was worse—a horrid existence in Bedlam or the hangman's noose?

To fill the time until the others finished dinner, she sat on the window seat and stared at the lake. She would keep trying to find the child until their last day at Mistwood Manor. Pushing her magic out to the water, Sera dropped lines through the still surface in the vain effort to find...something.

When the clock struck, she realised she had spent two hours fishing and had only managed to wear herself out. Time to go loiter outside the dining room. She peered around the open door and saw the others had finished their last course and were discussing where to take their coffee. With her thumb, she rubbed the mage silver ring wrapped around her pinkie and sent a whisper to Kitty.

Her friend pushed back her chair. "I find I am rather tired this evening. If you will forgive me, Lord Hillborne, I shall retire early."

The other women murmured their agreement and rose. As they neared the door, Vilma stumbled.

"Noemi, I do not feel well," Vilma whispered the words so faintly that Sera barely caught them from where she waited in the hall.

The woman's face drained to a deathly grey and a single bead of sweat trickled by her ear. Her eyes rolled up into her head as her knees buckled. Sera and Noemi lunged at the same time, the vampyre faster than Sera could imagine.

Noemi caught her companion and placed one hand on the side of her face. "Vilma? Stay with me."

Sera rushed into the room, propriety be damned.

"She is sickly! You did not tell me my cousin is ill. What is it? Nothing contagious, I hope." Lord Hillborne drew a handkerchief from his pocket and covered his nose and mouth as though someone had screamed, *Plague!* "This will be why I have felt poorly all day. It is all her fault."

"Miss Winters is overcome, that is all. There is a great sadness pressing on this house and she is a sensitive soul," Sera shot back at the viscount. Then she placed a hand on Noemi's arm. "Take her upstairs. We will join you shortly."

"You speak out of turn, girl. If you were in my employ, you'd be sacked with neither pay nor reference. Consider yourself damned lucky I didn't bring charges against you for striking me." He advanced on Sera. Apparently, his recent tangle with her had taught him very little.

Kitty stepped between her friend and the outraged lord. "You have suffered a great many horrors, my lord. To lose both your child and soon your wife. What husband and father would not be driven to despair by such events? As lord of this house, of course your grief is felt by all under this roof who care for you."

A footman lifted Vilma into his arms, and the contessa directed him out of the room.

Hillborne took Kitty's hand and pressed a kiss to

her skin. "You are a rare treasure, Miss Napier. How fortunate I am that Fate has brought you into my life."

"I can only hope that one day I will find a husband such as you, my lord. One who would give me many sons to occupy my time and lift the weight of managing my fortune from my shoulders," Kitty murmured, gazing up at the viscount.

Sera nearly choked, and thumped her chest where her friend's words lodged and she couldn't swallow them.

"I think the right man for such a robust and wealthy woman as yourself is closer than you imagine," he replied.

This charade had gone on for quite long enough. Bile surged up Sera's throat, and she coughed to relieve it.

Hillborne narrowed his gaze at her and backed away. "My cousin is spreading some sickness. That maid has it now. I want her gone."

"You do look a tad pale, my lord. Jones, come with me before more harm is done." Kitty nudged Sera's back and propelled her toward the door.

Twenty

Out in the hall, Sera linked arms with her friend. "You are, without a doubt, the most outrageous liar. It is a tragedy for England that you cannot pursue the law. What a performance you would deliver in a courtroom."

"I have the soul of a *lawyer*, not a *liar*. Nor am I an actress, but his greed blinds him. Any fool could see I was being facetious." Kitty wiped her knuckles on her skirts. "And he drooled on my hand."

They hurried up the stairs. Noemi had directed the footman to place Vilma in her larger room with its view of the lake—and the sunrise. Vilma lay on the bed, her eyes closed, her chest rising and falling in shallow breaths. The contessa fussed with the pillows. Kitty shooed the lingering footman away and said they would care for Miss Winters.

Sera found the potion she had brewed following

Hugh's directions. This one was to help Vilma's struggling lungs draw air. Noemi held Vilma's head while Sera used a tiny push of magic to dribble the nearly black brew past her lips.

"I have never seen her this bad. I fear my beloved will not dwell long in this realm." Tears misted the vampyre's eyes. Pain and love were written across her face. How could anyone think the undead woman cold and unfeeling?

Vilma stirred and licked her lips, then revived enough to take a few more sips from the vial. As the minutes ticked by, the wheeze settled and she seemed to breathe more easily. The folder of papers was forgotten in their concern for Vilma, and they remained where Sera had hidden them under the mattress.

The women waited. Noemi stretched out next to Vilma and crooned to her in Italian as she pressed a handkerchief to her damp brow. Kitty sat by a bedpost and seemed lost in thought. Sera perched on the edge facing the window, her hands curled into fists.

Useless.

She couldn't save Jake when he'd leapt from the rooftop. She'd failed to find Hannah in the lake. Vilma would die while she watched, and there was nothing she could do. Tears burned behind her eyes. It wasn't fair. Why give her such power and then render her impotent?

A pale hand reached for hers.

"Some things cannot be changed. Mother Nature has the final word on life and death," Vilma rasped.

"You are awake. Do not scare me so, *cara mia*." Noemi placed a tender kiss on Vilma's cheek.

"I think Lord Hillborne is convinced you have the plague." Kitty walked to the sideboard to fetch a glass of light ale.

"In my time back here at Mistwood, I have enjoyed my early mornings by the lake, in the company of a most wise mage." A slight smile tugged at the corner of Vilma's mouth.

Noemi arched one dark eyebrow at Sera.

"We talk of many things." Vilma found the contessa's hand and held it to her chest. "If you would still have me as your companion, Noemi, I am ready to close my eyes and jump into the unknown."

A frown wrinkled Noemi's brow, and she glanced from Sera to Vilma. "Truly?"

"I do not know what the coming years will bring, but I will embrace every day that I am given at your side. It is right to do this here. Mistwood has always been my home. I was born here and I would die here." She raised Noemi's hand and kissed it.

Noemi wiped a tear from her eye. "What adventures we will have together when you are restored."

Vilma struggled a little to sit up. "I am not afraid of death when it comes in your arms."

Sera pondered that while Mother Nature had the

final say on life and death, perhaps she was open to a little negotiation? Vilma would choose her own terms to slip from one state to the next.

"Does the process take long?" Kitty asked.

"Overnight, she will pass from the living realm into the one where I dwell. Then in the morning, Vilma will need to feed to complete her transformation." Noemi tucked a strand of Vilma's pale hair behind her ear.

Kitty's fingers tightened on the glass in her hand. "Feed?"

"Human blood will be necessary, but only a little. Then she can have her fill of the pig's blood I brought with me." Noemi waved to a small locked trunk in one corner of the room. Within, she kept bottles of the blood that sustained her.

Sera took the glass from Kitty before she dropped it and placed it on the table beside the bed. Her friend had already thrown herself at Lord Hillborne to give them time to search the library. It was too much to ask this of her, too.

"Vilma may feed from me," Sera said.

Noemi smoothed the blankets flat over Vilma. "No. Better not to let her first taste be that of a mage. I do not know what such potent magical blood would do to her. What if that were all she could drink afterward?"

Immediately Sera could imagine Hugh with a million questions. Chief among them being, would drinking a mage's blood create a gifted vampyre? Then she saw Lord Ormsby's face, red with apoplexy if Sera had to explain to him how such a creature had come into being.

Sera and Noemi gazed at Kitty.

She swallowed and wiped her palms down the front of her gown. "Very well. It appears I shall offer up myself and we will solve an ancient mystery—can a lawyer bleed?"

"Speaking of lawyers, perhaps we might remove the papers before you begin. Kitty and I can read through them while we sit with you tonight." Sera shoved her hand under the mattress and withdrew the folder.

"Yes. I would know what my father hid in the library," Vilma murmured, her voice fading away as her eyes fluttered shut again.

Kitty took the bundle and tugged on the ribbon. Flipping the folder open, she walked to the chairs placed before the fire. Sera joined her friend to give Vilma privacy as Noemi reassured her about what would happen over the next few hours.

Kitty dropped into a chair, her attention fixed on the papers in her hand. She muttered under her breath as she scanned the contents. Then she placed the folder on her lap to shuffle through the pages and odd loose sheets and cards.

Sera wrapped the room in a magical barrier to ensure no one inadvertently disturbed them while

Vilma turned into an Unnatural overnight. If Lord Hillborne or any staff, like Truby wanting to clean the fireplaces, wandered to the door, they would turn around thinking their task already completed. Next, Sera dimmed the lights and left only a soft amber orb glowing from the centre of the ceiling. The moon obliged, and sent ripples of silver over the surface of the lake to give Vilma a display to watch.

"We are ready to begin," Noemi called in a soft voice.

An internal dilemma surged inside Sera. Should she watch or not? At least she had some idea of what to expect, from when she had once controlled a mouse's mind and spied upon Noemi feeding from the other woman. Although that was before she considered them both to be friends. In the end, she decided to take up a position at the end of the bed, one hand resting on the post that held aloft the red velvet canopy.

Noemi sat on the bed by Vilma and gathered her companion into her arms. The contessa murmured in a low tone. Vilma tilted her head and bared her neck. The vampyre swept Vilma's hair away to expose alabaster skin. She seemed to inhale the scent of her companion, then tipped her own head back. Noemi opened her mouth and sharp canines extended from her jaws.

"Stop! You cannot do this!" Kitty rushed toward the bed.

The vampyre scowled at the interruption, her

fangs bared and her usually pale grey eyes turned midnight black.

"I am willing, Katherine. Do not worry about me," Vilma murmured and tried to wave the worried woman away.

"No, you don't understand. Your father left a will. It appears that a solicitor in the village drew it up, which is why his London man had no record of it." Kitty shook the handful of papers at her. "He has left you Mistwood."

"But that is impossible. The estate is entailed. Father could not leave it to me." Vilma stirred in Noemi's arms and the vampyre settled her back against the pillows.

Kitty waved the papers in her other hand. "If my interpretation of these documents is correct, the *estate* is entailed, but not Mistwood. The land actually attached to the title is situated up in Yorkshire and appears to have an old castle on it. From what I can gather from the deeds and correspondence, your family bought this place a hundred and fifty years ago and moved here. My father will need to confirm my understanding, but it appears *this* land is not entailed. Your father was free to dispose of it as he wished."

Tears misted in Vilma's eyes and she clutched at Noemi's shoulders. "He really did provide for us."

Noemi took Vilma's hand and held it to her heart. "Mistwood will be yours. Once you are strong again, you can sit by the lake and write your novel."

Kitty glanced from one woman to another. "The problem is, if you die now and become Unnatural, the law says you cannot inherit. You must wait, Vilma, until I can get these papers into my father's hands and we have other provisions taken care of. A few weeks, at most."

A weak smile touched the sick woman's pale lips. "For Mistwood, yes, I will hold on for a little longer. Can you, Noemi?"

The vampyre crossed her arms, and Sera wondered if she would sulk. One fang poked from under her lip and gave her the appearance of sneering.

Kitty shuffled the papers in her hands. "If I am right, we can snatch Mistwood out from under Lord Hillborne—and he will be banished to Yorkshire."

A grin bloomed across Noemi's face. "For that, and my *cara mia*, I am prepared to wait. What is a week or two when we have centuries before us?"

"There are also investments in this folder to ensure you and your mother had an adequate income. The annual dividends have been quietly accruing because neither you nor the current Lord Hillborne knew about them." Kitty shut the folder and held it tight.

"Your father knew you loved to hide under the desk behind the carved panel. He must have chosen its twin in the library, thinking you would find the papers there," Sera said.

"So, Lord Hillborne was right. Vilma's father *did*

have another source of income to finance the running of Mistwood," Noemi chuckled.

"How marvellous. To be able to return here. Mother will be mistress of Mistwood once more..." Vilma's voice trailed off as she stared out the window at the lake.

"You cannot tell anyone, though," Kitty cautioned. "He must not hear of what we found. We cannot risk him doing something stupid, like setting fire to the manor. When he hears that this estate is not his, we should have people in place to supervise him packing his bags and leaving."

"I will organise men to guard Mistwood." A hard glint entered Noemi's eyes. "I will not permit that horrid man to snatch her beloved home from Vilma."

Sera knew the perfect person to ask to act as supervisor—her aunt Natalie. How amusing it would be if Lord Hillborne tried his tricks with *that* formidable woman.

Once Vilma dropped into sleep, Noemi stood and drew Kitty and Sera to the fireplace to discuss their next move.

Kitty tapped the folder. "We must return to London as soon as possible. I need to get these papers to Father, and they have to be brought before the courts so Vilma and her mother may receive what they were always supposed to have."

"We will leave first thing in the morning. I will have a message delivered to where my men are staying in the village. For this, I will rise early." Noemi glanced at her sleeping companion.

"Lord Hillborne thinks Vilma has some illness that he might catch. Let us use that as an excuse for taking leave. We shall say we wish to return to London before she worsens. Sera, can you notify Hugh and Father?" Kitty retied the ribbon holding the folder shut.

"Of course. But there is little I can do to speed our return. We still have a two-day journey before we reach London." Vilma's condition worried Sera. Would she hang on long enough to see the estate back in her hands?

"My orchid may appear to be a thing of delicate beauty, but I assure you there is a stubborn streak under that surface. Death will not take her before she is ready." Noemi squeezed Sera's hand.

Sera offered a silent prayer that the vampyre was right.

Sera awoke early, despite having slept only a few hours. Since today was their last morning at Mistwood, she wanted to enjoy the lake one more time. They had decided the previous night to let Vilma sleep as long as possible while they packed and loaded their trunks onto the carriage.

She sat on the bench and watched the mist drift over the surface of the lake. The knowledge that nothing could be done for Meredith made despair crash over her. The slim possibility remained that Hannah lay somewhere under the surface, tangled in the embrace of weed. Sera preferred to think that Lord Hillborne had spirited her away somewhere, even if his horse said he had carried only the viscount that morning. As long as she held to the belief that he had given his daughter to an adopted family, the hope existed that she could be found. One day.

But that conflicted with what Meredith had said of a crow taking her daughter away.

Sera heaved a heavy sigh. She found no satisfaction in knowing the guilty party would hang. When she returned to London, she would be having words with Imogen. If the ghost had roused six months ago and told her to *help Meredith*, this terrible situation could have been prevented. Or if Warin had left London to visit his descendant, a protective gargoyle might have persuaded Lord Hillborne to change his ways.

Why had no one intervened? At least one bit of good news had come from their visit to Mistwood. After seven years, the final wishes of the previous Lord Hillborne had been found. The rambling manor would soon be in Vilma's caring hands and its staff safe from a predatory viscount. She hoped the castle on the entailed estate in Yorkshire had only elderly men wandering its cold halls.

A shadow swooped through the mist and cut a path toward her. As it neared, it called out. Not the child's restless soul, but a crow. She wondered if it was the same one she had spotted early in her visit—the one that had repelled her magic. The fancy struck her that it might be Elliot's friend, but what would that bird be doing this far from London? As she watched, the crow dived toward her, then flew to the nearby trees. Then it shot up to the sky and in a graceful arc, came around to fly at her again.

The way it turned its head made it appear as though it wanted her to follow.

Curious, Sera stood and walked through the damp grass. The corvid let out a long and low encouraging noise before flitting into the surrounding forest, where the house was quickly obscured from view by dense foliage. The trees were tightly packed, as though they stood arm in arm to protect the gothic manor. Her guide hopped from branch to branch, calling out if she lagged and directing her progress. Soon, the beech and oak opened out on a small clearing. Pausing, Sera leaned against a trunk and closed her eyes. She drew a deep breath, and serenity washed over her and soothed a fractious note in her soul.

A fluttering of wings drew her attention. The crow landed on the grass, and a wind stirred around its body, creating a tall, narrow vortex. In a flurry of midnight feathers, the bird grew in shape and size, becoming wider and taller within the swirling plumage. Feathers scattered like autumn leaves. When dust, leaves, and feathers fell away, they revealed a woman wearing a plain linen gown of deep purple. It was a simple and old-fashioned garment, similar to the kirtle medieval women had worn.

"A shifter. I knew it!" Sera pushed off the tree.

Twenty-One

The process of a shifter shedding one form for another fascinated Sera. She could imagine Hugh enraptured by the change and seeking to understand how a human could fit into a bird's body, and the opposite—how the bird expanded into a person. Did she have to regrow the shed feathers, and where exactly did her clothes come from?

Lycanthropes were always naked after changing from their wolf form—although with rather magnificent physiques to display. Or so she had read, having never seen one in person. She only had drawings in books to study.

"Lady Winyard, I am Erin Riley. Cousin to Elliot Brynn. On my mum's side." Erin would only have been chest height to Elliot and hadn't inherited his family's tall and lanky shape. She did possess the familial black hair, intense dark eyes, and golden skin tone. Erin held out one hand. When she turned it palm down, a length of silver ribbon dangled from between her fingers.

"This was one of a pair," she murmured.

"It was you," Sera gasped. It was similar to the ribbon given to her on her first morning in her house by a crow that had tapped at her window. She took the offered ribbon and wound it around her wrist. "It was you the other day, by the lake. I reached out with my magic, but you shook it off."

"No, that would have been one of my sisters. I've been to Soho, to find you. Elliot said you were here looking for a missing child and that her mother is in Newgate, accused of doing away with her." Worry pulled at Erin's dark eyes.

"Yes. Her ancestor is causing a disturbance at Bunhill Fields and insisting I *help Meredith*—Lady Hillborne. But I have failed in my task." Her time at Mistwood would always cast a shadow in her heart that she could do nothing. *Where are you, Hannah?*

"Is there no hope for Lady Hillborne?" Erin had a way of tilting her head that echoed her crow form's curious gaze.

Sera's breath left her in a sad exhale. "No. She will either hang or spend the rest of her days in Bedlam. I think that fate is worse. I had hoped we could prove that Lord Hillborne did away with little Hannah, but I have found no clues to connect him to her disappearance."

Erin shrugged her shoulders. A black fringed

shawl appeared from nowhere and draped itself around her. It seemed the crow could summon her clothing somehow. "That is because he had no hand in it. Her mother orchestrated the child's fate."

"Were you here? Did you see what happened?" A double tragedy had occurred by the lake that day. The distraught mother could not escape her abusive husband, and so had taken her child's life instead.

"Yes. We have a similar purpose, which is why I sought you out. Can you save her?" Erin clasped her hands together and in the speckled light, her gown rippled with bursts of green and black, like a feather.

Even if she could, Sera wouldn't. Not now that Erin had confirmed the mother was indeed responsible. Justice had to be served for Hannah. "The most we can hope for now is to keep Lady Hillborne alive in Bedlam for as long as possible, to stymie Hillborne's plans to remarry and make sure innocent people are never in his grasp again." Once Sera's hex took hold, marrying and fathering children would be beyond him.

"Hannah is alive," Erin whispered the words.

"What?" Sera spun on the woman, magic surging to the surface of her body. Meredith would be freed if they could present the child to the court. Then grim reality snagged the hope out of her chest and pulled it down into a dark well. What fate awaited the poor woman when she was thrust back into her husband's hands? Next time, no one would find either mother or child.

Erin held up her hands, the fringe of the shawl flaring out as though she flapped her wings. "She is safe, but all that we have done is for nothing if her existence is revealed."

Meredith's words made sense now. "When her maid found her, Meredith whispered that a crow had taken her daughter. I thought she meant her soul had been taken to the afterlife. She meant *you*." That was why Meredith was content to die. She knew her daughter was safe with Erin. That also explained why she didn't want Sera to find the girl. If she were discovered alive, she would be returned to her father.

Sera slumped to the ground and leaned her head against a solid oak. What to do now?

"Never before have we taken a noble child, but Meredith was desperate." Erin crossed to a purple beech and tugged free a strip of peeling bark.

"You *take* children?" The implication sank into her mind. How many other children had they snatched?

"As crows, we see much misery. When we spot a child in a desperate situation, and if we can help, we spirit them away to grow up free of whatever trapped them. They have always come from the lower classes. Children with no family, or no one to miss them. Or from places drowning in such sorrow, they assume the child simply ran away."

"Then why take Hannah?" A missing noble child raised many questions and concerns. What a sad commentary on their society, that so many could disappear with no remark from anyone. Then Erin's words echoed in her mind. "You said we have the same purpose, and that was why you sought me out in London. You know Meredith."

Erin sat on the grass next to Sera and brushed the papery bark across her palm. "Meredith is a friend, and she begged me to help her. I had to convince my sisters. We only wanted to save Hannah. I never intended for Meredith to be accused of the child's murder. We thought they would assume it was a terrible accident, but her husband was most insistent she be charged."

Sera's mind swam with the knowledge that the child lived and her mother had made the ultimate sacrifice to protect her. "How do you know Meredith?"

Erin flattened the bark between both palms and blew on them. When she opened her hands again, she held an ebony feather. "We grew up in the same village. She was so excited when Seth proposed to her. It was a lovely country wedding. Barely a week later, I visited her at the farm and she had a cut on her lip. Much like the one you have. When I asked her about it, she said she tripped."

Sera snorted. A more likely tale was that Hillborne had slapped her.

A sad smile flitted over Erin's face. "We know differently now. But at the time, I believed her. We never suspected the darkness lurking inside him. He was most charming when he courted her. They were only married a few months when he inherited the title. Taking up residence here freed his monstrous side."

Sera would argue that his beastly behaviour had begun long before he stepped inside Mistwood. "He evicted Vilma and her mother with nothing except what they could carry with them."

Erin pulled her knees up and wrapped her arms around them. "Greed is a demon inside him. Meredith was a fine bride when he was a gentleman farmer of the adjoining land. But for a viscount, he raged that she wasn't good enough."

Sera had an inkling of the new viscount's displeasure in his bride. "He could have attracted a fortune as an eligible bachelor in London. He still could if Meredith hangs. He was going to harm Hannah, wasn't he?"

"That day she lost their son, Seth also killed any love for him that lingered inside her. When she refused him entrance to her bedroom, he used the child to force her into compliance. But it was for nothing. Some months ago, Meredith overheard his plan to do away with her, to leave him free to remarry. Hannah, being a girl, was not required and indeed was an *unwanted expense*." The crow shifter spat out the words with a vehemence Sera shared. "She confronted him and he gave her a choice. If she threw herself from the highest turret or into the depths of the lake, he would let Hannah have a place in his *new* family."

"Sweeping floors or scrubbing laundry," Sera murmured.

"If Meredith believed him for a moment, I think she would have done it. But she feared what would happen to her daughter once she removed herself as an impediment to him remarrying. And there were the servants she protected. Every time I visited her here, we would meet in this glade. Each time, she had diminished a little more. Like a fire being extinguished, the life and vitality faded from her eyes. Yet still she remained determined to stand between him and those he tried to abuse." Erin tucked the feather behind her ear, where it blended in with her raven hair.

Sera searched her mind for anything that might save Meredith from impending doom. She needed time to think and to seek the help of her friends. Kitty and her father might know of some loophole they could exploit. There were so many questions she had for Erin. "You spoke of your sisters."

The crow stood and leaned against a tree. "This is why I have been pestering Elliot. I needed to know if you could be trusted, and if you knew of your history."

"Do you know my parents?" Had this particular crow carried her mother's soul to the other side and had some parting message?

"No. I came to tell you about the Crows. The three magical shifter offspring of a woman mage."

Erin leaned her head against the beech and stared up through the hanging boughs.

Sera laughed. This was no time for stories. The others would soon be awake and wonder where she had got to, and they were due to leave for London as soon as possible. They now had the dual mission of ensuring Vilma received the inheritance her father intended, and figuring out how to sneak Meredith out of Bedlam without her forever being a wanted criminal. "Mages cannot have magical offspring. It always skips a generation."

A smile tugged at Erin's lips. "Morag did. But you won't find her story in any book hidden in mage tower. It's a tale that's been passed from mother to daughter through the generations of Morag's family."

Sera crossed her legs, hoping there was some point to this tale. "What fairy tale is this?"

"No fairy tale. Your predecessor. And a tale they have scrubbed from your history."

Sera wracked her brain for the scant details of women mages in England. As far as she could remember, she was the first to live to adulthood in hundreds of years. She would have to travel back in time to the days of Romans and Druids to find another woman mage who had been treated as a priestess.

Erin smoothed her skirt over her knees and began her story. "Long ago, a girl mage was born. An old mage happened to be nearby at the time, and being more enlightened than his brothers and knowing what sad fate awaited the babe, he spirited the girl away to a magical forest."

"The only magical forest I know of is Sherwood." While Erin's story would be an entertaining diversion, Sera couldn't ascribe any truth to it. It was probably some regional fairy tale, whispered to children under cover of darkness. Although it did remind Sera of her own story, with her father snatching her away and seeking the protection of gargoyles to ensure she lived.

"In that forest she grew into a young woman, and the other mages and king could not touch her."

Sera huffed at that idea. How could one mage protect a child for years on his own, without any gargoyle assistance? Sherwood was rumoured to conceal a portal to the Fae realm. "He probably took her to the Fae and left her there until she was eighteen."

"Are you going to let me finish my story?" Erin spoke with a sharp edge that most definitely reminded her of Elliot.

"So sorry, do proceed." Sera mimed buttoning her lips together and drew her knees to her chest.

"The king called forth his most dangerous Unnatural assassin—and sent him to kill the woman mage and cut out her heart. Why would he do that? Are mage hearts different from normal ones?" Dark quizzical eyes fixed on Sera.

"No. Nor would it be needed as proof of her

death, as in that instance her power would be reborn in a new vessel."

"The assassin was a panther shifter, and he stalked the mage through the forest. He came upon her bathing naked in a river and was so struck by her goodness that he could not take her life. I think we can safely assume that if she was naked, it wasn't her *goodness* that struck him." Erin shared Elliot's earthy sense of humour.

"I doubt a shifter could kill a mage. Most likely she overpowered him." Sera imagined being attacked by such a creature and how she would defend herself.

"Whatever happened that day, he swore to be her protector. The woman mage sent a message to the king and said she would not bother him if he stopped sending assassins after her."

"I imagine that wasn't well received." Even in stories, women mages had to deal with annoying men.

"No. Then the king's heir fell gravely ill and no one could heal him. Except her. Showing mercy to the distraught king that he had never extended to her, she offered to cure the boy if the king left her to live in peace. With no other sons, the king agreed."

Sera wondered how she had cured the boy when their magic didn't extend to medical remedies. No wonder the tale had never entered the history kept at mage tower. A woman mage who escaped the control of the Mage Council and struck a bargain with the king? It might have given her ideas. "Where do crows come into this?"

"Mage and shifter fell in love, and lived happily in the magical forest. Over time, Morag bore him three daughters. Each was able to shift into a crow and each was able to wield magic. When they worked together, the three girls were as powerful as any mage." As she spoke, Erin brought her outstretched hands together and laced her fingers.

Sera leaned forward. "Impossible," she whispered.

Erin grinned. "No, it's not. Down through Morag's line, for hundreds of years, the Crows continue to be born to this very day. It's not quite every generation, as there is only one set of Crows at any time, rather like the number of mages being fixed. When the Crows are getting on a bit and their wings ache, the new Crows are born and their power is transferred."

"Do they die?" A mage's power needed death and rebirth to leap from one form to another.

"No, it is done by agreement. They willingly surrender their magic for the next generation, when the girls are of age."

Sera's mind reeled. If what Erin had told her was even partly true, it implied a woman mage could not only bear magical offspring, when male mages could not father them, but the power flowed through her maternal line undiminished by time. Ideas exploded in her mind. The few women mages born in Europe and Asia led a monastic life. They were allowed to practice magic and engage in scholarly pursuits, but they did not marry or have children. Was this why? To stop women producing magical lines that endured through the centuries?

Imagine if a male and female mage fell in love and combined their power into...a Nereus.

A child of Mother Earth and Father Sea.

Her heart pounded and her mind burst into a thousand bright sparks of possibilities. "What proof is there of this tale? If I assume you are one of these Crows, that means that, apart from being a shifter, you also possess magic." She had made clothing and a shawl appear and turned a strip of bark into a feather. But those could be parlour tricks that required very little magic. Certainly not a third of a mage's ability.

Erin held out her hand again and whispered under her breath. A single blue flame burst into life on her palm and with her other hand, she directed it in a slow dance up her arm. "Did you not wonder how we spirited Hannah away that day, unseen? We changed her into a crow and she flew with us."

Sera leapt to her feet. Too many words surged up her throat. They jammed on the back of her tongue, leaving her speechless. A mage with magical shifter offspring. All of them women. Almost as though Mother Nature thumbed her nose at the council and found another way to compensate for their abhorrent policy of smothering girls.

"Does the Mage Council know of you?" Sera

doubted it. If they knew a woman mage could have magical offspring with the right partner, they would have started a breeding programme to create Unnatural offspring. If a woman mage could create daughters who shared her power by a shifter father, how powerful would the offspring of two mages be?

Or did the council know? If there were never any women mages, they stopped any magical maternal lines. Lord Rowan would know, since he had advocated for her to live. Had any mages ever married Unnaturals and fathered children with them? As far as she could recollect, the mages only formed relationships with ordinary women. Lord Branvale had wed an Unnatural and had the marriage struck from the genealogy. Now her curiosity demanded to know *why*.

"Our family history is passed from mother to daughter. And sometimes to nosy cousins who can't figure out why they always lose at hide and seek." Erin closed her palm and extinguished the flame.

Sera let out a long breath. "You take a risk revealing yourself to me."

"You are the first in hundreds of years. But Morag's story should be known. Especially to a woman mage who could create others like us to endure for generations." Her eyes twinkled with mischief.

"Where are your sisters?" Questions fired in her head, demanding answers.

"With the children. I had to find you. To implore

you to save Meredith. She does not deserve such a fate." Worry returned to Erin's eyes.

Sera swept a hand through her hair. "I will do what I can. We return to London today."

"I will see my sisters and then find you there." Erin swept her shawl across her body and the swirling vortex enveloped her once more. This time, it shrank and dropped to the ground, revealing a crow. It cawed at Sera and took flight.

Sera gathered her thoughts. *Hannah lives.* The only way for Meredith to remove her child from her husband's grasp had been to feign the girl's death, and accept the charge of murder that followed.

She had never known of such bravery. Such love.

"I have to save her. Somehow." As she walked back to the house, ideas formed in her mind. While her magic had failed to save lives, it would allow her to take them. She would use that to her advantage. If Hillborne wanted to free himself of his wife and child, then Sera would find a way to make that happen.

Twenty-Two

Sera ran all the way back to Mistwood Manor, using her magic to make tree branches part and give way, rather than dodging around them. She thundered up the stairs, ignoring the startled looks of the staff going about their early morning chores. Bursting into Noemi's room, she found Kitty awake and reading by the fire. Vilma and Noemi lay on the bed, the young woman sheltered in the contessa's embrace.

"We have to go. Now!" She spoke in terse, low-toned words while still trying to convey urgency. Part of her wanted to scream out her discovery, but at the same time, she didn't want to disturb Vilma.

"What is this commotion?" Noemi sat up and opened lazy eyes. Vilma rolled over and cuddled into a pillow.

Sera swept her arms through the air in an arc and

created a silence spell. "Hannah is alive. We have to save Meredith."

"What?" Kitty was on her feet in an instant and rushed to Sera's side.

Even Vilma roused and murmured the child's name.

"We need to make haste. I will tell you all on the journey, and message Hugh to do what they can to stall the trial until we make it back to London. At least I have all those miles to figure out how to save Meredith without putting her back into her husband's control." Sera dragged over a trunk and then flung open the armoire doors. Deciding magic was far quicker, she gestured for the gowns to fold themselves up and tuck themselves into the trunk.

"I'm already packed. My trunks only need taking downstairs." Kitty walked to the velvet rope by the door and gave it a good tug. "I shall have a maid ready Vilma's things."

It took them an hour to dress and finish emptying drawers into their luggage. Sera took only fifteen minutes to fill her bag and tell Mrs Pymm they were returning to London.

Unshed tears glimmered in the housekeeper's eyes. "Miss Winters will be missed, but it was lovely to have her here again, even if only for a short time. What a shame your gift didn't locate Miss Hannah."

"I am certain that peace will be restored to this house and Miss Winters will return. When the opportunity arises," Sera murmured. As she took her bag out to the carriage, she wondered how long it would take for the previous lord's will to be verified. She hoped she could return to see the look on the current Lord Hillborne's face when *he* received an eviction notice.

The carriage pulled to the front of the house as Lord Hillborne appeared in the entrance foyer and the women descended the stairs. Noemi stood in front of him as Kitty and Sera ushered Vilma from Mistwood.

"Miss Winters is not well. We remove her to London, in case she spreads illness in this house. We already fear our maid has caught it," the contessa said.

On cue, Sera produced a coughing fit and made sure she jerked her body in Hillborne's direction.

His eyes widened, and he pulled a handkerchief from his pocket to cover his mouth and nose. "I should never have invited my cousin here. I see now that was a mistake. But I shall call upon Miss Napier when I am next in London," he called out as Kitty reached the door.

She turned and waved, then glanced at Sera and rolled her eyes. Lord Hillborne would find Miss Napier not at home, should he ever present his card. They took their leave, Vilma waving to Mrs Pymm, who stood under the archway to the stables and kitchen. Some of the other servants gathered around her, including young Truby. The maid waved at Sera in a shy manner, as though she didn't want the other women to see.

Sera returned the wave and wondered what she could do to improve the maid's lot in life. When Vilma reclaimed Mistwood, she would ask that Truby receive an education to expand her mind and prospects.

"I wish I could have told Mrs Pymm what we found," Vilma whispered. A little colour had returned to her cheeks with the potions and Noemi's special care.

"No one can know until it is settled. I shall impress upon Father that the matter requires urgency. It will not be long before you can return, I promise. This time you will be no guest, but its rightful mistress." Kitty patted Vilma's gloved hand.

Noemi agreed to push the horses as hard as possible and change them at regular intervals. While they couldn't reach London as fast as flying in a direct line, they could cut half a day from their return journey. Sera made a mental note to search the hidden library for any spells or incantations to turn herself into a bird. How much quicker travel would be if she could take flight. A kestrel, perhaps, in honour of her friend and their small investigative society. Or would a gargoyle be faster? She ought to discuss with Hugh which method of transport was quicker. Although any transformation would have to include retaining her clothing, or at the very least have some way to send luggage on ahead.

The carriage swayed like a small vessel on the ocean. Sera stewed over the problem of saving Meredith, and discussed defences and escape methods with the other women. None of them could find a way to free her, while at the same time keeping Hannah's survival a secret. Nor could they deliver the child back to an abusive father. The hex would sap Hillborne's body and stop his physical abuse, but words could wound just as deep. Hannah's faked death allowed the child a chance to grow up free of a toxic shadow.

Thinking of death, Sera regarded Vilma. Her complexion remained pale, but the alabaster no longer had the faint grey pallor of an impending demise. Odd, that her death would not only save her but also gift her a chance at a new sort of life.

Those words burrowed into Sera's mind. Somewhere in there hid the answer to her problem.

"Death," Vilma whispered, as though reading Sera's mind. "Death will save us both."

"Soon, *cara mia*, but not until you return to Mistwood as its mistress," Noemi murmured to her heart's companion.

"What if death could save Meredith?" Sera asked no one in particular. Saying it aloud gave the idea a more solid form in her head.

"The illusion of death has freed Hannah from

her father's machinations," Kitty said. Then a frown wrinkled her brow. "How do you know the child is safe and happy without her mother?"

She had no answer to that, other than she didn't know. "I have to trust Erin. She said she and her sisters provided a safe place for such children to grow, play, and learn."

"You're trusting a crow you've never met before?" Kitty arched a quizzical eyebrow.

"But Meredith knows her. She would not have given up her child if she didn't believe it was the best or only option." Though now that Kitty had raised the issue, Sera would find the Crows' secret nest and determine for herself the well-being of the children they spirited away.

"What a shame you cannot do something similar for Meredith. If Lord Hillborne believed her to be dead, mother and daughter could be reunited. Sometimes, it is only in death's embrace that we are returned to those we love," Vilma murmured while staring at Noemi.

The words sparked in Sera's brain. "Good lord, it's so simple. All Meredith has to do is die and she'll be saved!"

"You wish me to turn her into a vampyre?" Noemi tilted her head and appeared to consider the idea.

"No, I don't think that is a good idea." Sera could turn a blind eye to the vampyre transforming her companion into one of the undead to evade death. But if their numbers increased in London, she might have some explaining to do to the Mage Council and she had enough problems. "But like Hannah, we only need everyone to *believe* she is dead."

Kitty huffed. "But unlike Hannah, Meredith is in an institution surrounded by guards. Her corpse will need to be examined and pronounced dead."

"I will admit that makes it more difficult, but I still have many miles to determine how it could be done." Sera fidgeted on the seat. Ideas sprang into being and were teased into bigger ideas in her mind. Her hands itched to be in her little study overlooking her desolate garden. To test potions and whisper over a magical brew. To do something to ensure Meredith escaped the hangman's noose or the warder's fist.

She worried at the problem like a cat playing with the frayed edge of a carpet. How to take away Meredith's life and then give it back? This was a feat no mage could perform. Death held tightly to those it took. Even if such dark magic were possible, she doubted a book with spells telling her how to accomplish it would sit in plain view in the hidden library.

Lord Rowan would know. But that would mean involving another person, and what if he demanded the Fae bracelets in return for any spell able to take and restore life?

No, what she needed was a way to make Meredith *appear* dead, and for a doctor to pronounce her deceased. Or a surgeon. She scribbled notes to Hugh in her ensorcelled notebook, asking what signs a physician looked for when determining whether someone was alive or dead. She hoped such an examination didn't involve poking out an eye to see if the body reacted or cutting an artery to see if they bled.

After dark, they pulled into a coaching inn. Three of the women were ready to drop from exhaustion and even Noemi, who usually brightened up after nightfall, wasn't her usual exuberant self. They rose early the next day and continued on the road as the first tendrils of dawn blushed on the horizon. At least the innkeeper's wife had provided them with fresh bread and cheese, and the yeasty aroma filled the interior as they ate.

"We will make London by midday." Kitty squeezed Sera's hand.

"Hold on, Meredith," she murmured under her breath.

They travelled directly to Mayfair and the Napier home, where Hugh and Mr Napier waited. Both hurried along the path as the carriage rolled to a stop.

Hugh nodded to Sera, but concern wrinkled his eyes as Vilma stepped down, leaning heavily on Noemi.

"Miss Winters, how are you?" His large hands hovered near her form as though he could discern her exact condition without touching her.

"I still dwell in the realm of the living, thanks

largely to your most excellent tonics, Mr Miles." She patted his arm as she made her way into the house.

Hugh took Sera's hand and kissed her palm. "I am relieved to see your face once more."

"And I, yours. But we have much to do and little time." Her heart sang on seeing him. The words he had written in their shared notebook were etched in her soul—*I dream of you every night.*

"We have even less time than we thought," Mr Napier said as he showed everyone through to the drawing room. "Lord Hillborne has been busy with his correspondence. He is arguing that Meredith is of sound mind and given she has already confessed, needs only to be sentenced for her heinous crime. The judge has agreed to hear the case tomorrow morning."

Despair crashed through Sera. "Tomorrow? I can't do it that soon." She had worked for two days to craft the hex for Lord Hillborne and the outcome of that spell didn't matter as much as this one, nor was it a fatal curse. She couldn't afford any error in whatever she cast over Meredith to remove the appearance of life.

She turned to her friends as tears burned her eyes, and dropped to the nearest settee.

Kitty directed the footmen carrying in trays to place them on the table. "Of course you can. We have no alternative and you must use whatever you can concoct this afternoon."

"I will return to my home and have the horses

changed. Then you can use my carriage for this endeavour and, I expect, for the escape." Noemi had remained standing, one hand on the back of the armchair where Vilma had settled by the fire. "You stay here, Vilma, until I return."

With a curt nod, she took her leave to convey orders to her staff. As she left the room, Vilma's eyes fluttered shut.

Sera put one finger to her lips and drew the others to the card table. There was no role for Vilma to play in the next part of Sera's scheme. Indeed, the frail woman needed to conserve her strength to deliver the *coup de grâce* to Lord Hillborne.

Hugh cast the dozing woman a worried look.

"We are all concerned about her, but do not be fooled. There is a deep vein of stubbornness in that delicate form. She will rally to face another day," Sera murmured.

"Where are these papers you found, Katherine? I am of no use in formulating escape plans from Bedlam, and want to get started as soon as possible on having the late Lord Hillborne's will verified and executed." Mr Napier had a gleam in his eyes and he rubbed his hands.

Kitty fetched the folder with its papers and deeds, and her father spread the contents over the table. As the two legal minds worked on their strategy, Sera turned her chair to face out the window and watched the children play in the grassy area in the middle of the square.

Hugh knelt on the rug before her and took her hands. "You have all you need to craft your spell. Reduce Meredith's heartbeat to one per minute. Her breathing must be imperceptible. Add a blue tinge to her lips and a grey tone to her skin. As well, her body temperature must lower so she becomes cool to the touch."

An earnest belief in her shone in his eyes. In this matter, Sera only wished she shared his confidence. She had no time to practise and, unlike the hex she had embedded in Lord Hillborne, Meredith had to emerge unscathed from her spell. "What of her symptoms beforehand?"

"Convulsions. Eyes rolling up into her head. If you can produce foaming or blood from the mouth, that always keeps people clear and stops them from becoming too curious." He infused humour in his words.

She closed her eyes, but kept hold of his hands, not wanting to lose his warm touch as she ventured along a path to capture death. In her mind, she crafted the spell. One strand at a time was added to the whole, as though she embroidered a piece of cloth. When it spun in her mind with a kaleidoscope of colours, she added the last touch. Words to still Meredith's heart were wrapped around the spell and the colours muted, as though draped in the dark cloth of mourning.

Satisfied that she could perfect it no more, Sera opened her eyes. "I have it ready in my mind."

Hugh now sat on a chair next to her, leaning forward to keep their hands connected. Noemi stood beside Vilma wearing an outfit different from the one she had departed in mere moments ago.

"How long did it take me?" Sera asked, a moment of confusion clouding her thoughts. When she lost herself in the world of magic, time seemed to either pause or gallop forward.

"Two hours. Hugh refused to let go of you. I worried he would starve," Kitty joked as she placed a cup of tea in Sera's hands, and a plate holding a pie in Hugh's.

She sipped the hot beverage. A mage might stand immobile while casting their power inward to form spells and incantations, but it was thirsty work. Her limbs ached as though she had spent the afternoon moving large rocks, and her throat was as dry as if she'd slept all night with her mouth open. In a way, her tiredness reassured her. It meant she had poured all her magic into the spell now tucked away inside her, waiting to be unleashed on its target.

Outside the window, the light lengthened into afternoon. Soon, twilight would cast its blanket over the city.

Sera finished her tea in one long slurp. "We should go now. What if they have moved Meredith already, to face trial tomorrow?"

"They'll fetch her early in the morning. We just have to ensure she isn't there." Hugh swallowed the last piece of his pie, dusted his hands against one another, and then held one out to Sera.

"One way or another, she won't be." If Sera's spell failed and she couldn't resurrect Meredith, at least they would deny Londoners the spectacle of watching her dance at the end of a rope.

Twenty-Three

Hugh handed Sera up into the carriage. *Do not doubt yourself.* Their plan would work, because it had to.

Her friends clustered at the bottom of the path, worry and hope in their eyes.

"Bedlam," Noemi told her coachman.

They travelled in silence, a chill creeping into Sera's bones at what she was about to do. They all had a part to play in events that would unfold that afternoon, but Hugh's was the most critical. Before going to Bedlam, they stopped a mile away and waited.

"Who is going to meet us here?" Hugh asked, peering out the window.

"A friend." Sera would disguise her features. It wouldn't do for anyone to hear she had visited Meredith and hours later she was declared dead. But she needed a face Meredith would trust. Like the friend she had asked to take her child. She had dashed off a quick note to Elliot, asking him to send his cousin after the carriage.

A tapping of claws came from above them, followed by a caw. Then a crow peered into the window.

"Excellent. I need your help, Erin, if you would join us in here." Sera dropped the window, and the crow hopped inside.

The bird glared at Hugh with an unblinking midnight eye.

"He is a friend and I trust him with my life. He is also an amazing doctor and physician and someone you can call upon to help your children. Now, if I am to save Meredith, I need to borrow your face." Sera waved her hand in a circle and waited for the crow to shift forms.

The crow made a short, sharp noise, then jumped to the floor of the carriage. The windy vortex appeared and when it dropped away, Erin sat on the opposite seat in her indigo gown.

"What—how—" Hugh tried to speak but couldn't. Most likely due to too many questions trying to leave his mouth at once.

Sera reached out and took Erin's hand with a murmur of thanks. Then she closed her eyes and transformed her figure into one resembling the Crow.

Hugh looked from one to the other and then gave up trying to make sense of it. His only comment was an awed, "Brilliant."

"Thank you, Erin. The next time you see us, Meredith will be with us." Sera squeezed Erin's hand.

"We will be in your debt." The woman winked at Hugh and lifted her shawl up over her head. It turned into feathers that fell from the ceiling and covered the woman. As the pile shrank into nothing, it revealed the crow once more.

With Sera's disguise in place, they journeyed the last mile to the Bethlehem Royal Hospital. Sera and Hugh would enter the asylum separately. Sera, to say goodbye to her childhood friend; Hugh, to consult with the resident doctor about a matter of great urgency—the diminishing mental capacity of their king.

The guard eyed her suspiciously after she made her request.

"She is an old friend. We grew up together. I'd never forgive myself if I didn't get a chance to say goodbye." Then, remembering the form she projected to everyone else, Sera cocked one hip and lowered her dark lashes.

Erin did indeed possess magic. The guard swallowed and shrugged one shoulder. "All right then, love. I'll sneak you through."

Sera fell silent as they walked the chilly corridors. Damp seeped through the stone as though the walls cried out with the interred. Screams echoed along the halls. Shouts answered, but whether from the inmates or guards, she couldn't tell.

Her guide led her down another dim corridor. They were in the Incurables wing, where barred, rounded archways allowed a glimpse of those inside. Was this the path the curious trod when they paid a coin to stare at the madmen? They were on display like animals in the king's menagerie. Some were curled on the ground, hugging themselves and rocking back and forth like infants seeking comfort. One bashed her head against the stonework. More shouted and argued or barked and urinated in the rank straw.

"How can a damaged mind ever heal in such a place?" Sera murmured under her breath.

Fury flowed through her veins, dispelled the chill, and reinforced her glamour. Lord Hillborne would happily have continued his violent ways with his next wife, if not for Sera's intervention. Meanwhile, society turned a blind eye to his actions and those of other men like him.

Do one thing. She reminded herself of Hugh's words on a day that seemed long ago now.

She would do two things—the first in the asylum, the second in society.

Sera vowed that no more would women be trapped without the resources to either fight back or escape. During their trip back to London, she and Kitty had plotted what to do to help more women like Meredith. Kitty had the legal mind, Sera the magical. Together, the Kestrels would not only hunt murderers, but a different kind of prey—human monsters.

"This is the one." The guard stopped at a set of bars. He rattled the chain on his belt and selected a large iron key.

The amassed women had the colour drained from them. Their misery was now cast in tones of brown and grey. The guard unlocked the door and gestured to a group of women huddled in one corner.

"Mind you aren't too long—my supper will be getting cold," he said with a cheery wave for her to enter.

"Thank you," she said and laid one hand on his broad forearm.

"I'll be just along here." He backed away to stand by the barred door.

Magical wards had been embedded in the stone to stop any insane aftermages from causing more chaos. But they were mere annoyances to Sera. Whispering under her breath, she wrapped a protective spell around herself and searched the pitiful creatures for Meredith. The familiar form huddled in a corner, dressed only in a thin shift. Her knees were drawn up to her chest and her arms were wrapped around them.

Sera knelt beside her and teased out her protective bubble to enclose the other woman. With her back to the guard and the residents of the cell, she reached out and touched Meredith's shoulder.

"Meredith, do you remember me?" Sera spoke as though to a frightened child.

The woman raised a dirt-smeared face and confusion passed behind her eyes. "Erin. You should not be here. I am not afraid. Thanks to you, my girl is where he cannot reach her now."

Sera nodded as a lump formed in her throat, then she let the glamour drop for a moment to reveal her true face. "I know. I am a friend of Erin's."

Meredith drew a sharp breath. "Erin is a good friend. I do not blame her."

Sera considered what to say, hoping Meredith would catch the hidden meaning in her words. "You have many friends, and we are sorry we could not help you sooner. But death offers protection, does it not? Your child is happy where she is, and never again will her father hurt her. He cannot pursue what has been taken from him by death."

Meredith's eyes widened, and she rasped, "Yes. I only wish I could join her."

Sera smiled and took Meredith's chilled hands in her own. She needed the woman to understand her plan without announcing it to everyone in the room, including the guard. Even though she cast a layer around them, their interaction needed to appear normal while surrounded by madness. "I am sure that death will reunite you with your child, and you may be together in that place."

Silent tears rolled down Meredith's face. "I hope death will be so merciful."

Sera squeezed Meredith's hand. "I know she is. But you must be brave for what is to come. Trust in me and Erin, and all will be well."

"Yes. I trust you. Send me to Hannah," Meredith whispered.

There were echoes of what Sera had done to Lord Hillborne in what she did to his wife. She pooled all her magic around the spell, plucked the dark orb from her mind, and pushed it into Meredith. There, it would sit and wait. Although a much shorter time frame would elapse before it unfurled and snatched the noblewoman's life.

With nothing more she could do, Sera rose and returned to the barred door. "I have said goodbye to my friend."

The guard returned with a scowl on his face. "Who are you? You must think I'm stupid. I'm not letting you out."

Sera froze. In drawing on her power to send the hex into Meredith, she had let her glamour drop. He probably thought her an inmate, although a very clean one, trying to escape. She couldn't let him raise the alarm or someone might figure out what she had done.

Sera held her hands in front of her face and fanned out her fingers. "You didn't see anything unusual," she murmured to the guard. Mages weren't allowed to alter minds, but in an emergency she could blur things at the edges. She restored Erin's form over her own, and gave the guard the impression he had shooed another inmate away from the bars.

His expression went blank for a moment, then he

shook his head and grinned at her. "Ready to get out of here?"

HUGH WAITED a small measure of time after Sera had disappeared inside the building, then asked for Doctor Yule. He consulted with the other man for nearly an hour, before asking if he could tend to the inmates before he left.

"Yes, of course. Far too many for me to see to all their complaints. I'll have a guard accompany you," Doctor Yule said.

Sera's curse had left a mark on Meredith, one that only Hugh could see. As he walked the corridors and stared into the cells, he scanned each inmate for a ghostly red cross—the symbol they had agreed upon for the one who needed help.

Finally, he spotted the burst of colour in one seething mass of despair. A woman leaning against a wall bore the mark on her back, but it remained invisible to everyone else.

"I'll see what relief I can administer to this lot," Hugh said to the guard.

Once the man unlocked the gate, he moved among the sad group, worn down by the horrid conditions of the asylum. He dressed the open sores on one woman's leg. Another he tended had blood running down her face from bashing it against the brick. An hour had passed when a sharp cry from behind drew his attention.

Meredith clutched at her chest, her eyes wide with panic as one hand twisted in the fabric of her shift. Bloody froth bubbled from her lips and her body shook in convulsions.

"Here! She is having a fit!" he called to the guard outside the door.

The other inmates pulled back from her, like the tide retreating from a beach. None wanted to be splattered in the red foam lest they catch a contagion. He would commend Sera on that part later.

"Possessed!" one woman screeched.

He rushed to the woman as she struggled to draw breath into her lungs. He took her by the upper arms. Sera warned that if she fought the curse, it might not work as well. It would be better if she surrendered to it.

"Trust in death. Let go and you will see Hannah again," he whispered.

Meredith tried to nod as a tear clung to her cheek. Then, with a sigh, she let go of her hold on life. Meredith's eyes rolled up in her head and her body went limp.

Hugh swung her into his arms. "Quickly, man. Grab my bag, I must get her to the infirmary."

The guard rattled the keys and swung the door open. He snatched up the leather bag and then hastily locked the door once Hugh had passed through with his burden. The woman's convulsions stilled as they strode along the dim corridors. After a number of twists and turns, the guard pushed open the door to Doctor Yule's rooms and placed Hugh's bag on the floor. These were somewhat brighter, the overhead lamps casting an eerie glow over the narrow tables below.

Doctor Yule turned from his work at a bench. "Ah, Mr Miles, what interesting specimen have you brought me?"

"This woman has suffered some form of fit, and I believe her heart has given out." He laid Meredith on the table and leaned down to listen for any breath.

A brief moment of doubt tried to attack his mind. What if Sera had taken the woman's life, but could not return it? No. He waved the shadow away. There was no room for misgivings. Whatever unfolded in the next hour, Meredith was in a better place.

Doctor Yule made a harumphing noise in his throat. "Happens sometimes. Poor wretches simply give up on life. Can't say as I blame them. Would you want to spend years here?"

Hugh blocked the other doctor with his body, conducting his own examination of the prone woman's chest and throat. Sera's spell reduced Meredith's heart rate and breathing to imperceptible levels, but he couldn't risk the other doctor trying to make his own determination. Or picking up a scalpel for other purposes.

There was one factor in Hugh's favour—the other doctor's laziness and greed.

"Dead. Perhaps that is the greater mercy for the poor thing." Hugh brushed his hand over Meredith's face and closed her eyelids. "Shame to waste such a prime specimen, though, don't you think?" He had no skill at playacting, and Hugh hoped his colleague followed his meaning.

Doctor Yule laughed and greed shone in his eyes as he surveyed the woman. "While filthy, there is a good form there, and she has not become emaciated yet. This one will fetch a handsome price, indeed."

"I am writing a paper on the female reproductive system. I cannot tell you how *valuable* she would be in my research." His words were no lie. In consultation with Sera, he was turning his attention to issues that affected women, and ways to make their lives easier and to reduce the perils of childbirth.

"Oh, I'm sure you can place a value on her. I do have my regular contact to consider. I'm sure you can understand the position this puts me in." Doctor Yule picked up Meredith's hand and felt for a pulse, before placing it over her chest.

Hugh swallowed a surge of bile at being forced to haggle over the worth of the woman's body. As a surgeon who relied on cadavers to advance his knowledge, he was acquainted with the men who deposited bodies at a surgeon's door under cover of darkness, and had sought their services himself. Some of the bodies arrived in barrows, others wedged in wine kegs. He tried not to dwell too long on the startled look one had worn into death.

He dipped a hand into his pocket and drew out the coins Kitty had pressed on him. He held two between his thumb and forefinger. The glint of gold reflected in Doctor Yule's spectacles. "We are men of science who know the worth of our study. It is surely providence that this poor woman expired while I was examining her cell mates. I cannot let an opportunity such as this pass me by. I will naturally compensate you for the unusual nature of this exchange."

The other doctor practically salivated. "Well, it would save me the inconvenience of having to contact my man. But what shall we do with her until after dark?"

"Why, there is no need to wait. I have a carriage outside. She is a noblewoman. Have her put in a coffin, and tell everyone I am returning her remains to her husband." He rubbed the coins together. Despite the cold, sweat gathered between his shoulder blades and trickled down his back as time elapsed. Lying was difficult work.

"What if he enquires after her?" Doctor Yule stretched out a hand toward his payment, but hesitated.

"This woman murdered her child. Apparently, her husband, Lord Hillborne, has made it clear he wants nothing to do with her. She had confessed to her heinous crime, and was to be hanged. Her internment here was only a temporary reprieve while we ascertained her state of mind. Her corpse was to be consigned to a pauper's grave and, as we both know, would not have rested long there."

He fetched another coin from his pocket, this one a dull silver. "To compensate you for a coffin," he murmured.

Doctor Yule nodded and swiped the coins like a hungry dragon spying a meal. He curled them into his fist. "I have a coffin here for just such occasions as when an inmate does not leave my rooms on their own two legs."

He opened a side door that revealed a storage room. Against the back wall stood a long, narrow pine box.

Hugh and the doctor placed the woman within and tapped the lid into place. Next, he summoned a guard to help Hugh carry the load through the asylum.

At the outer gate, another guard stopped him. "Need to have a look, in case you're trying to help an inmate escape." He winked and chuckled at his joke.

"Of course," Hugh murmured. "This poor woman died of a fit. Doctor Yule has been informed that I am taking her body to her family."

They opened the coffin, and the guard peered within. A blue tinge crept from Meredith's lips and her skin had already turned grey. A fleck of blood congealed on her chin.

The guard jabbed her with a finger in the ribs. "At least she doesn't smell yet."

Hugh could scarce breathe himself. Even to his trained eye, Meredith appeared recently deceased. "We thought it best to move her before the rot sets in. Sometimes it drips through the timber of the coffin and makes quite the mess."

The guard screwed up his nose and, satisfied, he waved them through.

Twenty-Four

Sera paced the scruffy grass at the side of the packed dirt road, imagining a thousand different obstacles that might be playing out behind the stone wall. At length, the iron gate groaned on its hinges and gave way. Hugh stood at one end of a slim pine box. A guard held the other.

She heaved a sigh of relief and kept out of sight as the two men lashed the box to the rear of the carriage, then Hugh slipped the man a coin for his assistance.

He climbed into the carriage opposite Sera. "It is done."

The driver gave the word to the horses to move off and the carriage headed north and away from the sullen asylum. They travelled in near silence for an hour, before Sera judged it safe enough to stop for a peek inside the coffin. They stopped under a spreading tree and Sera cast an obscuring spell around them. The crow flew down and perched on the edge of the carriage roof.

Hugh and the driver set the coffin on the ground, then Hugh pulled up the lid. With care, he lifted Meredith from inside. She hung lifeless in his arms, her face with a grey pallor.

"It's a very convincing spell." He glanced at Sera, a hint of alarm in his eyes. He knelt on the ground and lowered Meredith, supporting her upper body in his arms.

She shared his concerns. What if she had actually killed the poor woman? "I have never done this before. I wanted to ensure both that it worked and that she didn't wake inside a coffin."

She placed her hands on either side of Meredith's face. Sera let her magic flow into the other woman's body, erasing the curse that slowed Meredith's heart to one beat a minute and chilled her blood. Bit by bit, she warmed the noblewoman from inside. When her colour appeared normal, she released the last trace of the spell from around the heart to allow it to beat regularly. Then there was nothing to do but wait.

Silence ticked by while worry nibbled at Sera. Then a thud sounded in Meredith's chest. Another. Then another. Letting go of her, Sera recalled her magic.

The other woman coughed. Then she sat up in Hugh's arms and looked around her. "Where am I?" she croaked.

"Safe." Hugh handed her a flask of water and checked her pulse.

Wide eyes regarded Sera, questions and hope simmering in their depths.

"You are with friends," Erin said from beside Sera. The Crow had landed and shifted form while Meredith shook off the enchantment.

"Erin!" Meredith gasped in relief and flung her arms around her friend.

Sera rubbed Meredith's back as she cried. "You and Hannah are dead to this world, but reborn in another. Hillborne will never harm you again."

"If you don't mind travelling at night, we'll make our nest before morning," Erin said to Sera, helping Meredith up into the carriage.

"I'd rather be far from here and see Meredith safe than wait for daylight to travel." Sera crafted a glowing orb and tethered it in the air in front of the lead horse.

Erin gave the coachman instructions and then changed form to fly home. She would alert her sisters that they were not far behind. Meredith slept in a corner of the contessa's soft cushions, while Hugh and Sera kept each other company during the long journey. Twice, they changed horses and Sera used the funds provided by Kitty to pay for them.

In the chill light of dawn, Sera's orb illuminated wrought-iron gates overgrown with ivy. As the carriage passed through, a crow perched on one of the pillars called out at their approach before taking flight. Trees brushed the vehicle as they passed, their growth unchecked by any gardener or regular traffic. The trees pulled back to reveal a stretch of lawn in front of a two-storey house built of pale stone. Smoke curled from chimneys at either end of the building.

Erin waited for them as they stepped down. "We're getting ready for breakfast. Some of the younger children are early risers. You must be famished."

Hugh's stomach rumbled, and Sera laughed as hers answered.

Erin took Meredith's arm and led the way through the house to a warm and cosy kitchen where dogs sprawled in front of the fire. Two women of similar appearance to Erin prepared breakfast. One stirred porridge, another made hot chocolate. Five children sat at the table. One leapt from her place and rushed at Meredith.

"Mama!"

The two embraced, Meredith's shoulders heaving in great sobs as she stroked Hannah's dark hair.

"How can I ever thank you?" Meredith said to Sera, looking over her daughter's head.

"I am sorry it was ever necessary, and no one helped you earlier." It was such a small thing, to give mother and child a chance to thrive away from Lord Hillborne. "Now, I think we all deserve a hearty breakfast. Then Mr Miles and I must return to London."

Another long day followed as Hugh and Sera

journeyed back to the city. The coachman deposited Sera at her front door before returning to the mews behind the contessa's home.

Elliot held the door open for her. "You've made friends with Erin, then?"

"Oh, yes. And she told me some very entertaining stories about young Elliot." Sera grinned at the footman.

He groaned as he shut the door. "I prefer her as a crow. She talks less when she's a bird."

Sera arched her back and tried to decide whether she wanted a bath or to head straight for her bed. The idea of bed won.

"Any sign of our messenger?" she asked, her hand on the newel post.

"Not yet." Elliot picked up the cloak Sera had shrugged off in the foyer.

"Blast. I had hoped he would deliver my key while I was away." If her secret correspondent kept Fae time, she might be an old woman before he passed over whatever she needed to cross Shadowvane. "No one is to wake me unless the house is on fire." Sera climbed the stairs, stripped off the minimum of clothing, and then crawled into bed. She barely had time to consider how marvellous it felt to be in her own bed, when sleep swept her away.

The next morning, she bathed and dressed before ordering a tray in her little parlour.

"Your letter box has been rattling while you were gone." Elliot gestured to the rosewood box with the brass corners as he set a laden tray on the desk for her.

While Sera had been away, the amendment to the Mage Act had been voted upon in Parliament. For once, Lord Kenwood stayed awake in the House, only to argue that she was a menace to society (and carriage wheels) who should be restrained. Thanks to the efforts of Mr Napier, the bill was defeated. Lord Ormsby and his supporters had failed to make her an exception under the Act and prolong her guardianship.

She was free.

But still, there would be no pleasing Lord Ormsby. He wanted her out of the public eye and most likely was already demanding to know where she had got to, even though he had approved her travel plans. Dropping into the chair, Sera pulled the wooden container closer and opened the lid. Papers were indeed crammed inside. Had a drain become blocked and none of the others wanted to soil their robes dealing with it?

After penning such replies as were necessary, Sera had Elliot hail a carriage to take her out to mage tower. Apparently not knowing what she was up to, and his inability to force another guardian on her, made Lord Ormsby nervous. A servant showed Sera up the spiral stairs to the Speaker's private study. He rapped on the door, then beat a hasty retreat.

"Lord Ormsby," Sera greeted the Speaker, her tone light as she entered his domain. Even in her triumph that his amendment had failed, she wouldn't rub salt into the wound by crowing about it.

"Ah. Lady Winyard." He gestured to the chair opposite his desk. Today, she was allowed to sit. "You dealt with the restless spirit, then?" Lord Ormsby peered over the rims of his spectacles at her.

"Yes. It was the great-grandmother of Lady Meredith Hillborne. The spirit was distressed at her great-granddaughter's charge of murder." On the return trip from the Crows' nest, Sera had had the coachman stop at Bunhill Fields. There, she had conversed with the spirit and reassured her of a happy outcome for all involved—except for Lord Hillborne, of course.

He made a noise in the back of his throat. "Terrible business, that, for a mother to take her child's life. Given that the woman confessed, what exactly did the spirit want you to do?"

"Imogen wanted me to find the girl's body, so she might be given a proper burial," Sera murmured.

"You failed, though, I hear?" Lord Ormsby scoffed, a trace of delight in his tone at finding fault with her.

"Sadly, the lake would not yield her body, but my attempt was sufficient to ease the spirit's distress. She has returned to her grave." Sera refused to rise to his bait and kept her hands in her lap.

"I hear the woman died in Bedlam. You wouldn't know anything about that, would you?" He narrowed his gaze.

"No. I understand Meredith passed before I returned from my mission in the countryside to find Hannah. I had intended to ask if she would reveal her daughter's whereabouts, but cannot now. Unless I were to try to reach her spirit." Sera met his stare with a cool, steady one.

Lord Ormsby huffed. "Well, her demise saved Lord Hillborne the stress of a trial and hanging. I hear he is taking it all rather badly, having lost both wife and daughter. They say the strength is draining from his body."

"Grief is a terrible burden to bear. I am sure it weighs heavily upon him." Sera dug her nails into her palms to stop from smiling. Her hex was doing its job.

"It is unfortunate you failed, and the viscount cannot bury his daughter. Now, to other matters. There is still unrest about your performance as Nyx, and I personally have grave reservations about your conduct. You have demonstrated a lack of maturity and require a guardian. Sadly, the majority of Parliament did not agree with those of us who are concerned for your well-being. However, what is done is done. I will consider how best to employ your skills now that you have returned to us." Lord Ormsby dismissed her like a chastised schoolgirl.

Sera managed to control her demeanour all the way through mage tower and out into the yard. Only when she was secure in the carriage did she burst into laughter. She had won one battle against the Speaker. They could not interfere in her life now.

It took some days for Mr Napier to dig through the documents they'd found at Mistwood and petition the courts to have the contents of the will upheld. Kitty and Sera delivered the news to Vilma, who lay on a chaise at the contessa's home.

"Mistwood is yours. We have only to evict the current occupant," Kitty said with triumph.

Tears filled Vilma's eyes. "Truly?"

"Yes. My aunt Natalie and Warin are only too happy to deliver the papers and oversee his departure. They leave tomorrow." When Sera had told her gargoyle protector all about it, Nat had volunteered to hand the papers over herself.

Although Sera expected she would be disappointed if she hoped that Lord Hillborne would attempt to bully her into submission or fight back. Warin would accompany Nat, then he would settle at the Crows' residence. Sera thought his protective instincts would be best served ensuring the children were kept safe, and she suspected their youthful joy might draw him back into the world.

"We can leave for Mistwood whenever you are ready, *cara mia*." Noemi took Vilma's hand and kissed her knuckles.

Kitty's eyes sparkled as she told them of the work

her father had done on Vilma's behalf. "Father has drafted your will and created a trust that will own Mistwood in the event of your demise. It will allow your solicitor to lease the property to someone of the trust's choosing. No matter how many years pass, it will always be your home. And Father will ensure he passes the administration of your estate and its income to a trusted solicitor when he retires."

The contessa had given Mr Napier charge of her affairs as well. Vampyres and solicitors were natural business partners. However, gargoyles who lived for a thousand years had yet to see the wisdom of long-term estate planning. Sera suspected that Kitty and her father had already hatched a plan to secure more Unnatural clients. All they needed was a change in the law so that they could deal with them in the open, without worrying about exposure to those who feared them.

The four of them made plans for a return to Mistwood under happier circumstances. As the women chatted, Sera fell silent, thinking on the sad events that had led to Vilma's return to her childhood home.

Hannah.

She etched the name into the back of her mind. In Hebrew, the name meant *grace* or *favoured*. To Sera, it now denoted a child so fiercely loved by her mother that the latter would challenge death itself to protect her.

If one day she were blessed with a daughter, she would call her Hannah.

Seraphina's journey to uncover the secrets around her continues in Feint and Doublecross...

Tournament of Shadows
Book 4: Feint and Doublecross

An unexpected move could place Sera in check...or will it be checkmate?

A strange beast stalks unfashionable Southbank, taking victims in a horrific fashion. Naturally the Mage Council sends Sera to track the supernatural killer, while pressuring her to marry one of their hand picked suitors.

With few clues as to whether the man was targeted or if it were a random crime of opportunity, Sera casts a remembrance spell that brings to the surface a similar crime. Set on the trail of a decades old curse that may have resulted in fatal consequences, Sera stumbles upon a tingle of familiar magic. Finally, she unravels long buried secrets about her history.

Then from the shadows, her opponent steps forward and makes a move. But with Sera distracted by revelations from her past, it could put her into a deadly checkmate...

Buy: Feint and Doublecross

History. Magic. Friendship.

I do hope you enjoyed Seraphina's adventure. If you would like to dive deeper into the world, or learn more about the odd assortment of characters that populate it, you can join the community by signing up at:
https://www.tillywallace.com/newsletter

Also by Tilly Wallace

For the most complete and up to date list of books, please visit the website

https://tillywallace.com/books/

Available series:

Tournament of Shadows

Manner and Monsters

Highland Wolves

About the Author

Tilly drinks entirely too much coffee and is obsessed with hats. When not scouring vintage stores for her next chapeau purchase, she writes whimsical historical fantasy novels, set in a bygone time where magic is real. With a quirky and loveable cast, her books combine vintage magic and gentle humour.

Through loyal friendships, her characters discover that in an uncertain world, the strongest family is the one you create.

To be the first to hear about new releases and special offers sign up at:
https://www.tillywallace.com/newsletter

Tilly would love to hear from you:

https://www.tillywallace.com
tilly@tillywallace.com

facebook.com/tillywallaceauthor
bookbub.com/authors/tilly-wallace
goodreads.com/tillywallace

CPSIA information can be obtained
at www.ICGtesting.com
Printed in the USA
BVHW091043311022
650744BV00015B/683

9 780473 656386